THE *Secret Lives*
OF THE *Four Wives*

by Lola Shoneyin

The Secret Lives of the Four Wives

THE *Secret Lives*

OF THE *Four Wives*

LOLA SHONEYIN

wm

WILLIAM MORROW

An Imprint of HarperCollins*Publishers*

THE SECRET LIVES OF THE FOUR WIVES. Copyright © 2010, 2011 by Lola Shoneyin. All rights reserved. Printed in the United States of America. No part of this book may be used or reproduced in any manner whatsoever without written permission except in the case of brief quotations embodied in critical articles and reviews. For information address HarperCollins Publishers, 10 East 53rd Street, New York, NY 10022.

HarperCollins books may be purchased for educational, business, or sales promotional use. For information please write: Special Markets Department, Harper-Collins Publishers, 10 East 53rd Street, New York, NY 10022.

FIRST WILLIAM MORROW PAPERBACK EDITION PUBLISHED 2011.

Designed by Lisa Stokes

Library of Congress Cataloging-in-Publication Data has been applied for.

ISBN 978-0-06-194638-7

11   12   13   14   15   OV/RRD   10 9 8 7 6 5 4 3 2 1

ACKNOWLEDGMENTS

I thank Olaokun for his patience, and his pleasure when things go well for me. My children—Mayowa, Kiisa, Leola and Jola—I thank because they put up with my tiredness at dawn, my tetchiness at bedtime, and my many broken promises. I thank my dad, Tinuoye Shoneyin, for his faith in me, and brother, Dele Shoneyin, for his support.

I thank Ike Anya, who has been my medical consultant on this novel. Anne Uzoigwe I thank because it was she who told me the anecdote that grew into this story. I am ever grateful to Bose Malomo, Nnorom Azuonye, Francis King, Simon Watson, Michael Peel, Emma Crewe, Diran Adebayo, Yatish Parmar, Felicia Green, Remi Raji, Pius Adesanmi, Clare Maloney, Adegoke Odukoya, Mojisola Ani, Ikhide Ikheloa and Abiodun Idowu.

I extend my deepest gratitude to my ace agents, Jessica Woolard and Ayesha Pande; and to my editors, Bibi Bakare, Carrie Feron and Rebecca Gray.

THE ALAO FAMILY

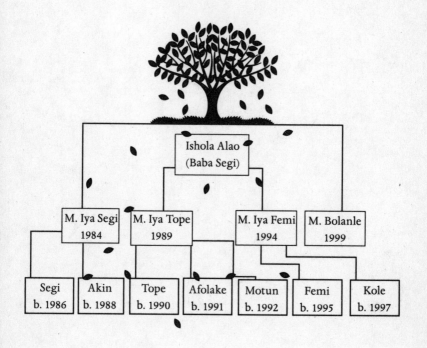

Ishola Alao
(Baba Segi)

M. Iya Segi
1984

M. Iya Tope
1989

M. Iya Femi
1994

M. Bolanle
1999

Segi
b. 1986

Akin
b. 1988

Tope
b. 1990

Afolake
b. 1991

Motun
b. 1992

Femi
b. 1995

Kole
b. 1997

CHAPTER ONE
POLYGAMIST

Bolanle

I DIDN'T JUST HAPPEN upon this room; I dreamed of the pale green walls before I arrived. Now the built-in wardrobe is mine and so is the ceiling fan. My window looks over a backyard with patchy but neatly trimmed grass. Damp clothes flap in the evening breeze and perfume the air with detergent. On the back wall, an iron drum is darkened from burned refuse. A tap juts from the grass and a weathered concrete slab lies beneath it. It is not a perfect view but it is mine. There are no flowers or trees, no fields, no rolling hills; just a vegetable patch where Iya Femi cultivates Jos peppers. I know that smell well. My mother used to cut them into fried eggs whenever she fell pregnant. The aroma from the frying pan would keep the rest of us on the cusp of a sneeze. Then one day, as Mama sat in the front yard wrinkling her nose, the babies would leak down her leg. Who could blame them? Maybe they heard her relentless nagging and decided that it was better to be born unformed. I must have covered my ears when I was in her womb, or perhaps she was quieter then.

Don't get me wrong, I didn't only come here to get away from my mother; I came to get away from the feeling of filth that followed me. If I stayed at home, I knew the day would come when Mama would come to my room and find pools of blood at my wrists.

After everything happened, I tried hard to continue being myself but I slowly disappeared. I *became* Bolanle, the soiled, damaged woman. Except that was hard too because Mama kept trying to make me do all the things the old Bolanle would have done. Don't you think you should get a job, Bolanle? Won't you apply for this bank job in the newspapers, Bolanle? Didn't you see the handsome boy that was looking at you, Bolanle! How could I tell her that I had failed to preserve my dignity? I was too ashamed to let her see the fickle shell I'd become. Inevitably, it became unbearable. The more she pushed, the more I resisted. I didn't want a job! I didn't want a white wedding! I just wanted the war between who I used to be and who I'd become to end. I didn't want to fight anymore.

Somehow, it all made perfect sense when I met Baba Segi. At last, I would be able to empty myself of my sorrow. I would be with a man who accepted me, one who didn't ask questions or find my quietness unsettling. I knew Baba Segi wouldn't be like younger men who demanded explanations for the faraway look in my eye. Baba Segi was content when I said nothing.

So, yes. I chose this home. Not for the monthly allowance, not for the lace skirt suits, and not for the coral bracelets. Those things mean nothing to me. I chose this family to regain my life, to heal in anonymity. And when you choose a family, you stay with them. You stay with your husband even when your friends call him a polygamist ogre. You stay with him when your mother says he's an overfed orangutan. You look at him in another light and see a large but kindly, generous soul.

After I first met him, I told my sister, Lara, that I'd found the perfect man for me. "You want to marry a polygamist and be part of a big, ugly family? Mama will go crazy! When will you tell her?" she cackled. She knew that for once it would be me on the receiving end of Mama's exasperation. Soon, I said.

Mama's reaction was predictable. She listened impatiently to my intentions and then said she would like to claw out the eyes of this man who had misled me. Just to hear him wail, she added. When she saw that I was unmoved, she tried her unique brand of persuasion. Your future will be futile and uninteresting, she said. Polygamy is for gold diggers and bush dwellers, not educated children brought up in a good Christian home. I thought this was funny because we'd never been churchgoers. Mama said it was shameful for a woman to go to church without her husband and Daddy said Sundays were supposed to be days of rest, as the Bible itself stipulated. By the time Mama was wailing about me embarrassing my bloodline, I was daydreaming about the peace I would have in my husband's house.

The day Baba Segi came to collect me, I scanned the bedroom I'd shared with my sister for twenty-one years: the powdery fadedness of the aquamarine walls; the window with missing louvers and rusted frames; Lara's waist beads, hanging from a nail above her bed; the small bookcase displaying my collection of Mills and Boon novels. I would miss the comforting tales of syrupy romance that I immersed myself in. I knew I couldn't take them all so I picked out six. Lara snorted in her sleep and I wondered what my nights would be like without the constancy of her breathing or her sleep talking. She fought Mama constantly in her nightmares. Whatever courtesies held her back during the day were discarded at nighttime.

It didn't bother me that I wouldn't have a tiered wedding cake, confetti, a veil or a highfalutin sermon from a practiced priest. I didn't expect any nuggets of wisdom from my mother, echoes of "look after our daughter" from my father, and certainly no mad dash for a final car-side embrace from Lara. Since I'd announced my departure date, Lara had withdrawn from me, as if I was a deserter. Every time she walked out of our bedroom, she would shut the door firmly, not slamming it, as I knew she'd have wanted to.

After a brief vote of thanks, Baba Segi waited in the pickup with his driver. I put my bags in the back and sat next to him. I must have looked uncertain as the vehicle picked up speed because Baba Segi turned to me with sympathy in his eyes. "Everyone is prepared for your arrival. Tonight you will sleep in your own bedroom." He ran his knuckles along my thigh.

The driver's eyes followed so I lay my knee flush against the car seat. I knew there was something I wouldn't like about that Taju fellow.

We dipped and dove along the rain-ravaged roads, jolted from side to side until we paused behind a battered blue Mercedes at Agbowo Junction. My insides felt as if they had been stirred with a heavy wooden spoon. While we waited for the traffic warden to wave us through, bread sellers descended on the pickup. Little fingers force-fed the car through the half-open window on the passenger side. I recoiled and leaned heavily on Baba Segi. Every hand clutched a clear polyethylene bag containing a loaf of bread and a bright-colored rectangular label: GOD'S WILL BREAD. JESUS'S BODY BREAD. HOME OF GODLINESS BREAD. MY DAY OF MIRACLE BREAD. ALTAR OF MERCY BREAD.

"Give my new wife one loaf each!" Baba Segi said.

The loaves dropped onto my lap and the tang of fermented dough rose to my nostrils. I resisted the urge to shake them onto the foot mat. If Baba Segi had known me better, he'd have realized how much I detested bread, the way it clogged up the throat and hardened the belly. I wondered how much my new family would like it when I appeared, arms laden with warm constipation. Baba Segi pushed twenty-naira notes into the children's palms and nodded Taju back onto the road.

"There are many things in this life to find joy in, so you mustn't be downcast. Give some thought to your husband."

I forced a smile.

Motorcycles darted through the traffic and pumped fading clouds of smoke into our faces. Baba Segi fanned his nostrils and belched. I looked away so I wouldn't embarrass him. He wasn't the most sophisticated man but there was time. He wasn't so old that he couldn't change. I told myself I would devote time to teaching him good manners.

"We'll be home soon." Baba Segi took my left hand into both of his and leaned forward, eagerly setting his eyes on the road ahead like a child.

"I am eager to meet my new family," I said, but the words came out flat and feeble.

Taju smirked and cast me a mocking side glance. I was right: I didn't like him.

"I am eager for my body to meet yours," Baba Segi whispered.

After a few more minutes of hand stroking, we turned into a short driveway. There was a tarpaulin sheet draped over four wooden poles. Three girls were playing ten/ten at the gate. They were dressed in smocks cut from the same cheap, checkered fabric. Wisps of braided hair met atop their heads like clasped fingers. As soon as they spotted the pickup approaching, they jumped into the air and cheered. Before long, more children had joined in the father-has-returned chant. An older boy appeared and pulled them out of harm's way.

The children couldn't hide their disappointment when they saw me but Baba Segi didn't appear to notice. He puffed out his chest and told the children to welcome their new auntie. The girls curtsied brusquely and the boys did hurried half bows.

"Baba Segi, they are the very image of you," I said to him.

"Who will leopard cubs resemble if not the leopard? Let us go indoors and meet the mother-of-the-home and my other wives." He slid a tinted glass door aside and there they were, his wives, lined up in a row, caught in the act of satisfying their curiosity.

I lowered myself onto my knees and greeted them. Only the one wearing dowdy clothes bothered to open her mouth to return the greeting. Then she glanced quickly at the other wives. The large one rolled onto her toes and gave me a hair-to-shoe examination. I guessed that she was the mother-of-the-home. She stood tall, hands on hips. The wife with crimson lipstick wore three gold bangles that jingled at her wrist. I'd never seen such a contrast in skin color. She might as well have been a zebra. While her forearms had a naturally deep hue, her knuckles were a sandy yellow. Purple veins rippled as she attacked a blackhead on her chin. She hummed a distant response to my greeting. They would need lessons in etiquette too.

I perched on a stool while the wives sat in large armchairs. The children shuffled around the room and whispered among themselves. To ease the uncomfortable silence, I told the wife with two-tone skin how gorgeous her skirt and blouse were. The fabric was 100 percent linen, embroidered with small violets. Even the buttons were shaped like flower buds.

"Uneducated women wear good things too," she retorted.

I'd have to start by showing them how to take compliments gracefully.

To take my mind off the awkwardness, I looked outside through the tinted glass doors. At that moment, a blazing sun ray struck the darkened glass and filtered into the room through a small chip. The chip broke the beam with its jagged edges and scattered embers all over the room. One landed on my foot like a fallen firefly. Then the sun crept behind a cloud and everything dissolved into hot air. But the chip remained, secretly concealing its radiance behind the small crack, shaped like the tick of a tentative hand. I took it as a sign. I was home.

"Will you women gape at my new wife until I starve to death?" Baba Segi asked.

"Not in this lifetime, my lord." The eldest wife, Iya Segi, moved quickly for one so generously proportioned. The floor shuddered with her every step. The other wives scurried after her.

LOOKING BACK, NOW THAT TWO YEARS have passed, I realize how naïve I was to expect a warmer welcome. I was foolish to think I would just be an insignificant addition when, in reality, I was coming to take away from them. With my arrival, 2.33 nights with Baba Segi became 1.75. His affections, already thinly divided, now had to be spread among four instead of three.

The women have not changed. Iya Tope is still cordial,

even kind when I am alone in the house with her. She doesn't say much except when she's talking about hair. Her eyeballs bounce around in their sockets and she uses her fingers to draw the hairstyles in thin air. I often ask her about hairstyles, just to hear a friendly voice that belongs to another grown woman.

The other two are a different story: they still have not forgiven me for the affection Baba Segi has for me. Iya Segi and Iya Femi shout, hiss and spit. They sweep the floor, all the time singing satirical songs to ridicule me. But it's not their fault that they are so uncouth. Living with them has taught me the value of education, of enlightenment. I have seen the dark side of illiteracy. So deep-seated is their disdain for my university degree that they smear my books with palm oil and hide them under the kitchen cupboards. I have often found missing pages from my novels in the dustbin, the words scribbled over with charcoal.

It is not as if I haven't tried. I offered to teach the wives to read. Iya Tope was keen to learn but then I found Iya Femi tearing up sheets from the exercise books to line the kitchen cupboards. When I reminded her why I'd bought them, she said I could crawl into the cabinets and teach the insects if I still wanted them to serve that purpose. I have tried to help the children too. I told them to assemble in the dining room so I could read to them. Only Iya Tope's daughters turned up the first day. The next morning, Iya Segi told me not to be in a hurry, that I should wait until I have my own children if I was so eager to become a teacher. Such is the extent to which they conceal their yearning for enlightenment. They try to throw me off by making as if their coarseness is a thing of pride but I see through the subterfuge. I will not give up on them. I will bring light to their darkness.

The children follow the examples that their mothers set them. Iya Femi's sons will not sit on a chair I have vacated. When I walk past them in the corridor, they turn to the wall and flatten themselves against it. No matter how many times I offer them sweets, they still treat me as if I have a contagious disease. I can only wonder what their mother has filled their young ears with. Iya Tope's girls are polite but distant. Sometimes, they bring my meals to my bedroom door. I know their footsteps. They shuffle around the house together, arm in arm like conjoined triplets.

Iya Segi has two children. The eldest, Segi, is fifteen. She is a dutiful sister to her siblings but I think she is afraid that I have come to take her place. I see her anger when I offer to help the other children with homework. She does not speak to me but I often see her shadow by the door. It is a wonder that she has not told Iya Segi that Akin, her brother, comes to my room when he needs help with his homework. Akin is my favorite. He knocks before he enters my room. He comes to help me if I have heavy bags. As he does with all the other wives, he greets me before I greet him. I have told him he was born with decorum. When he asks what decorum means, I tell him to look it up in the dictionary. He does and thanks me the next day.

One day, they will all love me. I will buy their affection

with the money Baba Segi gives me if I have to! I will bring sweets home for the little ones. I will buy Akin a brand-new satchel and get Segi one of those new velvet hair bands to harness that wild mane of hers. I will be a big sister to her. I will tell her everything I know about the world outside so she doesn't make the mistakes I made.

One day, they will all accept me as a member of this family. One day, I will have a child of my own and everything will fall into place. My husband will delight in me again, the way he did before my barrenness ate away at his affection.

CHAPTER TWO
BELLYACHE

W HEN BABA SEGI AWOKE with a bellyache for the sixth day in a row, he knew it was time to do something drastic about his fourth wife's childlessness. He was sure the pain wasn't caused by hunger or trapped gas; it was from the buildup of months and months of worry. A grunt escaped from the woman lying next to him. He glanced sideways and saw that his leg had stapled Iya Tope, his second wife, to the bed. He observed the jerky rise and fall of her bosom but he didn't move to ease her discomfort. His thoughts returned to Bolanle and his stomach tightened again. Then and there, he decided to pay Teacher a visit. He would get there at sunrise so Teacher would know it was no ordinary stopover.

As soon as his driver parked the pickup truck by the gutter that circled Ayikara, Baba Segi flung open the passenger door and reinflated his large frame. Without a word or a backward glance at his driver, he dashed down a narrow alleyway.

If his eyes hadn't been entirely fixed on Teacher's shack, he might have noticed that his driver had scrambled after him. Baba Segi stepped aside to make room for the schoolchildren on their daily pilgrimage. These children went to great pains to bid Teacher good morning, just to see him steam up the louvers with his response. "God mourning," the smoky-eyed sage hummed. The children waved happily and toddled off to school. Baba Segi shook his head. If their parents ever discovered that they had strayed from the dusty road that led to wisdom, stepped wide-legged over spluttering gutters and shifted between random buildings, those children would be in grave trouble. Teacher's shack was in Ayikara and Ayikara was not a place for children.

It wasn't a specific place but when you asked for directions, people looked away from their twirling wrists. There were three reasons for this. First, absolutely no one wanted to admit to knowing where it was, in case their neighbors were listening. Second, Ayikara didn't have distinct boundaries. Last, Ayikara was more than four or five parallel streets laced by lasciviousness: it was a spirit. The dark buildings were full of women whose faces glowed under ultraviolet lights. These women lived for other women's men. They cooked for them. Drank with them. Fought over them. Fucked them. Nursed them. Slapped them and loved them. And when the longing love caused made them ill, they surrendered their lives and died for them.

Teacher's shack, with its shiny glass windows and gleaming shot glasses, was sandwiched between two brothels.

Mostly, the skimpily dressed women brought their clients to drink of the shack-made whiskey, but on certain days they would get to the doorway and retrace their steps. These were the days when men glared at them through squinted eyes— the days that men came to meet men, to talk about women and the evil that they did.

These meetings were not prearranged; they just happened when two or three men were gathered. They started with one man lamenting his travails with a quarrelsome wife. And as more men ducked through the door frame, solutions were proffered: what worked wonders; what didn't work; what was worth trying; and what, if the man concerned wasn't careful, would eventually kill him.

Every man had his say but Teacher always had the last word. He was impressive; there was no doubt about it. Even as the men sat curling at the ears from the heat, enveloped by the miasma of both human and animal waste, Teacher would busy himself with his windows without breaking a bead of sweat. Gradually his eyes would smoke up and become teary. Only then would he speak, and only in the Queen's English.

Baba Segi was first warned about Ayikara when he was a young apprentice but the cautioner was female and unconvincing. Besides, he had just moved to Ibadan and his innocence had become a burden, the very kind Ayikara women helped to relieve. Four wives and seven children on, he'd grown weary of the stench and his visits had dwindled to once or twice a month. Still, these men had helped him through his darkest days.

Sixteen years before, when he was an impatient twenty-six-year-old husband, Baba Segi had sat with Teacher and two other men to discuss a predicament that was similar to the one he was in now. He had been eager for his sick mother to see the fruit of his loins but his wife's menstruation persisted. Teacher had suggested that he visit an herbalist and Iya Segi had lapped up the dark green powder her husband sprinkled on her palm. The medicine worked swiftly. Baba Segi cried with both grief and gladness at his mother's burial, six weeks after the birth of his daughter Segi.

THE DOOR OF THE SHACK stood ajar so Baba Segi entered the small room. He frowned. It annoyed him that Bolanle was the reason he had come, when just two years before, he had boasted of his conquest: how Bolanle was tight as a bottle-neck; how he pounded her until she was cross-eyed; and how she took the length of his manhood on her back—splayed out and submissive. He didn't quite know how he would tell the men that all his pounding had proved futile.

Inside the shack, Baba Segi was confronted with the same men who had pumped his hand when he first announced his intentions to marry Bolanle. They were talking to Teacher at a table by the window so Baba Segi dragged a stool over and joined them. They asked him what had brought him there so early in the morning and he told them of the agony that Bolanle's barrenness caused him. Teacher closed his eyes and shook his head while Olaopa, whose lips were perpetually browned from kola nut, let out a long breath. Although he also had four wives, he couldn't help remembering how the "educated wife" affair had overshadowed his own libidinal feats. None of *his* wives knew which end of a pencil to set to paper.

"Baba Segi, I think you should *drag* her to a medicine man if she doesn't follow you. You are the husband and she is a mere wife, and the fourth one at that! If you drag her by the hair, she'll follow you anywhere, I swear it!" Atanda licked his forefinger and pointed it in the direction of his maker. Even as he pinched a half-smoked stick of Captain Black from a tattered snuffbox, the expression on his face was unforgiving.

"Atanda! You want to land Baba Segi in jail? Who would dare to *drag* a *graduate*? When she opens her mouth and English begins to pour from it like heated palm oil, the constable will be so captivated, he will throw our friend behind bars!" Olaopa was a retired police sergeant and he knew, more than anyone else, that domestic violence was widely perceived as a waste of police resources.

"You are quite right, Olaopa." Baba Segi saw right through him. "Besides, these educated types were fed on cow's milk. We, as you know, didn't have that luxury. We suckled our mothers' breasts. If I lift my hand to her, the next thing I know, I could be conversing with Eledumare. No, we must never manhandle our women. Especially not someone like you, Olaopa, slight as you are."

More men had ducked through the low door frame into the crowded room. Everyone chuckled.

"Yes, but whose wife's belly is as flat as a pauper's footstool? I may be slight but I get the job done." Olaopa was a sore loser.

"Thank you for returning our mouths to the matter at hand, my friend." Baba Segi thrust the back of his head in Olaopa's direction and turned to the other men present. They stared back at him with sympathy in their eyes. An old night guard scratched away at the print on his T-shirt. It said 2001 IS MY YEAR OF INCREASE.

"Why are you running skelter-helter, Baba Segi?" Teacher's voice rang through the silence. The sunlight ripped through the torn mosquito net, hit a glass and shone a halo on the wall near his head. "You are running from post to pillar when the answer is there in front of your face. Since the woman is educated, she will only listen to people from the world she knows. The place to take her is the hospital."

BY THE TIME BABA SEGI arrived at his workshop, his shop assistants were waiting by the giant padlock. Their greetings were met with a dismissive grunt and they swapped knowing glances. It was going to be one of those days when Baba Segi would sit stone-faced in the back room with his head held up by his fist. Baba Segi knew it too. He sat at his desk, reached into a drawer and brought out the photograph Bolanle had pressed into his palm the day they met. As he thumbed away the film of dust on it, he thought how much her personality had changed, how she'd slowly lost her meekness and become full of quiet boldness, how discord had followed her into his home and made his other wives restless.

He remembered the day when he first met her. She'd accompanied her friend Yemisi to his building materials store. Yemisi did small building contracts for the married men she screwed; Baba Segi issued her the overinflated invoices she requested, and the goods. It was all part of the business.

"Just double all the prices," Yemisi urged.

Baba Segi had noted Bolanle's embarrassment and was greatly relieved when Yemisi rushed outdoors to take a call on her mobile phone. Within moments, she came back into the store and announced that she had urgent business to attend to. Bolanle offered to wait for her in Baba Segi's store.

After she left, there was a brief stillness and Baba Segi had taken the opportunity to let his eyes lick her unpainted fingernails, her lean face, her dark, plump lips and her eyes. Every blink was slow and comely. He became suddenly aware that he was inhaling the air that came from her and she was swallowing his. The gods have sent her to me, he thought as his eyes rested on Bolanle's bosom.

"Now that you and your friend have finished university, are you going to marry a man who will look after you?" he asked.

"When I find one," she replied.

It didn't seem like an opening for a middle-aged man with three wives and a home full of children, but he took it as one. He watched as Bolanle dipped her hand into her bag and brought out a tattered novel.

"Am I not an entertaining host?"

Bolanle snapped the book shut.

"Tell me when you alone will come this way again," he whispered quietly.

Bolanle fixed her eyes on the desk between them.

"Come tomorrow, come the day after. Any time I see you again, I will know the gods have favored me." Even he was surprised by his brazenness but he sensed her vulnerability.

"And will your wives not come and drive me out with a broom?"

"My wives do not visit my workplace. Your friend should have told you that. Why would they? They are taken care of; they have no reason to trouble me." Baba Segi felt an over-whelming urge to reach across the table and touch her but he hid his fists under the desk.

That was how it started. She came the next day, and then the next, and then every weekday until he had to bask in palm wine on weekends to make time pass quickly. He couldn't wait to have her, to show her off as his own. He wanted to be the envy of all his peers. True enough, many did not hide their resentment. They told him he was a fool to marry a graduate, that she was only after his money, that she didn't really love him and would leave him for a younger, educated man, after she got what she came for. Baba Segi laughed in their faces until, eventually, they came to terms with their own inadequacies.

———

A T   F I V E,   B A B A   S E G I   C A L L E D   Taju, his driver, and told him to start the engine of the pickup. His mind was made up. He would speak to Bolanle that night. It was Tuesday and he would be spending the night with her anyway. He flopped into the passenger's seat and stroked his hairless chin all the way home.

Taju honked twice as he drove into the large compound. The entire household poured out of different rooms to welcome their benefactor. Baba Segi's three sons lay prostrate, their torsos curled upward like mats rearing their edges. The daughters knelt before him. From the eldest child to the youngest, he called them by their names: Segi and Akin, a daughter before a son, from his first wife; Tope, Afolake and Motun, three girls born eleven months apart, from the second; and Femi and Kole, sons smugly birthed by Iya Femi, his third wife. Baba Segi looked lovingly into the faces of the older children and pinched the cheeks of the younger ones. He made each child feel extraordinary.

Midway to the sitting room, Baba Segi paused at the bogus archway as if it had suddenly occurred to him that the children couldn't have delivered themselves. Then, like he always did, he swung round and turned to his wives. And with unabashed flirtatiousness, he greeted them: "Iya Segi. Iya Tope. Iya Femi. Bolanle." Each woman curtsied, proud to be defined by her firstborn child, except Bolanle, who was *iya* to none.

The greetings done with, Baba Segi raised his arms so his *agbada* could be prised off by Iya Segi's deft fingers. She did the same with his *buba* and Baba Segi stumbled into the sitting area in his trousers and his vest, his eyes leading the way to his luxurious armchair. He stood with his back to it and, as always, he collapsed into it as if he had been struck by death. He tore at his watch and pulled it off his wrist. Before he placed it on the wooden stool beside him, Iya Segi had put her hand out to receive it. He smiled the way he always did. "Iya Segi, wife of my youth. Would I have breath if I had not married you?"

Iya Segi paused and turned to him. "May your breath be long, my lord. Where would *I* be if not for *you*?"

They were ritually joined in this reciprocal admiration until Iya Femi's bogus coughing interrupted them. The third wife could never stomach their display of old-fashioned affection. If any form of favoritism didn't involve her or her children, she was quick to register her disapproval.

Iya Segi brought a long wooden stool and placed it in front of her husband while her daughter, Segi, measuring her every step, carried in a bowl of hand-wash water. After steeping his hands into the bowl, Baba Segi dried them with the towel that was draped over his daughter's arm. He pulled the stool toward his crotch and proceeded to demolish the mountain of *amala,* morsel by morsel, catching every string of *ewedu* that dripped down his wrist with his tongue.

At the sound of a familiar melody, the children jostled for space in front of the TV and sang along to the theme tune of *Afowofa,* their favorite soap opera:

Talaka nwa paki
Olowo nwon'resi
Igbi aye nyi o
Ko s'eni to m'ola

The impoverished search for cassava flour
While the rich consume rice by the measuring bowl
The tide of the earth turns
No one knows tomorrow.

Like all good soap operas, it ended on a cliff-hanger that sent all the children into a frenzy of cushion slapping and teeth kissing. Baba Segi chuckled. "Tope, Motun, Afolake, Femi, Kole," he summoned, "come and share the tripe your father left on his plate for you."

The children assembled at his feet and tore at the tripe until they'd all wrenched a piece for themselves. Kole swallowed his portion in one piece and started hankering for his sister's.

"Iya Femi, Kole is as thin as an old man's cane. Why are you not feeding my son?" There was far too much concern in Baba Segi's voice for anyone to take him seriously.

"I feed him but the food disappears as soon as it reaches his belly. That boy would eat this entire house if you let him."

"Then cook him this house. And when he has eaten that, serve him the neighbor's too. My children must eat their fill.

It won't do for them to look like beggars when their father works so hard to keep the skin of their bellies taut. My Kole must grow big and strong so he can marry many wives and bear many children. Is that not so, Kole?"

"Yes, Baba. I want to be just like you!"

Everyone laughed at Kole's precociousness so no one heard Iya Femi whisper, "God forbid," under her breath.

Desperate to return to the center of attention, Baba Segi leaned onto one buttock and let out an explosive fart. The children looked at each other and giggled. Iya Segi, deadpan, inched toward him and asked if he needed some cold water to calm his stomach. Iya Tope stared unblinking at the TV while Iya Femi pinched her nostrils and turned her lips down at the corners. Bolanle, who had been wishing away Baba Segi's visit that night, shifted a little closer to Iya Tope's seat. Iya Tope saw her and moved to the center of her seat, as if to make room for her. Iya Femi sneered at the gesture from across the room.

Only Baba Segi's armchair faced the TV directly; his wives (except Bolanle, who hadn't earned her right to an armchair) kept their seats at the angle their husband insisted on. Baba Segi liked to observe their every facial expression: how widely they smiled at comedy sketches, how many tears they shed when they were gripped by agonizing dramas. The wives, knowing they were being watched, stared at the screen, never swiveling to look Baba Segi smack in the face.

As the show came to an end, everyone prepared themselves for the last ritual of the evening: the communal watching of the seven o'clock news. Before the newscaster even opened her mouth, it was obvious that she was a little off balance. She blinked in quick succession and a lump moved up and down her throat as she spoke:

A forty-year-old man named by the police as James Jerome has been detained after the plastic bag he was carrying was found to contain what medical experts have identified as three pre-term fetuses.

In April, the police launched a nationwide appeal for any information on the spate of ritual murderers. In the last year alone, the bodies of eighteen women have been recovered, all with fatal wounds to their pelvic region. The police are confident that Mr. Jerome's arrest will lead to the arraignment of the entire gang. Mr. Jerome used to work at the University College Hospital, Ibadan, as a mortuary attendant.

Halfway into her final paragraph, a short clip of James Jerome on a bench, handcuffed and dabbing a head wound, appeared on the screen. He didn't look at all remorseful, just annoyed with himself. Arranged on a piece of white cloth before him were three bloodstained fetuses, all head with scrawny little bodies. They seemed to come alive each time a strong wind lifted flakes of dry blood.

Iya Segi yanked her head-tie off her head and flung it across the room yelling, "Why? Why kill innocent children?" Iya Tope gripped her belly as if she were experiencing labor pains and Iya Femi, who proclaimed Jesus as her lord and savior, didn't sound at all like a believer. She pointed at the spot where James Jerome's face had been and cursed. "May you not miss your way to hell! May sleep possess you on the day Mercy is passing! May you leave your front door open on the day Death is on the prowl!"

The children huddled closer together and concluded that the news had induced maternal madness. Their father sat transfixed. Not caring that they might anger their mothers, the children looked to Bolanle with pleading eyes. Bolanle's lips trembled and a steady stream of tears trickled down her cheeks. After a few minutes, she got up and she fled the room.

Baba Segi felt his stomach growling and made to grab the bowl of hand-wash water. He missed the bowl completely and covered the cream-colored rug with his undigested supper. Iya Segi and Iya Tope ran to his side and fluttered around him like harried hens. They lifted Baba Segi by his arms and guided him to his bedroom, leaving Iya Femi to salvage the rug with soapy water and Dettol. They left him dozing under a light sheet.

LATER THAT NIGHT, BABA SEGI staggered down the wide corridor that the wives' bedrooms were cut from. Like he always did, he caressed Iya Segi's door on the right, touched the knob on Iya Tope's door on the left. He listened for voices at Iya Femi's door and finally paused at the threshold of Bolanle's door. He didn't knock; he just pushed the door open with his toe and brightened the room with the corridor light.

He wanted to see how much Bolanle had prepared herself for him. He wanted to know if she had covered her nakedness with a cloth, like the other wives did, or if she was wearing those accursed pajamas. His eyes caught the pink sleeves so he let out a short, sharp breath through flared nostrils. He often wondered why a woman would want to go to bed dressed like a man but he never mentioned it lest he appeared uncivilized.

Bolanle sat up in bed. Pretending to be startled, she rubbed her eyes and turned to acknowledge the looming silhouette by her bedroom door. Baba Segi's large gait was curled inward like a boxing glove. He reached for the door frame and rapped it with his fingernails. "Where did you read that a wife should leave the room when her husband is ailing?" he asked, as if Bolanle's education meant her every action was dictated by a manual. He didn't come in or close the door. He wanted every ghost that stalked the corridor to bear witness to her unseemliness.

"Like everyone else, I was sickened by what I saw." She threw her feet over the side of her bed and tightened a wrapper over her pajama top.

"What do you know about what you saw? A woman cannot know the weight of a child until she has carried one in her womb."

Bolanle was determined to deny him the pleasure of hurting her feelings. She lifted the bowl from her bedside table and pushed it toward his face so he got a full view of the rich, oxblood clay. Baba Segi glanced at the bowl and winced. Bolanle threw a handful of nuts into her mouth to conceal her satisfaction.

Baba Segi marched to her side and flopped onto the bed. "Tonight, I have come to *talk*, Bolanle." His weight made the sprung mattress uneven. "Yes, I have come to talk about the matter that threatens to turn us into enemies."

"I am listening, Baba Segi. I do not want to be your enemy," Bolanle said, relieved that sex wasn't in the cards.

"Your barrenness brings shame upon me. And I am sure that you are saddened by it as well. Every time I have suggested that we consult herbalists and prophets, you have called them con men and rubbished their powers. Well . . ." He inhaled deeply and raised his eyebrows. "I have thought long and hard about it and I think we should go to the hospital to talk to a doctor." He paused, expecting Bolanle to reject his proposal, but she just stared ahead, mindlessly throwing nuts into her mouth. "Tomorrow at six A.M., then." With this, he hoisted himself onto his feet using the bedpost for support and prayed that morning would wake them well.

CHAPTER THREE
HEAVY PERIOD

Baba Segi yelled frantically as he scrambled down the corridor to Bolanle's room. "Iya Segi! Help me! I can't find Bolanle! We were supposed to go to the hospital today! Where is she?"

"What have you lost, Baba Segi?" Iya Segi flung her room door open.

"It's Bolanle! She's gone! She must have run away in the middle of the night. All the money I have spent on her is wasted. My graduate is gone!" One leg was in his trousers; the other was caught in the waistband, so he was hopping along, sweat dripping from his bare chest.

"Have you looked in her bedroom?" Iya Segi tried to join in the panic but her words came out too slowly, too comfortably.

"I have looked everywhere!"

"These educated girls. They take your money and they

abandon you. After all you have done for her. What a wretch! She has run off with another man, no doubt!"

"Baba, she's here, asleep in the living room." Segi leaned into the corridor with soap suds all the way up to her elbows.

"Where? Let me see for myself! Bolanle! Bolanle!" Baba Segi hopped into the living room and his eyes fell on Bolanle, who was lying in Iya Tope's armchair with her eyes closed.

By now, the other wives too had gathered at the mouth of the corridor and were trying to make sense of the furor. They watched Baba Segi grab Bolanle by the shoulders and shake her. "She is here! Alive! Thank the gods," he exclaimed.

Iya Segi retraced her steps to her room without making a sound.

"I am awake now," Bolanle gasped, so Baba Segi wouldn't crease the pink stripes on her shoulder pads.

Iya Femi flicked on the lights and for the first time Baba Segi caught a glimpse of Bolanle's face. She had clearly been extra careful in applying her makeup. Her eyebrows were penciled in so they were symmetrical, not like the slapdash jagged lines Iya Femi sketched on her face. She had lined her lips with burgundy and used the tip of her pinkie to apply a sheer coat of gold to their fullness. Her skirt suit was well cut but two years without soft-scoop ice cream had made the waistband a little roomy. Her toes were edged into a pair of fuchsia slip-ons. Baba's hands shot upward as if the pink stripes were hot iron rods. Without another word, he stood up straight and marched to his bedroom. Iya Tope too returned to her bedroom. Iya Femi rushed after Segi; she wanted to know every detail. Bolanle just smoothed back her hair and smiled.

At six o'clock, Taju rapped on the metal door frame. Bolanle had fallen asleep again. The rapping grew louder until Iya Femi barged in from the kitchen making as much noise as she could with the keys. "I don't know how some people sleep like they are dead!" She tightened her wrapper over her bosom. "Let me open the door for you, Mr. Taju. Some people do not know that you are a *baale-ile*, head of your own household."

"Thank you, Iya Femi. Good morning. I hope you woke well."

"Let us just say that we woke and leave it at that." She shot a sweeping side glance in Bolanle's direction. "What about you?" The padlock came off and then the chain.

"Who would see your face and not wake well anyway?" Taju lowered his voice to a whisper and hummed his appreciation of her bare skin, glistening from the morning humidity.

"Mr. Taju, one would think you had not just prised your body from your wife's embrace. Anyway, it is good that you have come on time. I think Baba Segi wants to leave early this morning." They both laughed and Iya Femi walked back into the sitting room with Taju close behind her.

Taju had only ever been late once, about a year before, when he'd arrived with his shirt slung over his left shoulder and nail marks across his forehead. Ejecting a toothpick from between his teeth and pushing it into his Afro, he claimed that he'd beaten his wife senseless for letting his only son suck on a coin. This happened about a week after a male senator slapped a female colleague. The slap had resonated through all the quiet meeting rooms of the senate building and into the heart of every man on the street. It seemed to awaken a loosely fettered beast. Of course, the male senator blamed the devil for his actions and the two senators were soon seen embracing on national television. The same could not be said for the man on the street. Men were slapping their womenfolk as if it had become a national sport. At every street corner, disgruntled wives swung suitcases onto their heads, hoping to be persuaded to return home. At the marketplace, the Igbo fabric merchants tugged women roughly by the sleeve. Peeved taxi drivers prodded the heads of mothers who bargained with them; young girls were assaulted and stripped naked in the streets. Even in the labor wards baby girls were frowned upon by their fathers. Taju too was inspired to throw his best punch.

When Baba Segi finally summoned Bolanle, she was fast asleep, dreaming of Segun, a boy from her past. It was the same dream she always had. He was standing in the middle of a busy dance floor beckoning to her. She'd start making her way toward him but then he'd reach into his breast pocket and throw a fist full of small golden nuggets high into the air. Suddenly, all the women in the disco would abandon their partners for Segun's side and Bolanle would then be left standing there, unable to make out his physique underneath the mountain of miniskirts and low-cut tops.

"We must be there by six fifty!" Baba Segi opened the door slightly, rammed his words in and disappeared.

Before Bolanle could finish fastening the buckles on her sandals, she heard the front door slam shut. Baba Segi was talking to Taju through the open window of the pickup when she finally caught up with him.

"Get in," he ordered, barely giving her enough room to press through.

"Next to Mr. Taju?"

"If you don't want to sit next to me, you can sit in the back. Only the wind is uncomfortably cool at this time of the morning," Taju retorted.

Baba Segi looked at Taju and grinned. Bolanle might have been going to the hospital dressed like a graduate, but his driver could still put her in her place. As Bolanle squeezed between the two men, Baba Segi plotted ways in which he could keep her in the shadows, ways to keep her made-up face out of the daylight. He was determined to render her efforts useless.

As they approached the end of their street, the night guard saluted. He ordered them to wait and reached beyond the front tires to remove a plank that was riddled with long rusty nails. He raised the metal bar meant as a deterrent to the armed robbers who used to terrorize the neighborhood. Baba Segi took a fifty-naira note from a black leather pouch and thrust it into the night guard's hand. The guard took off his hat and waved.

They made their way toward Sango Road with the metal rails attached to the pickup rattling behind them. Taju knew the road well and navigated with the precision of a wasp. He skimmed the rims of the large potholes, throwing his passengers within an inch of their seats.

The minute they turned into Sango Road, they spotted policemen. One of them was putting out the flames on the kerosene-filled cans that had lit up their makeshift checkpoints. Two more policemen were emptying out the night's takings from their pockets and exchanging swigs from a portable bottle of Napoleon Chevalier. Their guns lay on the ground swaddled by black raincoats. When the policeman blowing out flames saw them approaching, he put down the lamp he was holding and raised his baton. "Hol' it!" he yelled. He didn't lower his baton or open his eyes until the pickup's hood was within half a yard of his worn black trousers. "Where are you going this early morning? Are you crimina's?" He peered at them through the passenger window. His eyes softened briefly when they fell on Bolanle but when she didn't engage his gaze, he resumed his interrogation. "Who are you? Identify yourse'fs!"

"Sergeant, I am Mr. Atanda Alao. We are going to UCH." Baba Segi smiled sheepishly as his hand crept toward his black pouch.

"Who is sick?" the policeman inquired, feigning interest. He too had spotted the bulging pouch and the tentative journey Baba Segi's hand was making toward it.

Both Baba Segi and Taju looked at Bolanle. The policeman's eyes were squarely fixed on the blue fifty-naira note edging toward his open palm. He looked in the direction of his colleagues. When he was certain they were still bent over the raincoats, he shoved his crotch into the passenger window and stuffed the note into it. His zip was within two inches of Baba Segi's face. Bolanle stared at the man's midsection, interested to see if he would top his own crudeness.

"Drive!" The policeman commanded, swooping on the taxi behind them.

When the policemen were out of sight, Baba Segi leaned out of the car and spat into a large pothole. There was no food in his belly but he still had to empty himself. Bolanle glanced at him but he rejected her concern and wiped his lips with the back of his hand.

Baba Segi could never keep things in. He was open-ended. His senses were directly connected to his gut and what didn't agree with him had a way of accelerating his digestive system. Bad smells, bad news and the sight of anything vaguely repulsive had an expulsive effect: what went in through his mouth recently shot out through his mouth, and what was already settled in his belly sped through his intestines and out of his rear end. Only after clearing his digestive system could Baba Segi regain calm.

Once when his shop assistants came to tell him that his shop had been burgled, he listened attentively while they read out the list of what had been stolen. Then, tensing his buttocks, he strode to the toilet. Within minutes, he reappeared with all tension gone from his face.

"All I can say is that what has happened has happened." This was not the philosophical response the perplexed employees expected; they looked at each other and wondered if Baba Segi was still suffering from shock.

BOLANLE HUGGED HER ELBOWS. TAJU had discovered a new method of rankling her. Every time he changed gears, he leaned his arm close to her breast. In the distance, an old train snorted and let out a gasp before it commenced its daily chugging. Sango Road was waking up. Minibus drivers were starting up their vehicles and spilling out of the over-crowded motor parks. Women with sleeping babies on their backs swept out their marketplace stalls and tut-tutted at the sight of cigarette butts and broken bottles: leftovers of the night's revelry.

The University College Hospital had a horrible reputa-tion. Patients being taken there would bid their loved ones farewell. The lack of government funding, coupled with the misappropriation of the little the hospital generated, had left the buildings dilapidated. Crucial medical tests were rationed and the doctors refused patients who hadn't brought their own medicine. The only reason people went there rather than the thousands of back-alley clinics was they could be sure the doctors had proper medical degrees.

Bolanle knew they were close as soon as she saw the palm trees that lined the main entrance and shielded early-morning mourners from the sun's unyielding rays. There were always tears at the gate because it was here that the news of death was passed on to brokenhearted family members: here, there was no risk of them throwing themselves over the hospital's many balconies. Besides this, the main gate was an awkward place for mourners to make a scene. There were too many people wrapped up in their own problems. So the mourners sat on big round boulders and wept silently.

"Where can I park?" Taju asked one of the security guards positioned around the gates to enforce organized grieving.

"Do I look like a parking attendant?" barked the man as he walked away.

"Sorry. I thought you were here to work. I didn't realize this was your father's living room," Taju hissed as he drove off, tires screeching. Before the guard could turn and wag a finger, they were negotiating the roundabout in front of the main building.

They must have driven around for ten minutes in search of a parking space before Baba Segi finally suggested that Taju let them out.

"There is a space there, sir," Taju said, pointing at an empty spot under a sign that said MORTUARY.

"Are you sure you want to park there?"

"No problem, sir. I will stay here in the car. Nothing will happen." Taju reassuringly beat his chest like he had dominion over the ghosts that lay beyond the big gray door and whatever mischief they might have in mind.

"Well, at least we know where to find you. We shouldn't be too long."

"Go well, sir." Taju ignored Bolanle. He ruffled his hair for a toothpick and inserted it between his teeth.

When Bolanle and Baba Segi reached the top of the first flight of stairs, the landing opened up into a long corridor that stretched out in both directions. Baba Segi glimpsed a figure in a white coat and ran to him. "Doctor! Doctor! I need somebody to help me. It is my wife's womb—" he panted.

The medic surveyed Bolanle's waistline and inquired if she was in labor.

"No," Bolanle replied. Before Baba Segi could further humiliate her, she added calmly, "We are here to seek medical advice."

"I see," the doctor said, nodding. "Is this your first time at UCH?"

"*I* have never had reason to come here before. Ogun bears witness," Baba Segi blurted.

Addressing Bolanle, the doctor gave them directions. "You'll need to go to the general outpatients department. Go to the end of this corridor and turn left, down the stairs, go to the end of *that* corridor and you should see a big sign that says 'General Outpatients.' It's written in blue. You can't miss it."

Furious at the way the doctor stared at his wife, Baba Segi grabbed Bolanle by the elbow. "Go your way! We'll find it ourselves!"

The astonished doctor watched as he dragged Bolanle off in the wrong direction. Bolanle snatched her arm from his grip and led the way. Each time they walked past a hospital clock, Baba Segi would tap the face of his watch and frown in bewilderment. Bolanle shook her head as they approached the sign that read GENERAL OUTPATIENTS DEPT. (GOD).

"The clocks have stopped, Baba Segi. It is not a miracle. Neither is it magic. The clocks have simply stopped."

Baba Segi looked at his watch one last time and lowered his arms to his sides.

A doctor was perched on the edge of a table in front. He turned linked fingers out above his head and yawned. Opposite him, a nurse sat upright on a plastic chair. The doctor yawned again and only made to cover his mouth as his lips were closing. One arm of his glasses was held in place with a Band-Aid and his beard was disheveled.

"So you are going home to sleep *all by yourself*?" The nurse placed her arms underneath her breasts so they jutted out. Her uniform was crisp and angelic.

They both turned when a well-dressed young woman approached, trailed by a huffing middle-aged man. The doctor scratched his head and headed back to his consultation cubicle.

"Can I help you?" The nurse's tone was friendly despite her small frown.

There were voices in the background—other doctors holding consultations with their patients.

"Sister, it is this wife of mine who needs your help," Baba Segi said.

"What is your name?" The nurse brought out a fresh pink folder from the desk she rested on.

"Bolanle Alao," Baba Segi replied.

"Date of birth?" The nurse looked at Bolanle strangely.

"January 19, 1976!" Baba Segi blurted again.

"Sir, is there a reason why she cannot answer herself? Is she deaf?" The questions were directed at Baba Segi but the nurse looked past him at Bolanle.

"I am her husband."

"That doesn't mean anything to us, sir. We want to hear from the patient. How old are you now?"

Bolanle moved toward the edge of a blue plastic chair and whispered "Twenty-five."

"And what brings you here today?"

She knew what Baba Segi wanted to hear. "I am barren."

"Is this your first visit to a hospital about this matter or were you referred?"

"This is my first visit."

"Address?"

"1 Saibu Street, Sango."

"Religion?"

"Christian."

"Level of education?"

"BA. University graduate."

The nurse looked up at her and then glanced briefly at Baba Segi. "Next of kin?"

For a moment, Bolanle went blank. All her life it had been her mother—the one person who would drop everything and run to her aid. Bolanle remembered the last conversation they had before she left for Baba Segi's house. "Have you lost your brain? After I scraped my salary together, month after month, to put you and your sister through university, you want to betray me?" her mother asked. It was four o'clock in the morning and she was due to move to Baba Segi's house later that day.

"Mama, I am doing what is best for *me*." Bolanle had rehearsed her answer.

"Is that what this is all about? Is it the prospect of stuffing fat into your mouth that has led you into this? If that is so, Bolanle, remember all the days that I slaved for you. Cast your mind back to all that I deprived myself of, for you and your sister! Have you not learned anything from the words that have fallen from my mouth all these years? Is your back broken that you cannot sow what you seek to reap from this man's table?"

"I'm doing what is best for me, Mama."

"PLEASE WRITE MR. ATANDA ALAO!" Baba Segi shouted now. "*I* am her next of kin. You should have stayed in your father's house if you wanted your mother to be your next of kin!"

Bolanle raised a palm to her mouth to prevent any more words from flying out; she hadn't realized she'd said her mother's name.

The nurse drew a line across what she'd written and started over. Her writing was swift yet leisurely, clear with no sharp angles. She handed the empty folder to Bolanle. "Go to cubicle five." She pointed to the empty cubicle even though the number 5 was emblazoned on a white A4 sheet and tacked to the door.

Baba Segi kept his eye on the pink folder. "Hold it tight," he mumbled.

The doctor's eyes were bloodshot but they responded to every sound in the room. As soon as the couple walked in, he stood up to take the pink folder from Bolanle and offered them the seats on the other side of the table.

"I am Dr. Usman. *My* job is to try to understand the nature of your ailment so I can refer you to one of our specialists."

"You mean we wasted our time coming here? Why can we not go straight to the special . . . special doctor? We . . . *I* am a very busy man, you know? And this is a very serious matter!" Baba Segi had jumped to his feet.

Bolanle put a hand to her face and kneaded her eyebrows with her fingertips. The doctor spotted it. She tugged at Baba Segi's sleeve but he threw off her hand. Dr. Usman spotted that too. Baba Segi slowly sat back down in his own time.

The doctor wanted so badly to roll his eyes that he had to raise his eyebrows to stop himself. He didn't want to appear condescending, if only for the sake of the young woman sitting opposite him. "I'm sorry, sir, but unfortunately, no specialist in this hospital will see you unless you've seen us first. That is why we are here and that is the way things work."

Baba Segi folded his arms and rocked on his seat, all the time mumbling.

"I presume you are husband and wife?" the doctor inquired, preparing to scrawl across a blank sheet of paper.

A fist moved to Baba Segi's waist. "Yes. She is *my* wife."

"Very good. So, Mrs. Alao . . . ?"

"Yes?" Bolanle responded tentatively. No one had ever called her that before.

"How long have you been married?"

"Nearly three years," Baba Segi replied.

"Bolanle, how old were you when you started menstruating?"

"I was thirteen."

"And how long do you normally menstruate for? How many days each month, I mean?"

"Four to five days."

"Heavy? Light?"

Baba Segi couldn't hold back. "Do you not know that you are talking to another man's wife? All these questions you are asking are meaningless. She is bar-ren . . ."

"Mr. Alao, I am conducting a medical investigation on my patient. The only reason you are allowed to be here is that she has permitted it." He shot Bolanle a sympathetic look. "If you cannot conduct yourself properly, I will have to ask you to leave."

"Just remember that she is somebody's wife."

"Now, I was asking about your—"

"They are always heavy," Bolanle replied.

"Very good. And are they painful?"

"No, not at all."

"Good. Do you and your husband have regular coitus?"

"What is the meaning of *coitus*? Don't think the two of you can bamboozle me because I did not go to university!" Baba Segi said.

Bolanle smiled wryly and shook her head.

"I was asking Mrs. Alao how frequently you have sexual relations."

"She gets her ration on Tuesdays, and sometimes she gets an extra day. No less, no more than any of my other wives. It is her womb that is not working."

"Co-i-tus, once a week." The doctor pronounced each syllable, then looked long and hard at Baba Segi to emphasize that his embellishment was neither required nor helpful. "So, there are other wives. And you are wife number . . . ?"

"She is number four." Baba Segi held up four fat fingers. "Number four!"

"I take it there are other children? I know it is bad luck to say how many but perhaps you could tell me roughly how many children you have."

"You dare to call my children rough?"

"No, sir, I mean approximately. An estimate. How many? Over fifteen? Over ten? Over five?" Dr. Usman exhaled sharply.

"Many more than five."

"But fewer than ten?"

"I would have had more than ten now if this woman's womb was not hostile to my seed."

The doctor leaned back into the old leather seat. The fabric was cracking like shattered glass. "Mrs. Alao, how long have you been sexually active?"

Silence. Bolanle's mind reeled. Did false starts count? Or was he referring to consensual sex?

"Mrs. Alao, when did you have your first sexual encounter?" the doctor asked again.

"I was . . . I was . . . the first? I was fifteen and eight months, four months before my sixteenth birthday."

"Ah!" Baba Segi placed both palms on the top of his head and began to hum at an unsettling pitch.

Dr. Usman threw his pen on the folder and tightened his brow. "Listen, Mr. Alao, you are obstructing this consultation. Plus, I believe you are . . . intimidating my patient."

"*Your* patient?" Baba Segi sneered. "She is *my* wife. *I* am the one who has married her. Why should *you* care?"

Dr. Usman often had to ask mothers, husbands, sisters to wait outside the cubicle, so he picked up the receiver of the phone and made to press a red button. "I'm afraid I am going to invite security to—"

"Please, Doctor, let us continue."

It was not so much the sound of Bolanle's voice but the volume that made Dr. Usman replace the receiver. "As you please, Mrs. Alao. Now, have you ever been pregnant?"

Baba Segi turned his entire belly toward Bolanle. A nerve shuddered down his leg and set his right foot in motion, making the sole of his slipper slap the linoleum flooring.

"Yes," Bolanle said.

The slipper slapping stopped abruptly.

The doctor continued. "How many times?"

"Once. The pregnancy was terminated." Bolanle stared ahead.

"Can you tell me where the procedure took place?"

"I don't remember. It was done by a nurse, somewhere near Mokola. I don't remember."

Dr. Usman braced himself when Baba Segi raised his hand; he thought he was going to strike his wife, but instead the older man opened his mouth and bawled, "Where is your toilet?" over and over again. Dr. Usman shoveled him out of the cubicle and in the direction of the men's room.

Back in the cubicle, Bolanle rummaged through her handbag and Dr. Usman pretended to read over his notes. Eventually, Baba Segi pushed the cubicle door open. He looked subdued and the strain was gone from his face. "I will be in the pickup," he whispered. "Doctor, when you buy guavas in the marketplace, you cannot open every single one to check for rottenness. And where you find rottenness, you do not always throw away the guava. You bite around the rot and hope that it will quench your craving."

"Mr. Alao, it is admirable that you have taken this attitude because this is by no means the end. We are hardly at the beginning. There is a lot to be done before you can even conclude that the 'guava is rotten.' There are tests we must do." Strangely, his heart went out to Baba Segi; he looked like he had been struck with a big whip.

"Tell *her* what she must do next." With that, he waddled out of the door and let it close by itself. The hem of his trousers mopped the length of the corridor.

"Mrs. Alao, I don't want you to worry," the doctor reassured Bolanle. "We haven't seen anything conclusive yet. We haven't even looked. But bearing in mind all you have told me, I have a few suggestions that might bring us closer to a diagnosis. You will need to have a pelvic ultrasound. There is always the risk of damage to the wall of the womb if the procedure isn't done by a qualified surgeon. This often leads to fibrosis—adhesions on the wall of the womb. As you can imagine, a scarred womb is not conducive to fetal development. Dr. Dibia is the gynecologist you will see. His clinics are on Mondays. I will give you a referral letter which you must take to the O & G department on your way out of here. They will check his timetable and book you in. When you return, be sure to bring the results of your pelvic ultrasound with you. You'll also need to do these blood tests. Bring those results as well." He glanced up from his form-filling to find Bolanle absentmindedly pressing a pimple on her face. "Mrs. Alao, there is no reason to be worried."

"I'm not. I am listening to every word you are saying."

"Good. Are you going to be all right? Your husband seemed a little agitated. Is there somewhere you can go?"

"I'll be fine. What more can he do to me? He can't humiliate me any more than he has done already. His other wives can't be any more hostile to me. He is my husband and I will return to his house."

"The environment you have described does not sound very healthy to—"

Bolanle didn't let him finish. "It is good that he has heard the things I said today. Perhaps they should have been said before. The world turns and we do too, within it. Who can say what sins pursue us?" She took the referral letter and the test request forms from the table. "Thank you, Doctor."

Back at the car, Taju could see that his boss was not in the mood for talking and he couldn't help but wonder why he was carrying the stench of loosened bowels. Bolanle, for her part, approached the vehicle with peace in her eyes.

"Take us home!" Baba Segi barked.

"I would like to be dropped off at Awolowo Road junction so I can visit my parents."

"Then we will take you to your father's gate."

"I think it would be better if you went home to change first."

Baba Segi looked at his trousers and shifted to the middle seat. He reasoned that it would be less irksome if he sat in the middle as opposed to sitting by the door. He didn't want to have to stand up to let Bolanle out.

Bolanle pointed her nose outside the window for fresh air. They drove past Sango and stopped at Awolowo junction. As always, there were girls standing under the tree hoping to flag down a taxi. No one wanted to brave the sun and trudge to the taxi stand.

Bolanle reached for the handle. Not caring that Taju was listening, she turned to Baba Segi, one foot firmly placed on the cobbled pavement. "We are to go back next Monday. Our appointment is at ten A.M. and we'll be seeing a different doctor." She flashed the appointment card and the test requests.

"When will you be back home?" It was still too early for him to return to anything related to doctors and hospitals.

"In the evening, probably around six."

"Do not be late for family time!"

CHAPTER FOUR
CRACKS

Bolanle

I SHUT THE VEHICLE DOOR FIRMLY. I waited by the roadside until they were out of sight before crossing. I had no intention of going to see my parents at all; I wanted to see what the market had in store for me.

Sango market was a long, muddy street. Shielded from the sun, the colors under the stalls' rusted iron sheets blended into a collage of dreary hues. The oranges dulled into maroon; the violets and greens smeared into navy blue. Wading through the stalls amid perspiring flesh was exhausting but I was not deterred. I strode directly to the crockery section. My little pleasures were of utmost importance now, since they angered Baba Segi and made him storm out of my bedroom.

It wasn't always like this. In the early days, I used to look forward to Tuesdays. I would wash my hair on Monday afternoon, oil and divide it into sixteen palm-measured mounds, each furrow revealing fine lines of glistening scalp. Baba Segi

liked us women to look like the old Oyo goddesses: queens
who contemplated the lifting of every limb; deities who,
when they heard their names, didn't just turn their heads in
one brisk, carefree movement but lifted their eyes from the
floor and let their faces follow their long proud necks by a
fraction of a second. I'd wanted so much to please him then
that I would rub myself with *osun* so that every strand of hair
dissolved into my skin. I'd go to the market, buy the biggest
snails and painstakingly rinse off their mucus with sea salt
and alum. Fry him a feast and then submit to him.

Things had changed. There was no pleasure in the pleasing, no sweetness in the surrender. Baba Segi only comes to
deposit his seed in my womb. He doesn't smile or tickle me.
He doesn't make jokes about my youth; he just rams me into
the mattress.

Just a month ago, he'd barged into my room. "Get
dressed," he yelled. "God has called a prophet to the moun-
taintop and he will only be there for four more days. Let us go
so he will lay hands on your belly and perform a miracle."

"One of those white-garment con men, no doubt," I said.
I told my husband that the only miracle the prophet would
perform was relieving Baba Segi of his hard-earned money.

"Listen to yourself!" he shouted. "Does your blood not
boil when you see other women carrying babies on their
backs? Do tears not fill your eyes when you see mothers
suckling infants? You of all people should be willing to try
everything! Offspring make our visit to this world complete! Do you want to remain a barren maggot?" He stood

over me, all six and a half feet of him, both arms flailing.

I covered my ears with my hands.

It must have been my vulnerability that turned him on because he returned at midnight to hammer me like never before. He emptied his testicles as deep into my womb as possible. It was as if he wanted to make it clear, with every thrust, that he didn't make light of his husbandly duties. He wanted to fuck me pregnant. If there was ever a moment when the memory of being raped became fresh in my mind, that was it.

I WALKED THROUGH THE MARKET and spotted the tiny second-hand bric-a-brac stall ahead. It was too small to have a decent roof so it was the only place in the market where vibrant colored wares could be honestly and accurately admired. My nose longed for the smell of old brass kettles, my eyes for the caustic stains at the bottom of aged bowls. As soon as my thighs brushed the table, I reached up for an old teacup and stroked the discolored cracks. I ran my knuckles along the chipped rim and felt the muscles in my neck loosen. Then my eyes caught an ivory bowl with embossed turquoise waves. Cherubs bearing goblets reached for the callused rim with stubby fingers. Their faces lit up as the waves washed them round the bowl's belly. I caressed it and my sadness fell away. This was my secret reprisal.

"Dat one come all the way from Italy," the bald crockery hawker shrieked. There were droplets of sweat racing down the sides of his face.

An irritable passerby pushed me toward him. "How much is it?" I asked.

The man swept his forefinger across his forehead. "I won't take a kobo more than five hundred naira from a beetifu' lady like yase'f." He smiled and shrugged his shoulders so that his collar licked the sweat that had gathered around his jawbone.

I dipped my hand deep into my bag, doubled up ten fifty-naira notes and pressed them into the hawker's hand. He looked around surreptitiously, nodded and handed me my prize in a black plastic bag.

When I first arrived in his house, I bought a large orange bowl and presented it to the wives. Iya Femi laughed when she saw it and said *their* husband only ate off white crockery, that he liked his food to supply color at meal times, that his food wasn't worth eating if he couldn't see the red of his palm oil and the green of his okra. I looked around the kitchen. True enough, it was filled with white plates and bland, gray dishes. But before I could snatch back the bowl, Iya Femi deliberately knocked it to the floor, breaking it in two. I picked up the pieces and rushed to my bedroom. Later that evening, Akin knocked on my door to call me for dinner. When I opened it, he handed me an envelope and walked off quickly. Inside was a tube of superglue.

BABA SEGI WILL HATE THIS BOWL, too, the way he hates all the other ones. I give him an eyeful of my decadent colors. It's the only way I get my own back.

I walked to the bus STOP on the far side of the market. Once on the bus, I opened the plastic bag and fingered the nail-sized stain at the bottom of the bowl. I poked it, pricked it and halfheartedly tried to peel it off. When it was clear that it was stuck fast, my stomach twisted with excitement.

Soon, I was on our street. It stretched before me like a lean arm and the Alao house waited at the end of it like a large muscular chest, the bamboo scaffolding flexed, dwarfing the puny lodges around it. As I approached the gates, I spotted an electricity pole that must have been felled by a rainstorm. A naked wire hung on a nearby tree like a stubborn strand of hair. When I get home, I must remember to slip Akin a note. If he comes to my room for help with his English homework, I'll tell him to warn his brothers and sisters not to go near the pole. He always does what I ask him. I won't say anything to the other children so Iya Segi doesn't shout at me.

CHAPTER FIVE
SHARING

Iya Tope

THEY SAY THE ELDER who soils the floor with shit imme-diately forgets, but the stench remains in the memory of the person who has to pack it. Some people are born to shit and some, like Bolanle and me, are born to pack.

Bolanle should have known how much her arrival would change our household. I remember the very day she stepped her foot in this house because it was our sharing night— the night Iya Segi distributed the week's provisions. That evening, our mother-of-the-home was quiet. The stone in her throat moved up and down like beads on a dancer's hip. Iya Femi's head was hot. She wanted the blood of this new wife who had taken her place as the newest, youngest, fresh-est wife.

My only worry was that Bolanle's arrival would disrupt the sex rotation. Baba Segi normally went from wife to wife, starting each week with Iya Segi. By Thursday, he'd start the cycle again, leaving him with the freedom to choose whom to spend Sunday night with. Baba Segi used this night to reward the wife who had missed her night because of her menstrual flow. Sometimes, a wife would have Sunday if he knew he'd been heavy-handed in scolding her.

Most weeks, Iya Femi got Sunday because she enticed him with her groundnut stew, her *ekuru* with shrimp sauce, her yam balls, her *asun*. Baba Segi's belly could not resist her. A more discerning husband would have been evenhanded with his Sundays.

Now that a new wife had joined us, one of us would have only one night a week. Perhaps Iya Segi had many thoughts because she knew this mantle would fall on her. She was the eldest. She'd had him for fifteen years and was approaching the age when enticing your husband to your bedchamber was unnatural. It wouldn't matter to her that she already owned his mind and did with it as she pleased. Some women just want everything.

We all sat around the dining table and Iya Femi made us leap by slapping the wooden surface. Her hands had a horrible yellow glow and her knuckles looked as if they had been scuffed with a stone. I don't understand why human beings are not satisfied with the color the gods have given them. A gold bracelet rested on the back of her hand. She wanted Iya Segi and me to see it so we looked away.

"Is it that our food wasn't tasty enough? Why would Baba Segi marry another wife? Has he condemned our breasts because they are losing their fists?" Iya Femi asked.

Iya Segi clawed at the jar of Gaga's Pomade and shook a dollop into three containers.

"Please, Iya Segi," I pleaded. "My daughters cannot sleep for dandruff. They scratch like lice-ridden dogs all night. Can you not spare me one more scoop?"

"Who cares about your daughters? Do you hear me complain when Iya Segi takes more milk for her children when mine are younger and *need* vitamins?" Iya Femi rolled her eyes and jerked her head in Iya Segi's direction.

At first, the older wife ignored her brazenness and began to rummage through a tin of Bournvita chocolate powder in search of the token that would earn her son a free Nigeria football jersey. When her fingers reappeared, they were coated in brown granules. "Iya Femi, you are in the habit of saying things that are too big for that little mouth of yours. If you are not satisfied with the way I share provisions, take your ingratitude to another man's house. Mind you, make sure you are the first wife and not a lowly third." She tucked the token into her bra.

"Who can tell what the future holds?"

To this, the older wife burst into noiseless laughter and hummed as she closed her mouth. I reminded them that Baba Segi would take care of us all but my words may as well have been the bleating of a goat. The clock in the kitchen struck ten. Not to tell a lie, it seemed strange that the woman Baba Segi was lying with was not one of us.

"I will not be cast aside because she is a graduate!" Iya Femi folded her arms over her bosom. "I do not want her in this house."

"You will trip over in your haste if you are not careful, woman. Your mouth discharges words like diarrhea. Let Bolanle draw on every skill she learned in her university! Let her employ every sparkle of youth! Let her use her fist-full breasts. Listen to me, *this* is not a world she knows. When she doesn't find what she came looking for, she will go back to wherever she came from." Iya Segi pointed to the door.

"Iya Segi, your words are like proverbs," I said.

"*Kruuk.* Let me ask you this: what does our husband value more than what fills his mouth?"

Iya Femi's eyes widened. "Children!"

"Ah! Wisdom at last," Iya Segi said. "When she fails to give him a child, Baba Segi will throw her out! We know she will not give him children so we should watch from a distance. I don't want to see anyone scratching her door frame with their toenails!"

Both women turned to stare at me.

THE NEXT MORNING, BOLANLE CAME OUT of her bedroom. The kitchen fell silent as soon as she cast a shadow on the door frame. She said good morning and winced as she curtsied.

"Your legs resemble those of a collapsible chair." Iya Femi pointed at Bolanle's knees and laughed out loud. "You didn't expect to get that sort of thigh thumping, did you?" She made her voice hoarse. "Tell me, does your back ache?"

"Careful, Iya Femi. Baba Segi has not left the house yet."

Iya Segi couldn't suppress the pleasure she derived from the taunting.

The poor woman looked like she would faint with shame so I offered a bowl of beans. "I just cooked them this morning," I said.

Bolanle looked at the bowl and said she wasn't hungry. She took a plastic cup from the drainer and filled it with drinkable water from a plastic kettle. I didn't blame her. After a night with Baba Segi, the stomach is beaten into the chest by that baton that dangles between his legs.

We all heard the yelp of excitement from the mat. Femi had found a stick and the object of his attention was a small wall gecko that was scrambling down the wall until it was less than a foot from Femi's reach. In a flash, Femi split its head into unequal halves. The creature tumbled down the wall and lay belly-up on the floor. Never in my life had I seen such wickedness. The boy is truly his mother's son.

It surprised me that Bolanle could speak to us after Iya Femi turned her like a spinning top. But they say a child who will play in the dark must first learn how to close its eyes. Bolanle wanted to play in the dark. She did not let Iya Femi's behavior move her eyeballs. The very next day, she came to the sitting room and asked if any of us wanted to learn how to read. Iya Femi stood up and hissed until she reached her bedroom door. Iya Segi's knee began to shake as if she would kick a hole into Bolanle's head but she just continued to count her money. I slowly lifted my hand. The look Iya Segi gave me could have thrown me from my seat. But what could I do? What would you do if you could not understand the words that your own children were reading?

The first day, I sat at the table and watched her show me how to write "A." Small "a" and big "A." I copied the letter out myself. Even though she said it was upside down and not quite right, my stomach was swollen with pride. Me! Writing!

That night, Iya Segi came to my bedroom and told me she would destroy my useless life if I ever sat to learn anything from Bolanle again. What could I do? On the right was the person who gave me provisions and held my life and the lives of my daughters in the middle of her palm. On my left was the wife who wanted to teach me to read and write, the wife who did not yet know that she could also be crushed by Iya Segi's powerful fist. The choices we have to make in this world are hard and bitter. Sometimes we have no choices at all. I did not go near the dining room at noon. In fact, I did not answer when Bolanle came to knock on my room. What would I do with reading anyway? Even if I learned how to read, what would I do with it? How would I use it?

That was how it was. Bolanle would bring suggestions. Iya Segi would listen and shake her knee and Iya Femi would hiss for the world to hear. I learned to keep my head down and sing in my mind so I would not hear the sound of their voices.

After a few months, the same Iya Segi who said we should watch Bolanle from a distance started to boil. She called me and Iya Femi to a meeting, saying that there were words to be spoken. These words were curses and insults. You see, the more Bolanle puffed out her chest, the smaller Iya Segi became. Iya Segi told us she had changed her plan, that it was no longer enough to wait until Bolanle's barrenness made Baba Segi chase her out. Iya Segi said we had to join hands and force her out. "Don't you see her high brow and unconcerned eyes? She thinks we are beneath her. She wants our husband to cast us aside as 'the illiterate ones,'" she said. "As a wife who has recently joined our household, it is her duty to submit herself useful to our wishes, not to think she can teach us!"

I pointed out that Bolanle was kind to the children. What I really wanted to say was that it seemed Bolanle had learned to keep her suggestions deep in her stomach. In recent weeks, she had been keeping to her bedroom, only coming out when she was summoned. Was that not enough for them?

"Iya Segi is right. She walks around as if she owns this house. Who made her queen over us?" Envy seeped through every word that came out of Iya Femi's mouth. "And look at all the lace Baba Segi buys her! What has she done to deserve it?"

"But our husband has always bought the same for us all!" I said. I was amazed that Iya Femi was still so bitter about Bolanle's arrival. Iya Segi and I hadn't despised her this way when she joined us.

"Why are you defending her? Is it the same blood that runs through your veins? Is your allegiance faltering? Or have you forgotten that we are bound by the same oath?" Iya Femi asked.

I opened my mouth but the words stuck to the walls of my throat.

"Let us only speak words that will push this matter forward. This girl has already been here five months but I know there will be trouble if she stays."

"Iya Segi, you must have the gift of the Holy Spirit. In my church, just last Sunday, a prophet saw a vision while he was praying for me. He said he saw a dark cloud edging toward me, heavy with rain. He said the cloud would blow past but when he looked in my direction, I was standing without a thread of cloth on my body."

My hand flew to my mouth. Nakedness was never a good thing.

"Now that we are all lying with our heads in the same direction, we must work together to blow this cloud away! These educated types have thin skins; they are like pigeons. If we poke her with a stick, she will fly away and leave our home in peace."

The first thing Iya Segi did was to talk to Baba Segi about Bolanle's armchair. Baba Segi had broken his rule for Bolanle. The tradition was that the comfort of an armchair had to be earned, which meant that unless you were pregnant with edema, breastfeeding or watching over toddlers, you were not entitled to one. To impress his new wife, Baba Segi spent thirty minutes in the dimly lit storeroom dusting, slapping and wiping before finally pushing another armchair into the living room.

Iya Segi and Iya Femi shook with anger when she sat

among us. I asked myself: what is in a chair? Is it not just to sit down? Did she not have a chair in her father's house? But Baba Segi soon started to grumble about the flatness of Bolanle's belly and Iya Segi seized this opportunity to advise him that comfort made the female form complacent. She reminded him that she would know because she was a woman. Bolanle's armchair was returned to the store the next day. When Bolanle came into the living room, Iya Femi could not contain her mischievous smile and offered her a cushion. Baba Segi avoided Bolanle's eyes the entire evening.

The second evil thing that Iya Segi did was banish Bolanle's friends from our house. After Yemisi and other friends visited for the third time, Iya Segi told our husband that they were bad role models for the daughters in the family, especially her daughter, Segi, who was at an impressionable age. Baba Segi jumped at the notion as if he had been looking for a reason to keep Bolanle to himself. He told Bolanle that he didn't want unmarried women near his doorstep. Bolanle received Baba Segi's instructions without a word. She never once looked at our husband with annoyance in her eyes. She just said she had things to buy at the market and quietly slipped out of the house.

IYA SEGI WAS WRONG ABOUT the skin of educated types. The more those two poked Bolanle, the more mercy her eyes showed, the more her hands opened to the children. I have never known anyone like Bolanle before. Even after two years of their wickedness, she still greets them every morning. What more do they want?

Just two weeks ago, my stomach was as hard as a fresh drum. For four days, I had not relieved myself. The more I ate, the harder my stomach became. Iya Segi saw me that morning but she did not ask me about the pain that drew tears from my eyes. She looked away and walked past me. Iya Femi saw my bloodshot eyes too but she just hissed, like she always does, as if I was an animal by the roadside. If not for Bolanle, maybe my stomach would have split open that day. She waited for the other wives to leave the house and came to knock on my door. She said she had seen that I was walking around like a woman pregnant with a grown man. I told her what was bothering me and she ran to the kitchen to fetch three glasses of water. She told me to drink them and wait for her.

I don't know where she went, but soon after she ran back with a shopping bag. The two tablets she gave me chased me to the toilet. I thought I would find my intestines on the floor. I sat there for a whole hour, but when I finished I felt like a human being again.

IT DID NOT SURPRISE ME when Iya Segi called a meeting on the morning that Baba Segi took Bolanle to the hospital. "That Bolanle is a troublemaker," she said. "She will destroy our home. She will expose our private parts to the wind. She will reveal our secret. She will bring woe." Bolanle always tied Iya Segi's tongue in a knot.

"What are we going to do?" Iya Femi asked. She locked her fingers over the dome of her head. "We must do something quickly!"

"Have we not done enough already? I don't think I want to be part of this anymore," I said. I don't know what came over me.

Iya Femi picked me up with her eyes and threw me to the floor.

Iya Segi shook her head and belched. "Listen to the fool who begs for crumbs from Bolanle's table! The lickspittle! It is all right for you to say you do not want to be part of us, after you have benefitted from my wisdom all these years. Now you wish to remove yourself? Well, you can't! You are bound to us. We are all bound together! And if you dare to open that stupid mouth of yours, I will ruin you myself. I will tell my husband things that will make him wring your neck in your sleep. Go! Take your small brain out of my sight. Imbecile!"

I left them in the sitting room so I don't know what they are planning. I fear for Bolanle but I am a coward. I know I should show Bolanle the arm of friendship. I should not pretend she is a stranger when the other wives are around. I should tell her to be careful but I can't. I am afraid of these women. I will just keep quiet and watch. What else can a shit packer do?

CHAPTER SIX
RAT HEAD

I F BOLANLE HAD KNOWN what lay in wait for her, perhaps she wouldn't have ventured to spend so long in the market, wandering from stall to stall. Before she spotted the small crowd gathered in front of her home, she smelled Mama Elepa's groundnuts burning. As Bolanle moved closer, she was sure she could make out Mama Elepa's fragile frame on their veranda, bent over from decades of carting firewood. Most of the women she saw were standing with their hands clasped behind their backs. Some had their hands on their heads and were hopping from leg to leg as if their bladders held them hostage. Taju was leaning against a pillar scratching his chin.

Iya Segi's voice was loudest. "Woe," she yelled.

Iya Femi was screaming in tongues. Iya Tope had an arm around Segi but the arm was limp like a wet cloth. Segi's eyes were red from weeping. Everyone looked around nervously.

"*She* wants to kill him!" Iya Segi pointed when Bolanle was within a few steps of the commotion.

"What did my father ever do to her? I am not married yet. She wants to kill my father with *juju* before he walks me down the aisle!" Segi flopped to the concrete floor and the spectators standing by rushed to her aid.

"Of what use is she? She cannot have children. Her womb is dead. She wants to kill our husband to save herself from shame. I am too young to be a widow," Iya Femi added.

As soon as Bolanle stepped onto the concrete floor of the veranda, the crowd went quiet. The bystanders parted and created a path for her. When she got to the sitting room, Baba Segi was in his armchair. His arms were slung over the sides, his great legs stretched out in front of him like logs.

"Good evening, Baba Segi. Why have you not changed your clothes?" Bolanle asked.

"Where have you been?"

"It is not even six yet. I am here on time like I said I would be."

"The question I am asking is: where have you been?" His voice was deep and hollow, like the aftermath of a drumbeat.

"So I can't even leave the house now?" It was a daring response.

In a flash, Baba scrambled up the back of his seat and leaped into the air like a gorilla in flight. He landed bang in front of Bolanle and gripped her throat with both hands. He squeezed hard and shook her, pressing his thumbs on her windpipe. "Who are *you* asking questions? Do I look like a fool? You said you were going to your father's house. Taju has just come back from there. Nobody there has seen you today! Where have you been?"

"The market! I went to the market." Her voice was hoarse from the pressure. "You can kill me, Baba Segi, but I only went to the market. Look at the bowl I bought."

Baba Segi searched her face and thought how strange it was that there was no fear in it, just pain. He glanced to the side and saw the plastic bag a few inches from her open palm. He let his arms drop to his sides.

Bolanle collapsed onto the floor.

Akin made to run toward Bolanle but Iya Segi's arm shot out from her side and held him in his tracks. His mother's arm was steadfast so he bowed his head and ran down the road.

Iya Tope knelt beside Bolanle. With Baba Segi towering over them, she slapped Bolanle's cheeks lightly. "Tell him, Bolanle. Tell him if you did it. Tell him. He will forgive you. We have all offended our husband before. He always forgives us. Confess to him."

Bolanle spluttered and grabbed her throat. The dry weather had split her lips and a solitary droplet of blood trickled from one of the creases in them.

"Tope, bring me some water." Iya Tope didn't take her eyes off Bolanle until her daughter returned with half a plastic cup of warm, recently boiled water. Iya Tope sprinkled some on Bolanle's face and placed the cup to her lips.

Bolanle looked up at the woman cradling her face in the crook of her arm. "Confess to what?"

Baba Segi marched to the stool beside his armchair and produced a see-through polyethylene bag. "This!" He spat, pinching the bag at the corner farthest away from what it contained. At the bottom of the bag, looking vaguely surprised by all the attention it was getting, was the head of a decomposed rodent, a large bush rat perhaps. "Tell me why I found this in my bedroom!"

There were bits of dried flesh stuck to it. Its mouth was bound together by red thread. A four-inch nail had been knocked into the crown of its head, shattering the skull at the point of entry, then driven all the way in until it protruded out of the rodent's throat.

Bolanle's face hardened. "How can I confess to something I know nothing about? Strangle me. Kill me. But first ask yourself if I would descend this low? Would I descend to this? Would I touch something so revolting? Do you really think I would go to a *babalawo*, let alone ask for something that would harm you? If I didn't want to be with you, would I not just leave?"

Iya Segi was by the door. She saw the opening and jumped in. "Who can tell why she would do this, Baba Segi? She wants to kill you first and then leave. She is a destroyer of homes! Why didn't she go to the abattoir if she was thirsty for blood? There is no blood for you here, Bolanle. There is no blood for you here. *Kruuk.*" She paused and turned to Iya Tope. "We have been suspicious for some months now, haven't we, Iya Tope?"

Iya Tope looked up at the older wife. She opened her

mouth but no words came out. She tried again but her lips just opened and closed like a fish anticipating a maggot.

"Iya Segi, I have never desired blood in my life." Bolanle felt tears welling up in her eyes but she blinked them back.

"Then why was *this* found in your bedroom?" Baba Segi's voice was calmer now. He was beginning to see that things didn't quite add up but he decided to see it through so he could observe her reactions. "Stand up and come and see for yourself. *I* will not touch it." He sighed with relief when Bolanle crawled toward whatever it was that Baba Segi had pushed beneath a stool. In a small calabash, there was a spool of once-white thread half-immersed in a pool of blood.

"Unspeakable!" Bolanle hissed. She turned and looked up at Baba Segi. "Do you think so little of me?"

Baba Segi looked away but Iya Segi would not let it go. "Oh, it is unspeakable now you've been found out! Who would have known that all those times you left the house, you were visiting a *babalawo*? Who would have thought that a *graduate* would stoop to something so *unspeakable*?" Iya Segi pronounced the word "unspeakable" like she was swallowing a single ear of corn. A clucking started deep within her double chin.

Bolanle put one hand on the side of her neck and grimaced. She let her head roll round in a full circle before turning to her husband. She shook her head and coughed to clear her throat. "I have nothing to say, Baba Segi, except that I do not know where these things came from. There must be some mistake. I have never seen anything like this before."

To the small crowd that had gathered in the sitting room, Bolanle said, "I say, I have never seen these things before in my life. Neither do I want to, ever again. Why would I want to kill my husband? If I become tired of my husband, there isn't a policeman in the world that can force me to stay with him. I am here because I want to be here!" She exhaled long and meaningfully. "I have lived in his house for two years and I want to continue to stay if my husband will have me. Only today, we went to the doctor to see how I could bear his children. I do not want to die barren. How is it profitable for me to become a young widow? Why would I want *my* child or any of these young children to be fatherless?" Her hands reached to brush Femi's head but he ducked.

Everyone looked on in sympathy and Segi wiped away her tears with the back of her hand. Iya Segi read the situation and stole into the crowd like a giant hen skulking to a secret stash of corn.

Just over his breath, Baba Segi said, "Bolanle, you can go to your room."

To everyone's surprise, Iya Femi catapulted herself toward him from the edge of the crowd. "Go to her room?" she shrieked. "Is it after she has killed us all that you will do the right thing? If this woman is allowed to sleep in this house, I will sleep outside with my sons. I will hold a night vigil and pray her out." She bounced on the balls of her feet, her upstretched arms exposing clumps of armpit hair.

"Iya Femi, you can sleep in the gutter if you want to." Baba Segi's voice was calm but anger had returned to his eyes.

"That is where you came from. My sons were not born to sleep in the gutter so they cannot follow you. Iya Tope, take my sons to bed. This woman's mouth will soon get what it deserves."

"Anyone who touches my sons may not live to tell the tale!"

"Has this woman's head scattered that she now scrubs my mouth? Have my words become so insignificant that they can now be contested?" He opened one of his hands to the crowd as if they would deposit the answers to his questions into his palm. "Iya Segi! Iya Segi!"

Perched on a crumbling concrete block by the side wall, Iya Segi remained still until several voices echoed her husband's call. "I am here, my lord!"

"This house is a mess. Clean it!"

"Right away, my lord."

Their voyeuristic thirsts quenched, everyone got the message and began to agitate for a speedy exit. The spectacle had been gratifying, the outcome glorious.

BABA SEGI COULDN'T BEAR to stay at home that evening so he drove himself to Ayikara. "I could have killed her with my bare hands. My own wife! It was as if a wild beast from inside me wanted to suck blood from her throat." Baba Segi didn't want the three men in the far corner of the shack to hear him. It didn't matter that there was an empty bottle of Teacher's whiskey on the table in front of them or that the few phrases

they exchanged were slurred and incoherent. This was a matter Baba Segi did not want to discuss with strangers.

"And you say she did not fight back?"

"No, she was calm. What fight can a fly fight when it is in
the clutches of a tarantula?" Baba Segi muttered and looked
away.

"Calm is not the reaction of someone who has been caught
red-fingered. Remind me. How did your other wives react to
this discovery? You mentioned that—"

"That is what I don't understand." Baba Segi cut him
short. "Apart from one of them who seemed as perplexed as
I was, the other two were adamant that Bolanle had planted
the *juju*. They were convinced that she was guilty."

"Hmm." Teacher smirked and nodded knowingly. "What
are relations like between Bolanle and these other wives?
There must be a reason why they were fighting tongue and
nail for her to confess."

"Well, in recent months, I myself have been hostile to
the young woman but only because of this question of her
barrenness. Her unwillingness to submit to my earlier solutions also hardened my heart. I have not been warm to her.
It has always been hard for me to hide what is inside. I think
perhaps my wives noticed this and copied me."

"So they want you to send her away and you think it a
reaction to *your* unhappiness."

"I know they do. They said so in my presence, in *her*
presence."

"Why have they not attempted to mediate? From what

you've always said about your first wife, I had come to believe she was of a more agreeable temperament."

"I would be lying if I said she wasn't. That woman knows every thought that enters my head. She knows when I am thirsty and when my belly is full. She knows I have been disgruntled about Bolanle and I suspect she just wants to relieve me of my troubles."

"But planting *juju* is excessive. Why use a hammer to swat an insect?" As if to illustrate his point, Teacher elegantly flicked a fly from his shot glass.

"It must have seemed reasonable to her given how displeased I've been. I agree with you though. It was as if Esu himself came to dine in my house yesterday evening. I tell you, I could have killed Bolanle." Baba Segi folded his arms and shook his head.

"Listen, Baba Segi, perhaps you are partly to blame for what has happened. Your partiality is the cause of these problems. Women do not hesitate to become cannibals when they are hungry. That is why I have never kept one. Some people laugh about this behind my back but what they don't know is this: he who does not have a head has no need for a cap."

"Indeed."

"But back to the trouble in your household: it is my belief that the solution lies with you. And I can tell you that her being educated is not helping matters either." His finger rapped on the side of his glass.

"I don't understand."

Teacher took a sip from his whiskey and winced when

he swallowed. "What I mean is that she is different. It may well be that your other wives are slightly *uncomfortable* about this. They may think it gives her an edge." Teacher chose his words carefully.

"What sort of edge? I do not sleep with any one more than the others!"

"It is more complicated than that. It could be that they are envious."

"That, I can rule out." Baba Segi was afraid that Teacher would suggest that he too was prone to such.

A smile tickled the corners of Teacher's lips but he didn't submit to it. "If you are sure that this is not the case then it all lies in your hands. Treat your wives equally. Blacken the kettle as you blacken the pots."

CHAPTER SEVEN
QUEEN

Iya Femi

WHEN A PLAN DOES not go right, you plot again. One day you will get it right. One day you will be able to damage the person who hurts you so completely that they will never be able to recover. I have told Iya Segi this on several occasions. I keep telling her that we need to find a permanent solution but she does not have wisdom. She says we should continue to humiliate Bolanle until she runs away. "Let us cut her feathers," she says.

Well, the bird has shown that she can fly without feathers. I knew we should have gone for her throat. We should have bled her into a hole in the earth!

Yes, I said finally. I have suffered too much in my life to let that rat spoil it all for me. So what if she is a graduate? When we stand before God on the last day, will He ask whether we went to university? No! But He will want to know if we were as wise as serpents because that's what the Bible says we should be.

If we let Bolanle ruin us, then we would all have failed before God. I reject failure in Jesus's name. I will not fail. The prophets in my church have seen that this rat has an evil spirit. I can't say God has not revealed it to me too. He shows Himself to all who serve Him in spirit and in truth. I'm glad Iya Segi has come round to my thinking. She has now seen that we need to do something. Now that Baba Segi has decided to take the rat to the hospital, time is short.

When Bolanle first arrived, I scrubbed Bolanle's tongue with bitter leaf! Ha! I made her understand who was in charge of this house. I showed the sting of hot peppers. If she comes to this world again, she will run if she hears the name Iya Femi.

Let me tell you one of the things I did. Laughter kills me when I think of it. I don't think she had been with us for a year when Baba Segi asked me to make *aso ebi* for the entire household. The neighbor's birthday was in two weeks time and he wanted us all dressed in the same fabric from top to bottom. "I want you all to look like queens," he said. I looked at him and wondered why, if he wanted wives that looked like queens, he married a woman like a toad and a scrawny rabbit that nibbles at Bolanle's burrow.

And that Bolanle! Is that his idea of a queen? Being a graduate does not make you beautiful. I know true beauty. And it is in pale yellow skin. I was born darker than this but I use expensive creams to make my natural beauty shine. I take my nails to a proper nail studio. I buy good makeup, unlike that Bolanle, who wanders around with her face as haggard as a sack. Ha! Queens indeed!

Anyway, on the day I went to collect the clothes, I came out of the house and heard Bantu's "No More No Vernacular" screaming from giant speakers on the neighbor's fence. I danced into the pickup, leaving the entire family waiting in the sitting room.

The tailor's store was only twenty minutes away but I stopped at a few places. By the time I got home, even my sons were sweating from anticipation. I rushed into the sitting room, arms laden, and surrendered the pile of clothes to the stool by Iya Segi's feet. The witch sniffed the air around me. She must have picked up the scent on my thighs.

I heard Baba Segi's voice. "I was waiting for the tailor to put finishing touches to your clothes," I said. "Would you have preferred it if I came home without them? It is wonderful that we will all be dressed the same!"

Ha! Sometimes I wish I could pat myself on the back. My cunning knows no bounds!

For a few moments, Iya Segi stared at the outfits. The children couldn't conceal their impatience. "Mama, the clothes!" Akin pretended to cough as he spoke so his mother wouldn't think him wayward.

Iya Segi cocked her head with interest before reaching for the pile and placing it on her lap. The witch touched all the clothes before anyone, as if she wanted to render them secondhand. She fingered the plastic buttons and touched the threading before giving each outfit to its respective owner. One by one, everyone stepped forward to collect their outfit. Iya Segi told Iya Tope to drop Bolanle's clothes by her bedroom door. She said everyone should return to the sitting room in thirty minutes so we could set off to the party.

I got dressed quickly and headed to the sitting room so I could see everyone come in. Iya Segi caught me in the corridor as she came out of the bathroom. She ran her eyes over my outfit. "Such beautiful gold thread! Such fine sequins!" she said. Her throat was thick with fury.

"The tailor said he ran out of sequins when he started to sew yours. He said the girl who sold them to him was in confinement. But if you want, let us exchange. I'll wear yours and you can wear mine." I even started to unzip my blouse at the side. Ha! She would be lucky if she could fit just one of her breasts into my entire blouse. She hissed and turned into her bedroom.

Baba Segi joined me soon after to inspect us the way he always did. As the children walked in, he looked with pride at the parade of red stars against royal blue. He nodded as his eyes went from face to face.

Iya Segi soon waddled in. Her dress resembled a pillowcase with long sleeves and a ruffled collar that extended all the way up to her ears. That neck of hers is an embarrassment. If she always wore clothes with high collars, maybe she would eat less. Maybe she'd stop grunting like a pig when she eats.

Iya Tope, for her part, looked no different from her three

daughters. Did she not behave like them? Was she any cleverer than they were? I told the tailor to sew the skirt two sizes too big, and her blouse baggy and without darts. The neck gaped and slid off one of her shoulders. As usual, she didn't say anything; she was more concerned about Bolanle, who had just emerged from her bedroom.

Bolanle's outfit looked like it had been knocked together by a roguish hand. To be honest, I sewed it myself. I watched the tailor on a few occasions and made the skirt from the discolored ends that he did away with. Instead of the square meter that the rest of the wives received as headgear, Bolanle's head was bound by a bright purple strip of cloth about eight inches wide. I don't even remember where the cloth came from. Her face was bland as if there wasn't a single thought in her head. Who knows what the lizard was thinking! Everyone stared at her. Iya Tope drew her palm to her lips but Iya Segi's eyes began to twinkle. Ha! I knew she would like it!

My husband finally asked me to stand up. You can trust me. I gave him the queen he asked for. My skirt was fitted and the slit rode just above my knee. My blouse was adorned with crystals and the darts shaped my figure and lifted my breasts. I was well accessorized too: matching court shoes and bag; coral beads on my wrists; and a large, gold crucifix around my neck. It was a good day.

Back to the present problem: Iya Segi and I decided to meet on our own after the rat head incident.

"That stupid Iya Tope ruined it all!" I said.

"Let us thank the gods that she did not tell Bolanle

beforehand. I thought she would drag Bolanle to her bedroom to breastfeed her! Iya Tope's foolishness could start a village war. The only chance we had was to be united. Now see how Bolanle marches about the house gloating." The stone in Iya Segi's throat was traveling up and down like a man's. "Iya Tope is like the demon who accused the gnomes of mischief. He woke up to find his sword inside his own belly and there was nothing he could do! Nothing! He lay in the forest with his blood clotting at his side, too weak to stand, too frail to shout."

"Iya Segi, forget about Iya Tope! Let us take care of this matter ourselves. We have the wisdom and the strength. Between the two of us, we can restore this home to what it was."

"You have spoken well, Iya Femi. You have spoken the truth."

CHAPTER EIGHT
TRADE

Iya Segi

THE BLOOD THAT RUNS through the daughters that Iya Tope brought into this home of mine is dirty. Her children are sickly. Not long after Bolanle arrived, Iya Tope sat in the sitting room looking for pity. She likes to sit around the house plaiting her daughters' hair like a beggar in the marketplace. Motun had a fever that morning and Baba Segi insisted that she stay at home. When the other girls heard that they would be separated from their sister, they sobbed and wept. The middle one, Afolake, strained and wriggled in her seat. Tope begged to stay at home so she could look after her sisters. I do not tolerate such rubbish so I told the older two I would whip them all the way to their classrooms if they did not get into the bus.

"I don't understand these children of yours," I told Iya Tope. "The affection they have for each other has become unhealthy. They are like forsaken triplets lost in a forest. *Kruuk*.

Each unable to survive without the others. They want to eat from the same plate, wear the same hairstyle, speak with the same voice! Will they marry the same husband?"

After dropping the children at school, I returned home to find Iya Tope in the sitting room. As I stepped onto the veranda outside, I heard Bolanle asking Iya Tope if the child was better.

"Much better, thank you. I swathed her in a wet cloth for about ten minutes. My children do not cope well without sleep. They scratch their heads all night. Look!"

As I entered, Iya Tope was parting her daughter's hair with the wooden comb to reveal a line of scalp that was scabby in parts and freshly clawed in others.

"I have hair cream that is good for dandruff. Let me get some for you," Bolanle suggested.

"Iya Tope, why are you begging for hair cream?" I asked. "Are you not satisfied with what your husband gives you that you now have to scrounge? You should be ashamed of yourself!"

"*I* offered," Bolanle said.

"I am the one you should come to when you are in need! In fact, I think Baba Segi should hear of this ingratitude!"

"I did not ask for hair cream so there is nothing to tell Baba Segi." Iya Tope reached behind her daughter and produced a container with nothing more than a smidgen of cream in it.

Iya Tope shifted a fraction of an angle in her seat; it was clear she was no longer receptive to Bolanle's company, or her conversation. She busied herself with her daughter's hair and said nothing. Bolanle noticed it and left the room.

It is important that the wives know their place in this house. They must know what they can and cannot do. They must remember that I am the only one who can do business, not that they've shown a desire to—Iya Femi has sworn never to do another day's work in her life and Iya Tope doesn't have a head for trade. What am I saying? She doesn't have a head for reasoning!

I had to use all my wisdom to force Baba Segi's hand. After giving birth to Akin, my second child, a son for that matter, I knew the ache in Baba Segi's balls would subside. That's when I made his head spin with worry.

It started with the sighing. I would lie next to him in bed and sigh. He didn't seem to take notice so I'd sigh, sit up and shake my head hopelessly. I had to do this on several occasions before it finally occurred to Baba Segi that he may not be a perfect husband if his wife is saddened. Men are like that. They think they sit in the center and the world turns around them.

When he inquired what was causing my distress, I told him it was nothing and blew my nose into my wrapper. After a few weeks of this, I took to crying. I thought thinking sad thoughts would bring tears to my eyes but I found I couldn't evoke any. It was as if my mind had decided that my life had been without adversity. I had to use onions—my hands always smelled of them anyway. One night after Baba Segi had climbed off me, I smeared my eyeballs with onion juice.

Baba Segi couldn't take my sniveling; he sat up and turned on the light. "What is it that has twisted your insides, my wife?" There was both weariness and earnestness in his voice.

"It is nothing, my lord." The time was not exactly right.

"That is all you say! Nothing! Nothing! Nothing! Yet you weep like a mourner!"

"It's nothing." I cried silently so I would not wake my children in their cots.

"Is it the house?"

I shook my head. *Almost.*

"Is it me? Is there something you want to do?"

"My lord, my hands itch for work."

"Work? Are your hands not full with the children you are taking care of?"

I dropped to my knees and told him of my wish to have a small stall where I could sell sweets wholesale, interact with other women and learn of new recipes, the best household detergents on the market, better ways to please a husband. I slipped it in when I noticed each blink weighed down his eyelids longer than the one before. "I also want to attend driving school."

He raised both eyebrows and widened his eyes.

"I will be able to take my children to day care without them sweltering in the heat like poverty-stricken orphans."

Shutting his eyes tight, he stretched up his arms and yawned. He lay back down, slid his bottom down the bed and covered himself with a sheet. When he'd sufficiently burrowed into his pillow with the back of his head, he asked, "If

I permit you to do these things, will a man be able to sleep in his own house?"

"Long and soundly, my lord. Long and soundly."

Within months, I informed him that wholesale sweets were no longer lucrative and that a wise woman had advised me to try selling cement. A few weeks later, this same mysterious woman (who lived her life for her husband) advised me to extend my stall and build a proper shop. Before the year had run out, I was talking of a second shop, but only so I could be nearer to the children. Men are so simple. They will believe anything.

"Does your friend approve of this?" Baba Segi asked as he undressed one night.

"Which one?" I asked before thinking, but corrected myself quickly. "You mean my friend from the market? Did I not I tell you that she died?"

"Died?"

"Yes, just like that. She just . . . er . . . slumped and died. The lucky woman has departed this world of sin and strife."

"This is very unfortunate. Did you attend the funeral?"

"You forget that I have two children and a husband to look after. She was a Muslim so they buried her the day after. Let us pray the wind that carries her soul to heaven will be a gentle one so that the journey will be without turbulence."

That is how I started my business. And that is how I learned to drive. Men are like yam. You cut them how you like.

One day, about three months after Bolanle arrived, I was in the sitting room, counting my money. I wouldn't usually be at home at this time of morning but I wanted to rent a new shop space, and the previous owner demanded payment that afternoon. I had shops in most of the major markets—Mokola, Dugbe, Eleyele, Sango—but I wanted to have one in Ojoo, too. Rather than rush to the bank and endure hours in the queues, I decided to take from the stash I hid under my mattress at home, to save time.

The banknotes were old, crumpled and dirty but that has never bothered me. I sat in one of the armchairs and crammed a stool into the little small space between my knees. I handle money with great affection. I like the feel of it on my palm so I turned each note meticulously until I could see the man in all of them.

I didn't know that our stray hen had brought friends until I heard them rattling down the corridor. I pulled my skirt over the stool. They greeted me and I greeted them back. "I hope we will see you again soon," I said. I meant to address both visitors but I couldn't stop my gaze from returning to Yemisi. As soon as the door closed behind them, I jumped out of my armchair and looked through a hole in my clenched fist so I could see Yemisi's perfect form. Ah, if only desire didn't always carry trouble on its back. Now is not the time, I told myself. There is a time for everything.

CHAPTER NINE
IYA TOPE

NINE YEARS AGO, I came home from the farm to find Baba Segi sitting in my father's hut. I was twenty-three years old, I remember. It was later in the year that my older brother declared that I was ripe for marriage. My mother did not tell him to mind his mouth. Instead, without raising her face from the heap of melon seeds, she added, "Truth be told, she is bordering on decay." I cannot forget that day. Not because their words did not cause me sorrow but because I remember thinking how unjust it was that the gods had blessed *them* with such wondrous eyes. How was it that they could see the womanhood that I—on whose body it was plastered—could not? Within me, I was certain I was still a child. I thought like a child and enjoyed childish pleasures like pursuing ants as they carried away sugar lumps and scratching hardened scabs from the edge of my old wounds. I even conversed with friends that only I could see.

My father was from a long line of cassava farmers who learned to hoe cassava mounds before the age of three and hacked the brown nuggets from the soil until the day they too were planted in fertile land. Unlike most villages, ours did not have a school or electricity. The nearest school was six miles down the expressway. Elders scowled at the more eager pupils. The time it took to walk to school and back could be better spent, they said. By the time hair sprouted from the armpits, most children had their own cassava stalls on the edge of the highway. As for electricity, we didn't send gifts to the local government chief like other villages. We were simple people: what the ground didn't give, we didn't yearn for.

Most people looked forward to the planting season but I hated it. I detested the hoeing and wished away the heavy watering cans. So when it was time for planting, I complained of backache. I lay groaning on my mat while my brothers and sisters unfastened their hoes from the nails that jutted out of the hut wall. As I rolled from side to side clutching my back, I dreamed of the day weeds would cluster around the cassava shoots. Weeding, I loved. I loved the feel of the small leaves, the strength of the stems. I loved shaking the soil from the roots and laying them in a row. Sometimes I liked to hawk them to my imaginary friends. Good fresh spinach! Buy your fresh spinach!

My father called me one day and asked when exactly I planned to finish weeding the family vegetable patch.

"Soon, Baba. And when I finish, I will start again," I replied.

"Your age-mates are planting, grinding, drying and sell-ing, but you creep around the farm, sweating over weeds until your shadow lengthens."

"I am thorough, Baba. With weeding, you must be thor-ough."

"My daughter, men want women who can work beside them on the farm, not behind them! Your younger sister has suitors who would climb a thousand trees to win her hand. Are you not concerned that no one has turned their mouths to talk of marrying you?"

"Maybe the men you speak of have not seen how thor-oughly I can weed."

"Have you not heard the words I have spoken?" He let out a long breath and seized his walking stick. Without another glance in my direction, he drew lines on the earthen floor: a cluster of strokes and then, about a yard apart, one stroke standing all by itself.

In those days, it was common for wealthy men who owned *gari* factories in Ibadan to dazzle village farmers with their big cars and big money talk. They leased farmland and paid the villagers to tend the crops that grew on it. Their goal was to reap the yield from crops that they had never nurtured. My brother said that was the way of the rich.

The year before, my father had been greatly pleased when he waved good-bye to two trucks full of hefty cassava tubers. He received more money than he had ever seen and he kept the wad of crisp notes in his trouser pocket for days, smil-ing every time his knuckles brushed against them. Baba Segi had returned for another prosperous harvest the following year but he was met by fidgety fingers and eyes that darted downward, sideways, then upward to the gods. My father was afraid so he gave Baba Segi the news in full view of the entire village.

Sitting on a bench next to my father, Baba Segi looked like an insatiable demon. His skin was oily and supple whereas my father's was flaky and dry like *orogbo* shells. Baba Segi's shiny face didn't show any reaction to the news but his toes flapped in leather slippers like the ears of a dog. Then, quite unexpectedly, he looked around and seized a boy by the arm. "Take me to the toilet," he begged. Every eye watched Baba Segi as he barged through the door of the unroofed pit latrine. We heard every rumble, every gurgle, every fart and every splutter. When Baba Segi emerged, he reoccupied the space on the bench and told the dumbstruck villagers that everything happened for a reason and that he was thinking of a new business anyway. He added that the ways of the gods were mysterious.

The truth was that the rains had punished the village of Borode by refusing to fall and the sun had dealt mercilessly with the cassava shoots. Instead of standing high and cooling the soil with their broad green leaves, they stooped and coiled until they were toasted like bristles. The ground hardened and split from the heat, forcing anxious villagers to journey to the forest in search of water to moisten the soil. Even my father, with his bent back, followed the trail of water fetchers. He got on his knees and scooped sand until his fingers touched water.

I was frustrated too. No water meant no weeds. Since the sun denied me my joy that year, I hid under the pile of mats at home, as far away from its wrath as possible. It was only when I heard the wind carrying voices home from the forest path that I abandoned my hiding place to help them ease calabashes off their heads. My father's wives sneered at my helpfulness and my mother hid her face behind her wrapper.

On the day Baba Segi was to cart off his bad harvest, my father sat on a stool outside his hut and stared at the miserable baskets, six in number. His legs were stretched out in front of him and his chin rested on his walking stick. When I surfaced from my mother's hut to slice okra, I greeted him. He didn't respond but followed me with his eyes. He made me feel so self-conscious that I took my okra back into my mother's hut. Soon afterward, Baba Segi's pickup appeared at the end of the dusty road. My father shouted my name and instructed me to turn out a large mound of *amala* to be accompanied by *efo* made from the freshest spinach leaves I could find. My father didn't wait for Baba Segi's feet to touch the ground; he scooped him out of the pickup and into the darkness of his hut.

It did not take me any time to prepare the meal so when I finished, I joined my mother and her co-wives in the shade of palm fronds. My siblings sat there too, slapping off gnats that perched on their bare shoulders. I found it strange that they were being so quiet. They normally talked with their mouths, their arms, their necks, their eyes and their lips. They talked about everything from the texture of snake meat to the oval guavas by the riverbed. Sitting in the middle of this strange, heavy silence, I wondered whether I should seize the opportunity to say something. It didn't look like they'd cut me short and take over my voice the way they usually did.

Just when the sun began its journey into the treetops, my father summoned me. I was surprised to find him and Baba Segi sitting so close together, their arms touching as they drained the bottle of schnapps that was normally only sipped at weddings and funerals. My father told me to bring the food in and I returned with a wide tray but as I stooped at the door frame, the men stopped talking. Baba Segi inspected me as I placed the plates on a low stool and fetched cool water from the earthen pot. He examined my face as I poured it into two plastic cups. My father watched him watching me.

"She is not a great beauty," I heard my father saying as I closed the door. His discretion had dwindled with the schnapps. "But she is as strong as three donkeys. And thorough too. What she loses in wit, she gains in meticulousness. This is a great virtue in a woman. I have three wives so I speak from experience."

Even a child would have worked out why my father was extolling qualities that had previously vexed him; I was compensation for the failed crops. I was just like the tubers of cassava in the basket. Maybe something even less, something strange—a tuber with eyes, a nose, arms and two legs. Without fanfare or elaborate farewells, I packed my bags. I didn't weep for my mother or my father, or even my siblings. It was the weeds I didn't get the chance to uproot that year that bothered me. I should have known something unusual would happen that year. The drought did something to my ears: whenever I spoke to my spirit friends, their words were muffled, as if spoken from a plot on a faraway land.

Taju threw my belongings in the back: two plastic bags and two tubers of yam. I sat between the two men in the pickup and stared ahead at roads I had never traveled before. So this was Ibadan—the big city where all our secondhand clothes enjoyed their first outings, the place where cars honked, engines roared and bus conductors screamed. I covered my ears. Everything was so urgent, most unlike the leisurely pace at which things bumbled along in the village.

In the middle of all this noise, Baba Segi asked me if I was happy about being his wife. I couldn't utter a single word. I wanted to say something. I should have said something but I couldn't. It has always been hard for me to speak my feelings. Even now, when I try to say things, my mouth opens and closes like a fish waiting for a hook. I choke on words, I swallow them. I didn't have to worry about this in the village because my family could read my mind. Just before I left, I went to my father's hut and stood by the door. I didn't need to say anything, the same way he didn't need to look at me. "I have made my decision and it's final," he said.

When we arrived at Baba Segi's house, he pushed me toward Iya Segi and warned me that I should show her great respect. He said I should be grateful that I was in such good hands. Iya Segi smiled, but I could see her chest thumping beneath her *buba*. Her neck had a scarf of skin wrapped around it. She squinted at the lacy dress my mother told me to wear for the journey. It was more suited to a fifteen-year-old but I liked the way it rustled when I walked. Her eyes swept across the tiny fruits on my chest, which had never been groped or suckled. If not for fists drawn like daggers at her sides, it would have been impossible to tell what she was hiding behind the creased eyes and set smile. She was not happy to see me and by the time her husband finished the introductions, the lamps in her eyes were dead.

"Come to my room," she said. "I have good soap that you can wash yourself with. I will also give you clothes to wear. Your rags cannot stay in this house." All the time her lips moved, her dead eyes were fixed on Baba Segi so he wouldn't miss a word. Then, slinging her son onto her hip, she admonished me for my silence. "You are a wife now, not a child. Say thank you to your husband and follow me."

Several months after, she knocked on my door in the middle of the night. She must have crawled out from under Baba Segi because back then it was just the two of us. She had Baba Segi four times a week and I had him thrice. I would have happily given up *my* nights as well. There were weeks I ached so much I could hardly sit.

"Get pregnant quickly or he will soon start to force-feed you bitter concoctions from medicine men until your belly rumbles in your sleep," she said.

For many weeks, her words kept me awake at night. Then, one day, as she had predicted, Baba Segi asked me what was wrong with my womb. "If your father has sold me a rotten fruit, it will be returned to him." *His* words bothered me even more than Iya Segi's. I didn't want to go back to the village; in Baba Segi's house, I did not have to plant and harvest cassava. Apart from the daily chores Iya Segi allotted me, all I did was plait and play with Segi's hair. Her hair was jet black, every strand stubborn and strong. Combing it was like weeding; it took time and nimble fingers but the results were beautiful.

I will not mention the name of the man I met because I am ashamed. All I'll say is that he was the meat seller Iya Segi sent me to every Wednesday. Although his meat was always tasty, I still asked him whether the cow that was opened up on the table was killed on the day. He replied that his meat was always fresh and scraped some orange marrow into his mouth to prove it. He smiled. His teeth were not white but they looked like they could crack many bones. His tongue was pink and his eyebrows met above his nose. He was from Iwo; I could tell from the incisions that darkened his cheeks. He nodded and cut five hundred naira worth of meat into small cubes, all the time listening to another butcher's anecdote with one ear.

It was not until I untied my wrapper that I realized that the money wasn't where I'd knotted it. What grown woman throws away money her father does not have like that? I felt like a child again. For a while, he watched me scramble and search the muddy ground. Then—I think when he was sure I was not pretending—he asked me to stop troubling myself. Markets are dangerous places and women were often disgraced for such misdeeds, so I was lucky. I offered to leave the meat and return later with the money but he insisted that

I take it with me. He said he would be at his stall until four o'clock.

I gathered all the money Baba Segi had given me over the months and quickly explained what had happened to Iya Segi. "Make sure something worthwhile comes out of all this foolishness," she murmured. "The days are passing quickly and your village calls you!" She emptied the diced beef into the kitchen sink and waved me away. I caressed Segi's hair for a few seconds and left.

He was already scraping his table down with a knife when I got there. "I did not doubt for a minute that you would come," he said.

I let him see that I had brought more than I owed and pressed the money into his hand. I held it there and took his eyes into mine. At first, he looked surprised, but then he closed his fingers around the money and told me to sit and wait for him to finish his cleaning. My heart rejoiced. So there were other people on this earth who could tell what was on my mind! He led me to his home and took me. I will never forget that day or any other that I spent with him. He made my body sing. He made me howl when he bent me over; he made me whimper when he sat me on his belly. And when he took me standing up, it was as if there was a frog inside me, puffing out its throat, blowing, blowing and blowing until *whoosh*— all the warm air escaped through my limbs.

Even when my belly was rounded, I continued to go to him. I couldn't help myself. There was something he gave me that I wanted constantly, endlessly. Three days after I gave birth to my first daughter, I waited for Baba Segi to leave for his new building materials store. As soon as Taju drove him away, I tied the infant to my back and sat on a boulder outside the meat seller's home. When he arrived, he asked me if the child was a boy or a girl. I completely forgot that I even carried a child on my back. Please do not blame me. It was eagerness; I had not been with him for a week. By the time he had hung up all his tools, I had removed the baby and my clothes and laid them down in a neat pile on the floor. Tope was a good baby; she did not cry. He asked me if I had brought him some money. I wondered if he lay with me for the money alone.

For three years, that was how I lived: three days of pummeling from Baba Segi and a day of healing from the meat seller. Those afternoons were worth life itself and it was not until one morning, after I'd given birth to Motun, my third daughter, that I realized how little of life remained outside those afternoons. Iya Segi burst into my room, her brow folded with anger, the skin around her throat rippling. "Can you not hear the infant crying?" she shouted.

"Oh, my thoughts were far away." I got up to lift the child out of her cot. Her small eyes were glazed from crying. I placed my nipple into her mouth. As I looked around for my other children, Iya Segi's eyes followed mine. Afolake was sitting in a corner pushing what was leaking out of her nappy into Tope's nostrils. Tope was fast asleep; all her clothes were inside out.

"Too far away!" Iya Segi pinched her nose and perched on the edge of the bed. "Last week, our husband asked me if

you were sick. He said there was a bad smell in your room."
She looked around suspiciously as if something catching
would jump out of the walls. "I will not let you destroy this
home with your excesses. You have allowed the concubine to
become the husband. I have not known anyone to worship
a penis the way you do!" She stopped to take a long breath.
"Listen carefully to what I have to say because if I am forced
to say it again, it will be wedged between curses. You will *not*
see this man again. You are like a child who has not developed
the temperament for secrets. You are lucky we have a husband who believes he is more than all women and most men.
If he were more discerning, more like a woman, say, he would
have seen through your madness. And anyway, a new wife is
coming, so brace yourself. I just hope *she* has some sense in
her head." She left the room dangling Afolake by the arm. I
heard her yell Segi's name and instruct her to scrub the child
thoroughly in the backyard where the dirty water would be
absorbed into the ground.

I sat there quietly and watched Motun twitching in her
sleep. She was six days old. Her mouth had abandoned my
breast. She looked so small and so unloved. A deep, damning
shame came over me. I could not believe that I had neglected
the children who bought me the easy life I lived. There and
then, I decided to become a good mother to my children.

I would be a liar if I said I wasn't tempted to visit my meat
seller. I was. The yearning was hard to bear but each time
the urge came, I bit my bottom lip and rocked myself to sleep
with a pillow between my knees. The body quickly remem-

bers how to die in the face of pain. I cast all sweetness from my mind and drew my children close to fill its space.

Iya Segi was right: a new wife arrived. She was tall and lean yet you could see that she had whipped her life onto the road of her choice. She had great strength in her forearms and she did everything with determination. Iya Segi spoke sourly of me and referred to me as *apoda*—the stupid, slothful one—behind my back. Tope, my daughter, told me so. It would not surprise me if they were plotting to throw me and my daughters into a well.

Iya Femi, the new wife, soon gave birth to a son and there was much celebration. The new mother clapped her knees together when she sat and strutted about like her womb was a gold mine. That was to be expected but it was Baba Segi's words that made my ears ache. He spoke as if Femi were a jewel, as if he were the first child to be born to the family: "A daughter can never be like a son," he said. "Only a son can become a true heir."

Iya Segi promptly reminded him that he already had an heir in Akin, her own son.

My daughters were born with eyes in their stomachs so they are quick to digest all that they see. They cling to each other for comfort and move together like a single wave. When one cries, the others cry too, and when one laughs, the others smile before asking what is amusing. Sometimes I feel like *I* am one of them. We look after one another and I have taught them all I know. "Do not commit adultery," I tell them. "Follow the path that is good and right," I say. And when they forget to do their homework, I ask them if they want to be educated ladies or useless tubers with arms and legs. They giggle when I say this.

One day, I had a thought and shared it with them. I said it would probably be better for me to hang myself after they marry and leave home. They crumpled into a pile on the floor and wept. "Mama, we would never leave you here," they cried. They understood so much more than I ever did. Like I said, they have eyes in their stomachs.

Bolanle does not deserve the treatment the other wives give her. They bark at her as if she were a child: "Don't sit there!" and "Don't touch that!". All day long, they are at it, yet she does as she is told and never complains. We both do as we are told. One of these days, I should talk to her. I must think of the words that I will say to her. Perhaps it is too early. And the other wives would call me a traitor. They would eat my flesh and the blood from their lips. I think I will watch her a little longer. If fate says we will speak to each other, then one day we will.

I have a secret. I have started weeding again. I do it when Baba Segi comes to lie with me. He doesn't like it; he keeps clasping my hands high above my head to stop me but when he is in the throes of humping, I wiggle one arm out of his grip. I close my eyes and scrape the soil. I push aside the leaves; I prod the stem and pinch the bud. My mind goes to the meat seller so I pull slowly, very slowly. Then, quite unexpectedly, the plant is uprooted and pulsing at my fingertips. I do not open my eyes. I don't want to see Baba Segi looking at me.

CHAPTER TEN
ROGUE

Bolanle

IN THE TWO YEARS I've been living in Baba Segi's house, he has never apologized for his mistakes. He makes peace his own way and it involves tattered brown envelopes bursting with fifty-naira notes, thrust beneath doors at dawn. I'd been ruffled by the red-thread incident and I could think of no better way to calm myself than to spend the day at Dugbe market. I walked the length of Dugbe market, then decided to visit the bric-a-brac stall around lunchtime. My intention was to buy something really ostentatious like a copper plate but when I got there, I found neither bell nor bell ringer.

"You better keep walking," a woman who stood with her back to me warned. "The police might be watching from afar to see who comes looking for him. Keep walking. We are talking about *stolen* property, you know?" The woman was unpacking cheap aluminum pans and cutting up cardboard boxes with a giant pair of tailor's scissors; she didn't turn round to face me.

I wondered if she was addressing someone else. "Sorry to disturb you but I am looking for the man who sells imported tableware."

"Move closer to my stall. Didn't you hear me? He has been arrested. Yesterday, a rich man came to buy some plates. When he got to your friend's stall, he immediately called the police. It turns out some of the plates on sale were his very own. Within minutes, your dish seller and his stolen wares were bundled behind the counter at the police station."

"You mean *all* the crockery was stolen? But he said they were imported by Italian merchants!"

"Italian merchants?" The woman burst into laughter. She clutched her enormous breasts before doubling herself over, as if she feared gravity would lug them off her chest. When she sat up straight, there were tears streaming down her face. "My sister, you make me laugh! Did you expect him to say he got the plates from so and so's house? Or maybe you expected him to give you the address they were stolen from. My dear, he confessed within minutes; he didn't even wait for the sergeant's third slap. Sister, the sun is high. Go your way. You are blocking my stall. Unless of course you want to buy pots. Mind you, these ones are made in Nigeria."

"No, thank you." I shuffled along with the ebb of evening buyers. I felt like a stupid fool, but more than that I felt like an accomplice.

I rushed home as soon as I could, wondering what to do with the bowls. Apart from the fact that their splendor now seemed iniquitous, they were evidence, stolen goods, and I knew I had to dispose of them.

The bats were on their daily pilgrimage; the sky was awash with them. As a child, I'd always marveled at their fluidity, how, like dirty water, they poured onto the graying sky in organized chaos: a chosen few dropping to the flanks, floating awhile before rejoining the rest of the cloud.

"Why do bats travel at dusk?" I once asked Mama.

"Because they are witch birds. Witches fly at dusk."

This was not a satisfying answer for a nine-year-old. "But how can a bat be a witch?"

"Because they hang upside down. If you hang upside down what will happen to you?"

"Would I die?" I asked. The good beans dropped through my fingers into the bad beans pile.

"Of course you would. But *they* wouldn't. They can sleep upside down because they have evil powers. Stop talking and sort the beans, Bolanle. We have to finish quickly. The landlord's wife wants us to grind them as well." She whispered, "It's her husband's birthday party tomorrow."

"Can we go? I want to see the cake. Lara found some in a plastic bag last year."

"Did she eat it?" Mama's hands stopped moving and crept to her waist. Her jaw stopped too, which was a bad sign because she never completely swallowed her bitter kola. She always swirled a diminishing nugget around her mouth.

"No. Yes." I knew I'd said too much. Mama forbade us from scavenging.

"Will you children never learn?" Mama turned to her left and then her right as if she was addressing an invisible audience. "Look at me sitting here sorting beans! Do you think I don't have better things to do? I agreed to pick these stupid beans to secure the roof over your head, so *Madam* will not tell her husband that I am unhelpful, so *her* children will not see *my* children carrying their belongings out on their heads like wretches after *they've* served *us* a notice."

"I know, Mama."

She wasn't finished. She tucked her hair into the black hairnet and pulled her right earlobe in my direction to indicate that I should open my ears to their full capacity. "I don't want to see you going there begging for food. If your father wants to go there, lick their bottoms and beg for beer, let him. I am not bringing my children up to be beggars. I am working myself to death because I want you and that glutton sister of yours to own houses and cars. I am bringing you up to be able-bodied women who will fight for prosperity and win. No one enjoys success if they do not work hard for it."

"I hear you, Mama."

She still wasn't finished. "Will the taste of cake improve your lot in life? Is it nourishing?" Mama also asked ridiculous rhetorical questions when she was annoyed. The problem was that they required contrite monosyllabic answers.

Mama lifted her hips off the stool. I knew there was more trouble to come from the look on her face. Her features had become pinched and distorted with anger. "Let me go and find that Lara. She will hear it from me today. Why must she follow her long throat wherever it beckons? And was she not supposed to help us sort these stupid beans? Where is she now? Lara! Omolara!" she bellowed.

A few moments later, I heard Lara screaming. Mama had yanked her from the mattress she was curled up on, pulled her outside by her ear, all the time slapping her over her head. A slap for every syllable. "You are a la-zy girl. Who will mar-ry a glut-ton like you? Why is it al-ways you? Why can't you be like your sis-ter?"

Through tears, she glared at me, her large seven-year-old eyes full of malice. I could only stare back; my eyes were also brimming with tears. Lara did not speak to me for three weeks. When I entered a room, she walked out. When we were forced to sit together, she made sure our legs didn't brush against each other. It took six balls of *akara* to appease her. And even then, when I handed them to her, she just wolfed them down without saying so much as thank you.

As soon as I got home, I ran to my bedroom and pulled on a pair of worn jeans. I forced my arm under my bed and pulled out an old cardboard box. Then, one by one, I knelt before my stack of crockery and crushed them against each other. *The Long Honeymoon* tried to flee my fingers when I groped under the bed for it; I threw it in the box. I gathered all the mementos I'd kept over the years: the single earring that Segun, the landlord's son, had given me when I turned eighteen. Just wear it like a pendant, he said. In went the hairpiece

Baba Segi said looked like a horse's tail. All the love letters I'd written to myself were the sort I'd have liked to receive. I tore up every one and sprinkled the pieces around the box like confetti.

When I was finished, I hauled the box onto the top of my head. It was heavier than I had thought it would be but I'd learned to endure that sensation of my neck disappearing into my shoulders. Years before, Lara and I had been forced to fetch buckets of water from a nearby well because the landlord had complained that the human traffic to the bore-hole on his property unnerved him. When the cold water splashed over our shoulders as we trudged home, we cursed the Water Corporation that denied us tap water in the first place.

I heaved past the other wives in the sitting room. They stared at me and then at one another in puzzlement. I pretended not to see them and marched ahead to the desolate spot in the backyard where the old drum was. Charred bits of metal and melted plastic that had been pushed into the ground by rainfall protruded from the earth like gravestones. The ground around was scalded, the stones discolored by soot.

I eased the cardboard box onto the ground with a clatter and gave the blue keg a generous jiggle. The liquid trickled from paper to pottery and immediately the air around the box distorted the patterns on the crockery. It took only two matches to set the box alight. I stood there and watched the fire cremate my past, even when the heat drew sweat from my face. When the fire died, I gathered scattered shards, dug a hole in the warm soil and buried them.

Back in my bedroom, I surveyed the open spaces that rolled out before me. Now there would be room for a cot, I thought.

CHAPTER ELEVEN
IYA SEGI

I WAS AN ENORMOUS child. My mother said I made her back curve like a cat's tail. She said she didn't know what to do after my father left her so she just ate and ate. After I was born, she consoled herself by eating more. She ate and ate and what she couldn't eat she rammed into my mouth till I was rolling on the floor, beckoning sleep. She said she was forced to wean me because I shamed her in front of her customers by demanding breast milk. Let me suck, I am hungry, I whined, to the surprise of the old women. My mother sent me to day care the next day, like every other four-year-old.

The food my mother ate seemed to toughen her: her arms and legs could rival a man's for strength. She said so herself. And she was the only woman who turned *fufu* and sold it wholesale. My youth was filled with the smell of fermented cassava, my nails brittle from immersion in water.

I never knew my father. "Your father left me for a beautiful woman. I told him I was pregnant but he didn't want to hear it. He sliced me like okra and left. He pursued another woman's hole and died inside it," my mother said. When she spoke of my father, a small Adam's apple bounced around her neck like an erect nipple under a loose blouse. "Men are nothing. They are fools. The penis between their legs is all they are useful for. And even then, if not that women needed their seed for children, it would be better to sit on a finger of green plantain. Listen to my words. Only a foolish woman leans heavily on a man's promises."

My mother had a friend who sold dye. We called her Mama Alaro. Her fingers were always stained violet and the soles of her feet were black like burned rubber. Even though she knew that children were afraid of her, she insisted on stroking the head of every child who greeted her. She was a widow too and she had just one child—a son called Ishola. Iya Alaro and my mother were great friends. Both of them were fat and callous to the eye. When they sat on a bench under the guava tree, it was as if two elephants were swaying on a branch. The children around the village would summon each other, just to look at the spectacle. Some of them could not hold their laughter. "May that laughter choke you," Iya Alaro would curse.

By the time I was eighteen, Ishola, who would be my future husband, had gone to Ibadan to be a bricklayer's apprentice. I had become quite adept at making *fufu*, and like my mother I had a stash of money under my mattress. But it was a small mattress, in a small room, in a tiny two-bed house. I troubled Mama about getting my own quarters; I was tired of squeezing past her at every doorway. "I have told you before that you cannot buy land and build your own house. The village men will say you are ridiculing them, doing what they can't!"

"But it is just a house, Mama!"

"And they will tear it down and burn it, daughter!"

My money grew until I had to hide it in old water pots in my room. Every night, I would light my kerosene lamp and sit with my buttocks against the closed door. Even if I had counted the day before, I counted the money all over again. My fingers liked the feel of money. My eyes liked to see the piles of money swell. I worshipped money. Even when boys teased me over the flap of flesh that circled my neck, I was not bothered. I looked at them and sniggered, knowing their fathers' fathers could not have a fraction of the wealth I had accumulated.

My mother grew weaker until death shone in her eyes. I could see it without looking. I was twenty-three and my breasts had bulbed and sagged. It wasn't until the day I went to call the carpenter to repair our bench that I realized there was a whole path in life that I had never trod. The carpenter was about my age and as I described the extra reinforcement I wanted for our new bench, I noticed that he was looking at the buttocks of the tomato seller walking by. As if she knew, she turned to him and smiled. "You want it?" she asked.

"Only if you are giving it away for free."

"Nothing in this world is free, let alone a woman."

"Tell me the price and let me consider it."

"It is beyond your means." The girl swung her hips like ripe mango on a tree.

I could not stop looking at her. Her walk, her filthy tongue, her short-cropped hair, her bare feet—everything about her fascinated me. I was awash with lust.

"Lady, I cannot afford you but here is somebody who can," the carpenter shouted after her. He was guffawing and his front teeth protruded in my direction.

The tomato seller looked at me, kissed her teeth and chuckled.

I returned the next day and sat with the carpenter with a list of new furnishings for him to construct. I'd hoped that the tomato seller would hawk through the same route but she did not return. Her brazenness meant she probably wasn't even from our village. I walked home with the new bench balanced on my head. I was disappointed.

I went to bed scattered and perplexed. That night, I did not help my mother put balm on her rheumatism. And when she knocked, I lay still. I couldn't get the girl out of my mind. For comfort, I started to count money, but before long, I was lying dreamily on the bed. There was money everywhere, spread liberally over my thighs, my neck, my upper arms. This is how my mother found me—bathed in money, wearing the notes like a garment—when she barged in at midnight. She was equally alarmed to find me naked but for my underwear. My clothes were strewn all over the room. Mama concluded on the spot that the root of my madness was money. "You have made money your husband," she said.

From then on, marrying me off became her life's ambition. "Child, did you see Baba Elepo's son? He asked of you when he passed just now," my mother would ask. It was as if she wasn't the same woman who'd said God gave men bollocks for the weight they lacked in brains.

"I do not want her to die alone like me," I heard my mother saying as she lifted the skin of her thigh to scratch the inside of her knee.

"She has entered the age of shame," Iya Alaro replied in agreement.

"Money has taken over her senses. She does not even care about bearing children."

"Did I not warn you? Now men mean nothing to her. She's grown up hearing you rip them to shreds!"

"I just wanted her to know the truth."

"Ah, well, she knows it too much now."

"Come, my friend, where is your son? Will he not return?"

"Look at me talking about the holes in *your* roof when mine is leaking. My son is twenty-six. Every time I ask him when I will see my grandchildren, he tells me he has to make the money he will use to feed them first."

"You mean he has not found a wife after all this time?"

"He says Ibadan doesn't have wifely women anymore, only women who are after money."

"Then why doesn't he come and take a wife from here, in Omi Adio?"

"You have spoken wise words, my friend."

"We have been friends for a long time. I am dying. Why don't you take my daughter and make her yours? Let me give her to you with my blessing. Let your son take her from me and I will watch over them from the next world."

From my bedroom, I heard my mother sobbing, which was strange because the prospect of death did not usually upset her. She said she wanted to go to heaven and kill my father all over again. She was desperate for me to be married.

Mama Alaro looked at my mother and made a decision there and then. Although she worked as hard as my mother, she was not as wealthy. "Whether we accompany our palm oil with yam or we accompany our yam with palm oil, the most important thing is to have a good meal of oil-soaked yam. We must help each other."

Even listening in on their plans for me did not take the tomato seller off my mind. After searching for days, I traced her to the farmland on the edge of our village. When I saw her, courage failed me. My liver weakened and I could not bring myself to talk to her. I abandoned my *fufu* and stalked her, overjoyed to be breathing the air she was breathing. I saw every man she teased. A gasp escaped my lips every time she rolled her hips and jiggled the beads that adorned her waist. Sweat was dripping from my neck like rain from the awning. I can't explain why but I wanted her for myself. I wanted to build a house for her and keep the key between my breasts. I wanted to dress her in the finest *aso oke* so she could parade herself for my delight alone. I wanted to lock her between my thighs.

When I got home that evening, I opened my bedroom door and immediately the shadows cleared from my eyes. My room had been ransacked and all my money was gone. My heart beat so loud that the sound filled my head. I couldn't scream lest demons rush out of the forests so I opened the door of my bedroom to report the tragedy. Mama was standing there filling up my doorway. "It's *all* gone," she said. She was standing erect without leaning on the doorpost. I had not seen her like that in two years. "I have given it to the man who will be your husband. He will need it to look after you."

"My husband? Mama, women don't need husbands." I quoted her own words back to her.

"*You* do. You need one to bear children. The world has no patience for spinsters. It spits them out."

"Is this all so I can bear children?"

"It is every woman's life purpose to bear children. Do you want to become a ghost in the world of the living? That is not how I want to leave you in this world."

I did not hold her words against her but nodded approvingly throughout the wedding festivities. Omi Adio will never be able to boast of a more lavish marriage. Both my mother and Mama Alaro did not hold back in spending money. They bought three cows and eight bags of rice. They invited the chiefs from all the neighboring villages.

"Come and see the splendor of the woman who was abandoned for mere beauty," my mother said as she welcomed guests.

I surrendered because I knew it was the prelude to her death. The celebrations were her last dance with the living. She could no longer stand up unaided and when she sat back to survey the caliber of the wedding guests, each breath sounded like a long drawn-out fart. I knew, as many did, that she would soon breathe her last.

My new husband observed me with interest but I looked ahead and turned my ear to him. I could see the tomato seller dancing with the carpenter. A small crowd had gathered around them. The moments of notoriety made the carpenter euphoric; his teeth were high up in the air and he rolled his hips in jerky movements. My husband followed my gaze, perceived my repulsion and decided it was time for us to get up to thank the guests at each table.

"*Eyin Iyawo o ni m'eni.*" They prayed for a fruitful union.

"*Ase o!*" he replied, rubbing his palms together and looking at me mischievously, as if to warn me that I would soon bear lashings from his penis.

As I prepared to accompany him to Ibadan the following day, I knew he didn't know the source of the money his mother had stuffed into a belly bag. From the way he held his head, it was clear he believed it was a great gift from his mother. On the bus to Ibadan, his arm rested on mine. It was as if someone had placed a twig on my wrist. He was a thin man in those days, so slight that a whirlwind could have swept him away. I looked up at him and found him smiling at me. I smiled back, with all my teeth. My weight may have made me the butt of many jokes but my teeth shone like light through leaves.

Later that night, at his one-bedroom hovel in Ibadan, he wriggled between my thighs and marveled at the size of my breasts. He said they would do him for a lifetime. It was my first time so I hardly heard his words. The pain in my belly spread through my back and up my neck to my ears. That night, I dreamed of the tomato seller. She was sitting on top of a huge tomato shrub yelling, "Where are you, carpenter?" The carpenter was hiding behind a tree nearby, pelting her with little red tomatoes. Every time one hit her, it splattered and left a red ring on her skin. When I woke, I told myself that my heart had stopped aching for her and that she could have the carpenter if that was what she wanted!

My new husband turned to me. "I am pleased you are here with me, if only to fatten me up a little," he said.

"I will follow you anywhere, my lord." I raised my buttocks and let him fill me again. I would follow my money anywhere.

After two years, his business began to flourish and he bought a piece of land. He rallied cheap laborers and our house rose from the ground very quickly. For a time, he seemed happy. I was certain that I satisfied him. Men! They always try to swindle you out of what is yours.

When he brought home other wives, I did not complain. I did not say a word. I did not even show that I feared for my money. I just kept quiet and watched him. Who can tell what madness makes men go in search of things that puncture their pockets? *Kruuk*. But that was the path he chose, and I accepted it. Women are my husband's weakness. He cannot resist them, especially when they are low and downcast like puppies prematurely snatched from their mothers' breasts. I do not blame the women either. They too are weakened by the prosperity he offers.

Besides, apart from that Bolanle, whose nose is so high that it brushes the skies, the other wives do not offend me. They are like humble maidservants who live for a kind pat on the head from the mother of the house. They know that *I* am the true provider. My husband only thinks he controls this household and I let him believe that he does. I *want* him to believe he does but *I* am the one who keeps this household together. Good things happen here because *I* allow them. *I* alone can approve vengeance and only *I* know how to bring calm.

As a baby, Segi clung to me as if the spirits had warned that I would one day run away and leave her. She has grown to be a loyal daughter. When I knew the damage that Bolanle would do to our home, I warned her. I told her that a girl who abandons her mother's breast for another woman's will be cursed. I told her that she must be my eyes, my ears, my nose and my hands when I am not in this house. She has been faithful. She tells me everything that happens in my absence. I have told her that she must cling to me until the day she leaves to rule her own home. She will not falter. I have trained her well.

Akin refused my milk after a year and cried for morsels of food. Rather than be bound to my back, he preferred to walk beside me. All day, he sat next to me at my first cement stall. Never did I have to wipe a tear from his kind eyes. He entertained himself: watching me as he fed himself, smiling each time I tucked money into my belly bag. Now I have eight cement shops in Ibadan alone and my wealth swells by the day. Do not say I am greedy because I am not. It's just that as my money grows, my path to freedom becomes clearer. Everybody wants to be free from whatever binds them. Baba Segi will breathe his last one day and my money will return to me. I will pile it on top of the money I have now and the heap will be as hefty as the hills of Idanre. Then, I will leave this city and return to my village. I will buy a big marble headstone for my mother. I will burn down her bungalow and build a four-story building in its place. From the top balcony, I will watch hawkers come and go.

I will not let Bolanle turn my future upside down.

CHAPTER TWELVE
THEATER

Bolanle

S T. GABRIEL'S ULTRASOUND CENTER was not what I expected. The building was in a small compound in Yemetu and there was a sign that pointed visitors in the direction of the top floor. The front wall was decorated with large stones cemented together so it looked as if the building had been sculpted from a mountain of granite. From the gate, I saw women sitting on benches, their backs leaning heavily against the iron rails that enclosed the balcony. There was a drugstore on the ground floor where a garage should have been but no windows to shed light on the boxes of tablets bundled together on the shelves. It looked dark and dingy. A large yellow fridge held the garage door open. A young woman sitting outside on a bar stool called to me, "Auntie, cool yourself down with a bag of cold pure water."

I ignored her; I wasn't thirsty. I'd hailed a taxi on Sango Road and instructed the driver to take me directly to my destination. The taxi driver peered at me through his rearview mirror, probably wondering why an ordinary-looking woman was wasting money on such an extravagance. As if to pay me back, he tried to overcharge me. "Two hundred naira," he said, fiddling with some wires behind his steering wheel.

"Fifty!" I asserted.

"Madam, pay a hundred. Each passenger pays twenty naira from where I picked you up. And this car carries five passengers."

"I will give you eighty. You are only supposed to carry four."

"Madam, you must help us poor taxi drivers. If we don't carry five, how will we feed our children?"

"By not trying to swindle your passengers." I counted four twenty-naira notes and placed them in his open palm.

The man looked at the money. He contemplated haggling some more but relented when he saw that I had folded my arms and cocked my head to one side, daring him to do so.

The stairs were steep and cumbersomely coiled. I reached the top to find an array of women: different heights, different widths, different stages of pregnancy, all of them huffing and puffing, most of them emptying small plastic bags of water into their mouths. They all looked like they were set to leak from every orifice and flood the faded rubber tiles.

I saw the waiting room through a wall of windows. Every space on every bench was taken. Beside a wooden counter, a door inside opened into a corridor. I looked down the passage. There were two doors on either side; three were signposted with doctors' names, one was baldly labeled TOILET. There was a small queue at each door but no less than nine women clenched their thighs outside the lavatory.

A nurse in a gleaming white dress assessed me as I approached the counter. She was short and heavy hipped, but her ebony skin glowed. Her teeth were white with a sizable gap separating the two front incisors. I spotted the gap as soon as she spoke; my passion for blemishes had not left me. She took down my name and deftly stapled my request forms to the ultrasound center letterhead.

"You have to sit down and wait. Drink some water. It makes it easier for the doctor to see everything he needs to see. We recommend three bags."

"How long do you think I'll be waiting for?"

"It is impossible to say, but if you leave, you will lose your place. You are number seventy-eight; number twenty-three just stepped in now. Have a seat and wait, like everyone else."

I scowled and walked out onto the balcony without making eye contact with anyone. Did I say I was different from everyone else? I reflected on her abruptness as I picked my way down the stairs. I snubbed the drugstore again; I wanted a bottle of water. The thought of scrunching bags of dubious water down my throat held little appeal. As I walked out of the gate, a policeman in his faded black uniform caught my eye. He stood across the road from me and was filling his tank with a small keg of gasoline. There were more policemen sitting on a bench under a trimmed almond tree. Squatted before them was a young girl measuring boiled groundnuts into old milk tins and transferring them into newspapers that had been folded into neat triangles. The policemen were in a jolly mood; they kept falling forward in fits of laughter.

I walked past a fragrant roasted-plantain stall; a woman in a lacy low-cut blouse fanned the coal with a sheet of cardboard. The smoke made my eyes water so I quickly crossed the driveway of a mechanic's workshop and stopped in front of a pharmacy. From outside, I could see that the pharmacy was brightly lit by fluorescent bulbs. The windows were closed too, which meant it had air-conditioning.

Back at the ultrasound center, I sat on the hard wooden pew and shifted my weight from buttock to buttock. I didn't seem to have as much cushioning as the other women. I reasoned that pregnancy must be kind to the backside. I glanced at the women's fattened nostrils and marveled at the immodesty with which they displayed their swollen ankles. As they waddled out of the dark corridor, I tried to guess who might be carrying twins, triplets, a boy, a girl or a stillborn child. After all, some of the women left with bloodshot eyes and bits of tissue stuck to their faces. Why else would they be so bereft? It was a tedious game but it helped to pass the time. The women probably thought I was in my first trimester; the thought awakened butterflies in my belly, not the sorrow I anticipated.

My eyes caught a sign on the wall: IF YOU HAVE ANOTHER BABY GIRL, BLAME DADDY! I was just thinking of Iya Tope and her desire to give birth to a son when it registered that my number had been called.

122   ❖   *Lola Shoneyin*

"That's me," I said, standing up hurriedly. My forms fell from my lap.

"Go to room three and *wait* until you are invited." The nurse frowned and eyed the forms as I retrieved them from the floor, as if to be certain that I picked up every single one.

The doctor was pleasant looking. His chin jutted out slightly, giving his face a glum appearance. The armpits of his tie-dye shirt were darkened from perspiration even though cool air was blowing from a noisy air conditioner hitched into a rectangular hole in the wall. His eyes did not leave the scan monitor.

"Your forms, please," he said, motioning to me. I handed them over to a nurse holding out her hand.

The doctor's fingers were long and his nails were bitten into the cuticles. He flashed me a reassuring smile as he splattered a globule of gel onto my belly. He called out figures and letters to the nurse. She repeated everything he said and filled out the blank spaces on the forms.

"Turn onto your left side, please," the doctor requested. He held out his arm so I could grasp it and change position; he pressed my belly with three fingers.

It was mildly uncomfortable but I did not let out a sound. When the examination was complete, he told me to change in the adjoining room, all the time sealing his findings away in an envelope. I wanted to ask questions but decided not to. Whatever the news was, it was best to hear it at once. I took the envelope and went in search of a diagnostic laboratory.

———————

TEN YEARS AGO, I STOOD beneath that same *agbalumo* tree not far from here. I was alive then. I was head girl of my secondary school, head of the school literary and debating society. I knew I was the daughter every parent wanted. I could tell from the way they asked my opinion of their children's conduct in school. Those were the days when I was Mama's beloved child. Mama said my sister Lara was so lazy that she'd need a maid to lift food into her mouth. I was the good daughter.

That day, it rained so hard that birds' nests fell from the trees. It was impossible to stand by the roadside without being edged downstream by the currents. There was muddy water everywhere, swishing around people's feet and sweeping along scrunched-up newspapers and plastic water sachets. The wind had turned my umbrella inside out and my clothes were wet to my skin. As was the case when it rained hard, the taxis didn't respond to whistling or *pssts*. They preferred to preserve their carburetors rather than brave waterlogged potholes. I'd never come home late from singing practice before and I knew my mother would soon start worrying. I hadn't even done my chores. I kept looking at my watch with the hope that the second hand would tick a little slower. I reassured myself that at least Awolowo Road was safe, a place where rich, decent people lived.

I was looking at the palm trees peeping over the fences crowned with shards of broken glass, when a Mercedes screeched to a halt, reversed and parked about a yard away from me. Hoping it would be one of my school friends, I ran to the car and poked my head through the window. The face I saw was unfamiliar so I apologized and took two steps back. My mother had warned me about kidnappers.

"You are going to get swept away by the rain," came a soft voice from the driver's seat. "Where are you going?"

I took another step back and looked in the direction of the passing cars. Maybe he'd drive on if I looked away.

"Are you waiting for someone? Look, you are the only person standing here in the rain. If you are waiting for a taxi, I could give you a ride farther down. There are lots of taxis at Osuntokun junction."

I moved a little closer. I glanced at the car and then at him. He looked respectable, not like the thugs my mother had described. I could smell his cologne; it was like freshly cut grass. His face was handsome and his fingernails were filed to perfection. He was wearing a polo shirt with a crocodile on the left breast. His jeans were clean.

"My mother has told me not to accept rides from people I don't know," I said as I reached out to the door's handle.

"I am not a stranger anymore, am I? My name is Thomas and I'd say we've already been having a pleasant conversation." He grinned.

When he got to the roundabout, he took a sharp right instead of taking the second exit.

"Sir, you said Osuntokun."

"Are you in a hurry? I just want to make a quick phone call to my sister in the U.S. She's in the hospital. I live just round the corner. As soon as I am done, I'll run you down to

Osuntokun. I may even be able to take you home. Where do you live?"

"I live in Agbowo. The problem is that my mother will be worried."

He sniggered. "Big girl like you, mentioning your mother in every sentence. You sound like a baby. Are you a baby? How old are you?"

"I am fifteen. I am not a baby." I held my head high.

He turned round and looked at my face, then his eyes dropped to my breasts. "You don't look fifteen. Are you really?"

"Yes."

"What kind of music do you like?"

"Anything."

"Anything? Well, this will be to your taste then. It's perfect for people who like anything." He took out a Wasiu Ayinde CD and inserted it into the car deck, which swallowed it and belched a familiar drumbeat.

He turned up the air conditioner. I felt its coolness blow up my bare arms and through my damp blouse. It smelled like rain hitting hot pavement. It was a comforting smell. I sat back and relaxed against the velvety seat.

He turned into Lower Awolowo Road and sped down a close. He jumped out to open the gate, thrusting the key through a makeshift hole in the thick iron.

After he drove in, he locked the gate behind us.

"I won't be a minute," he said, and ran indoors, shutting the car door.

I looked around me. There'd been a power cut so it was dark. The deafening blare of generators came from the houses on either side. From the lamps in the house next door, I could make out bloodred hibiscus, rows of potted partridge pea plants lined the walls.

The man suddenly rushed out of the house with an umbrella. He was now wearing a pair of khaki shorts.

"I want to put the generator on. I can't see a thing inside. It's one of those cordless phones and I don't know where it is. Why don't you get down and help me look for it so we can be on our way?"

"No. I'd rather wait in the car. Thank you."

"But you'll get bitten by mosquitoes. There's more music inside."

I huffed and left my bag in the car to show that I had no intention of staying long. I was inquisitive. I had never been driven in a Mercedes before. My father owned an ancient Peugeot 504 and my mother had hopped on and off buses for as long as I'd been old enough to note it. Part of me wanted to see how this man lived. I wanted to see the inside of his house, see the kind of chairs he sat on. I wanted to know if he had the wall-to-wall carpeting my friends at school often described. I wanted to smell wealth and glimpse the lifestyle I aspired to, the luxury I would live in when I was older and rich.

Soon after his generator started roaring, he reappeared and I followed him into his kitchen. He held the door open for me and locked it behind us. "Security," he reassured me.

The kitchen was covered in white tiles. A large chest freezer hummed in the corner. The spotless gas cooker had six burners; I'd never seen one like it. The work surface was tiled, all white except for a few drops of what looked like black currant juice.

His sitting room walls were light green. Cream leather armchairs were arranged around a square rug that had acacia trees around the edges. There were oxblood cushions every-where.

"Just wait here while I search the bedroom."

He knew I was taking everything in. It was probably obvious from my clothes that I was unfamiliar with this sort of bounty. I sat on a sofa and looked ahead at the big-screen television. I got up first to touch it and then to switch it on. I couldn't tell what button to press so I squatted to look at the diagrams. I didn't hear him creep up behind me.

"So, how about a little fun before you go?" He had taken his shirt off and there was a mass of curly hair petering out as it reached his boxer shorts.

I covered my eyes. I perceived something uncompromis-ing in his tone. It unsettled me and my heart began to race.

"Come on, don't waste time. Isn't this what you came for? You think I don't know your type? You just came to fuck. Didn't you? You want to be fucked!"

"No, sir. I just want to go home. I don't want anything else, sir," I whimpered.

His hand shot upward and his fist connected with my

cheekbone. I staggered. The wooden stool behind me stopped me from falling to the ground. I regained balance and stood up straight. I covered my face with my hands and burst into tears. "Please, sir, have mercy on me. I don't want anything else; I just want to go home." I cried, but I knew no one could hear me. I could barely hear myself over the din of the generators.

He moved closer to me and with great accuracy, he struck both my shoulders with his knuckles. My arms fell to my sides like logs and I fell to my knees from the pain. He grabbed a handful of my hair, dragged me into his bedroom and threw me on the bed. He climbed on top of me but I clamped my legs together and pleaded for him to stop. My resistance annoyed him and he pulled a pillow over my face. I was sure I was going to die because I couldn't breathe. I could hear my heartbeat slowing. My arms were still limp and I couldn't even scratch him. When he finally lifted the pillow off my face and laid it beside me on the bed, I barely had the strength to inhale; I was paralyzed.

"If you don't want to die, lie still with your legs apart!" he barked.

I saw the glint of desperation in his eyes. Was this the man who had helped me out of the rain? Where had this monster come from? Those were my last thoughts before I blacked out.

There was a splash of icy water on my face and for a moment, I thought I was back by the roadside. Then I felt pain deep in my groin. There was wetness between my thighs. I burst into tears. What had he done to me?

"Don't exaggerate. It's not that bad. Go to the bathroom and clean yourself up. It's getting late and you should be home." His voice was soft again.

I summoned all my strength and stumbled through the open door. The first thing I saw was my reflection in the mirror above the sink. I touched my face, thankful that the swelling was hardly noticeable. What I had hoped to save for my husband had been wrenched from me and all I had to show for it was an excruciating ache and dishevelled hair. When I rested my arms on my breasts to button up my blouse, I felt how tender they were. I took a peek and found fading teeth marks all over them.

The toilet roll sat on top of a pile of magazines. The cardboard sphere revealed a naked woman's open legs. I wet the tissue and wiped off the streaks of blood on my thighs. I noticed that my skirt was still bunched together at my waist so I freed the hem and ironed it down with wet palms.

The man was dancing in his seat and singing along to the music in between cigarette puffs. It had stopped raining. He raced down the Oyo Road toward Agbowo. Throughout the journey, I stared out of my window, trying to reconcile the person I was now with the girl who stood, cold and wet, beneath the *agbalumo* tree. I caught my face in the side-view mirror. Who are you? I asked myself.

"You should be smiling," he said, tapping his fingertips on the steering wheel.

"You can drop me off right here. I will walk home." We were in front of the university gates, three streets from our flat. Before facing my family, I wanted a little time to compose myself.

"I mean it. You should be happy. You are a woman now. You should be thanking me." He parked very close to the curb.

"Thank you," I spluttered as I climbed out of the front seat. I didn't know what else to say. I didn't look back at him; I did not want to remember his face, his eyes, his jaw. I wanted to forget him. I walked as briskly as I could and disappeared into the throng of plantain sellers.

AT THE LAB, THE SIGHT of my blood coloring the syringe brought back memories of the operating room. It had been more of a hut really—planks knocked together, covered with corrugated iron sheets. There was no ceiling so the sun had an unfair advantage. Segun was bent over me, clutching my hand. He was nervous; his hand kept reaching inside his breast pocket for a handkerchief that wasn't there.

"You know it's best to do it here, don't you?" Segun tried to bolster me, praying he was answering the questions my eyes were asking. "The risk of being seen is too high anywhere else. God forbid that one of my father's friends should recognize me. What would I say I was doing in a hospital? With a woman!"

"This place is fine," I said. I didn't want him to think that I wasn't grateful. I don't know what I would have done if he hadn't had the good sense to bring me here. It didn't matter that he was sleeping with me and therefore horrified by the thought that the child might be his. Things had happened quickly between us. He said he wanted me and I gave myself to him. The affection he showed me was everything.

"Of course, this place is fine. I have been doing this for twenty-five years. If all the women of Ayikara are satisfied with my services, you should also set your mind at rest." The midwife had traipsed in wearing an oversized lab coat. She had a metal pan in one hand and a stainless steel instrument in the other. Her gloves had droplets of blood on them and her pinkie peeped through the rubber.

"Mister, you will have to leave now. Wait outside, please."

Segun brushed my arm as he walked away until our fingertips were the only parts of our bodies touching. The anesthetic was swift. I slept with Segun's face before my eyes.

I dreamed that I was on a roller coaster, which was strange because I had never even seen one before, except on TV. A stranger sat to my right with a noose around his neck. To my left, a man sat with a pillowcase over his head. It was as if we were bound together by fate because as our carriage soared, sank, dipped and climbed, we were gripped by the same fear and all of us pleaded to be let off. The man on my right suddenly began to bang his head against the metal guard that held us in place while the one to my left ground his teeth relentlessly. I made to slap sense into both of them but iron bars appeared from nowhere and pinned my arms to my sides. I couldn't move any of my limbs. "Please, let me off! I promise to be strong!" I screamed. I didn't know why I was uttering those words. They were meaningless to me.

I never came off the roller coaster. Instead, I opened my eyes to find Segun holding me down with all his body weight, his chest on top of mine. From the corner of my eye, I could see the midwife wiping down the steel beak-like instrument with cotton wool and bloodied water. Tears ran down my face and into my ears. My heart raced and I was unbearably thirsty.

When I tried to sit up, I expected my arms to be buckled to the examining table but they were as they always were: free. There were drops of diluted blood everywhere. The nurse had stuffed a clump of cotton wool into my under-wear; it looked like white pubic hair. Segun helped me into the back of the Honda his father had bought him for his twenty-first birthday. He propped my head up with the packet of sanitary towels we'd bought on our way to the nurse. "Stay down so no one sees you. I will drive to a quiet spot so you can rest for about an hour. There isn't much time. Your mother will soon be back from work. Remember, I can only drop you at the junction; you will have to walk home by yourself."

AT THE DIAGNOSTIC LAB, the nurse deposited my blood into the labeled vials. Tears made the back of my eyes ache but I was determined to shed them in the safety of my bedroom. They escaped as soon as the sun warmed the top of my head.

How could I hold it together when my destiny hung before me like the proverbial mangoes? "Hear me," the king pronounced, "the flesh of these big yellow mangoes gives eternal life. But beware! The tree has roots of poison. Only the strong and the brave can eat the mangoes and live." But could anyone boast of strength and bravery before they'd eaten the mangoes and lived?

CHAPTER THIRTEEN
IYA FEMI

Your father and your mother are gone." The man whose lips mouthed these words was my uncle, my father's only sibling. His eyes were bloodshot and swollen. He had lived with us for as long as I could remember. When my father went into the deep forest to hunt bush meat, it was he who watched over me and my mother. My mother didn't need watching over. Whenever my father stepped out of the house, she sat on the porch and wove baskets until he returned. Many said their dying together was God's mercy.

"Gone where?" I asked. My parents didn't go anywhere without telling me. My tears demanded it.

"They are dead." My uncle shook me by the shoulders as if to ensure that the words he'd spoken sank into my belly. I fought off his fingers. I leaped into air, aiming for the wall with my forehead. It took three grown men to hold me down.

Somebody must have put a curse on them. People in our

village didn't like to see others doing well. "Why else would a log slip from a lorry and crush them on a road they traveled every day?" This was the question I asked the perplexed mourners who came to pay their respects. My parents were good people, hard workers. Our house was built from concrete blocks; my father always said we deserved to live like royalty.

They were buried on the day they died, the Muslim way. I was their only child but I was not allowed to see them. The men did their best to hide their corpses from me but I saw red streaks on the white cloths they were bound with. Blood leaked from their broken heads as they were lowered into the ground. *Kai!* What a terrible appetite this ground we tread has! It eats blood and bones heartily, no matter how good they are.

"We have found work for you in Ibadan." My uncle did not have the courage to say this to my face, so instead he sent the ugly witch he was courting. My mother despised her; she said the woman had the disease of the eye: everything she saw, she wanted.

"I don't want to go anywhere. I want to stay in Oke'gbo where my parents are buried. This is my home."

"Wipe your eyes," she said, passing me a rag. "It has been a month since your parents died. This is not your home and it will never be. A girl cannot inherit her father's house because it is everyone's prayer that she will marry and make her husband's home her own. This house and everything in it now belongs to your uncle. That is the way things are."

"Everything belongs to my uncle?" It was as if the witch had rammed a fist through my chest. If I had a knife at that moment, believe me, I would have sliced her belly wide open.

"Yes, your uncle. What will you do with this house anyway? You cannot live here alone. Even your grandmother has said it is better for you to go."

She was lying. I'd seen my father's mother on her way to the market. She was half-blind. From the way she was walking, gingerly greeting passersby, it was obvious she hadn't been told of her son's death. It would have killed her and another funeral would have been expensive.

"So you and my uncle will live here and use all my father's belongings?" My uncle had worn my father's hat to the burial.

"Go and pack. The people you will work for are coming to collect you this evening."

"I cannot believe my uncle would do this when he knows how much my father wanted me to go to school! He wanted me to be educated. Baba, can you hear me? What kind of misfortune is this that has befallen me?" I placed my hands on my head and invoked my father's spirit.

"Listen to the words coming from your mouth. Your parents have spoiled you. Maggots crawl beneath your skin. Your uncle has found you a household where they have promised to send you to school if you behave, yet all you can talk about is the misfortune that has befallen you. Many people who are older than you have not tasted the sweet life you have enjoyed since birth. Your parents should be ashamed!"

I do not know when and how my teeth found her ear but they refused to unclench, even as blood dripped from her lobe into my mouth. My uncle heard the wailing from where he was hiding and ran to her rescue but I was knotted around her. The hand pestle my uncle used to knock my mouth open broke one of my front teeth. I didn't care. What is half a tooth to half an ear? She would think twice before speaking ill of my parents again.

When the woman who came to collect me arrived, they eagerly told her that I was an untamed animal. They told her to watch me lest my madness drive me to bite the bark off neighborhood trees.

"There aren't many trees where we live," the woman said. "And if there were, she would be too busy sweeping the leaves under them."

As they drove me away, I glared at my uncle through the rear window and licked my lips. He should have known I would return one day, but that is the problem with evildoers. They forget that the world turns, like the people in it. I was indeed pampered but I was not spoiled. And although my mother washed all my clothes for me, there were no compromises when it came to cooking. She knocked me over the head with the wooden spoon if my *amala* was either too soft or too dense so I spent many nights nursing an aching forehead. It was at the Adeigbes' household that I learned how soda bites the finger and hardens the palm.

As soon as we got to Ibadan, the woman snatched my bag, pressed two check dresses into my hands and told me I was to call her Grandma. She said only her children called her Mummy and I was too lowly to emulate them. "Here," she said, "the house girls wear uniforms." She showed me a tiny space under the stairs and pointed to a mat that was wedged beneath three wooden planks. "This is where you will sleep. Let me warn you, I don't want to see any signs that someone slept here when I come downstairs in the morning. I will burn anything that is out of place. If that means you'll walk around naked, then so be it."

I served the Adeigbe family for fifteen years. I served Grandma and her husband; I served their children and then their children's children. From the day I got there, I was a house girl and my status did not change. They pillaged the most fruitful years of my life, all the time treating me as if they'd found me in a pit latrine. Grandma slapped me if a drop of oil fell from the ladle to the cooker. If I didn't answer the first time she yelled my name, she shaved every strand of hair on my head. If I ever overslept, she would cut me all over with a blade and rub chili powder into the wounds. Once, when she saw me speaking to the gateman, she stripped me naked, rubbed chili between my thighs and locked me out of the house for a whole day. She did not even remember that I was eighteen years old with a chest full of breasts and thighs full of hair. All I could do was weep with shame.

It was Tunde, Grandma's first son, who first climbed between my legs. I was not allowed to retire for the night until everyone who lived in the household was within its walls, so I would doze on the stairs while I waited. On this particular night, he came in drunk as usual. He said he'd had a bad night and I should have mercy and let him fuck me. I didn't scream like Grandma's daughters did when they brought men home on hot afternoons; I lay down quietly and hid the pain beneath my skin. When he had finished, he embraced me and told me my body was worth paying for.

"I don't know what you're doing here," he said as he washed himself in the kitchen sink. He emptied a handful of detergent onto his palm and scrubbed his penis with his fingertips. Then he patted his pubic hair with a dishcloth. "You're not going to serve my family for the rest of your life, are you?"

I remember this conversation because I was twenty-one years old at the time, yet it had never occurred to me that I could leave. Although the prospect of freedom excited me, the thought of escaping made my heart pound. In my child-ishness, I decided to give Grandma a chance to redeem her-self, so I reminded her that I would like to go to school one day. She cursed me for my ingratitude and took away my mat for three days. The floor was so cold that I never mentioned it again. Although Tunde's words often came to my mind, I tried to forget the possibility of a future, a marriage, a family or a home of my own. I became convinced that laundering other people's clothes, cooking three separate dishes every mealtime and comforting babies (that weren't mine) was my life. I was a fool to think Grandma would be interested in giv-ing me the opportunity to improve my lot.

It wasn't until the day Grandma sent me to the market to

buy two cans of sweet corn that the impulse to flee returned. Grandma had had me chopping, roasting and frying since three A.M. that morning. It was one of her grandsons' birthdays and birthdays were a grand affair. I suffered from fatigue after every one. My limbs would ache and my head would boil for days and there were times when it took me a week to recover. I never let Grandma know this. If she saw me resting, she'd punish me.

It was surprising that she even allowed me to go by myself because she preferred to do all her grocery shopping herself. I normally walked two steps behind and struggled with the carrier bags. And although it was *her* memory that had failed her the day before (she'd stupidly ticked sweet corn off her shopping list even though she hadn't bought it), *I* was the one who was sent into the hot sun. She didn't even permit her driver to take me; she said such luxuries would make me aspire to a status that was beyond me. I was on the verge of collapse when I got to the market. The top of my head was baking and I could feel the warm sand through the holes in my flip-flops.

Anyway, there I was, propped up by one of the walls at Bodija market, when a man asked me if I knew Jesus. From the little time I'd spent in primary school when my parents were alive, I knew that Jesus belonged to the Christians. Since I wasn't allowed to go to church with Grandma and *her* family, He was indeed a stranger, so I answered, "No."

The man shook his head, looked up to the skies and then at me.

"I was born a Muslim." I hadn't asked for his sympathy.

"Then let me buy you a Coke and tell you what happens to those who die without confessing Jesus as their Lord and Savior." He had a Bible wedged in his armpit. His shirt was faded and his trousers were at least two inches short. He himself looked like he could do with Jesus's blessings so I was suspicious of his eagerness to save me yet moved by his generosity. I drank my first full bottle of Coke in fourteen years and it bubbled in my stomach. Its sweetness spread to my feet and my fingertips. The preacher spoke of love and all its virtues but I just watched his mouth twitching from side to side. Perhaps he sensed that this idea of universal love was ridiculous to me or maybe I just wasn't responding to his words the way he'd hoped, because his tone suddenly changed. It became firm and no-nonsense. His eyes bulged when he warned that I would go to hell if heaven rejected me.

"But why would God reject me when I haven't done anything wrong?" I thought perhaps I had fallen for the charms of a lunatic.

"We have all sinned and fallen short of the glory of God," he said.

"But what about people who sin every day? What about the rich who take and destroy?" I was curious to see if his God would be partial to Grandma because she was wealthy.

"Hellfire!"

"Are you sure of this?"

"Sister, all sinners will burn." His eyes flared on the word "burn."

His intention was to put the fear of God in me, but instead the thought of Grandma burning excited me. In my mind's eye, I saw images of hell: flames, melting faces, singed limbs. When he asked me to repeat the Sinner's Prayer after him, the sound of Grandma's wailing and gnashing of teeth drowned his voice. I imagined my uncle and his woman sizzling in a bonfire of my father's possessions. *That* was a particularly exciting thought.

"Congratulations!" he shouted. "You are now born again. Now you too must spread the gospel of good news. For saving another soul, God has just added another room to my heavenly mansion." He drew a map of his church on the back of a tract and handed it to me.

"Thank you," I said as I walked away. I was glad he got something out of it too and tucked the paper into my bra.

From that day, I prayed early every morning and late into the night. I created an altar beneath the stairs and laid the map of New Beginnings Church on it. A Jehovah's Witness booklet with images of heaven on the front cover sat next to it. Whenever Grandma slapped me for being absentminded, it was comforting to remember that *I* would be welcomed into the new Eden while she was banished from the glorious gates and condemned to hell. Praise God!

About two months after I received Jesus, Grandma scorched me with the iron because I'd burned a hole in one of her silk blouses. As I spread a film of Vaseline over the naked flesh, I decided that it was simply not enough to edify myself with thoughts of her body crackling in hell. Something more drastic needed to be done. For hours every night, I would chant: God, send Grandma and her family to hell but spare Tunde, her son. Tunde was still slipping money between the folds in my mat. I wasn't sure if he was paying me for the sex we now had frequently or if he was just petrified that I would confess our trysts to his mother. I had no time for telling tales when there was so much praying to be done.

After seven days of fervent prayers, Grandma slipped in the bathtub and broke her leg. My initial joy was shattered when I realized that she used her immobility to find me more work. She became an invalid: I had to bathe her and towel her dry as well as everything else. Was Jesus punishing me? Or was he pushing me to use the reins he'd handed me? I chose the latter and started stirring urine and then a few drops of toilet water into Grandma's goblet. It wasn't long before she was admitted into the hospital for terrible diarrhea. How weak are the stomachs of the wicked! All the time I lived there, I was only allowed to drink tap water. Grandma said it was wasteful for me to drink from the family supply that *I* boiled and filtered every morning.

Since the day my uncle had sold me, this was the first time Grandma hadn't been able to send me on errands. I soon began to believe that I too had dropped from between a woman's legs! While her husband and children spent their days by her side in a private hospital, I wandered beyond our fence. There was a new house being built across the road and that is where I met Baba Segi. He was supplying the plumbing materials and he looked powerful yet kind in his yellow safety helmet. I offered him Grandma's precious boiled water. He accepted it and thanked me. The next day he brought me a basket of oranges. It was Taju who delivered them. I didn't waste time in telling Taju I was looking for a man to marry me. I was desperate; I didn't want Grandma to come back and find me.

"Baba Segi is the one who has enough money to marry many women," Taju advised me. "The *one* I have complains every day."

"Then *make* him marry me. Convince him and put me in your debt forever. I have no relatives so there is no one for him to pay homage to."

"Did you drop from the sky?"

"Even farther up than the sky! Wait here and I will bring you something." I divided the money I had stolen over the years into two and forced one half into Taju's hand.

I don't know what he told Baba Segi but he did his job well. Less than a week later, Taju came alone in the pickup and parked across the road. It was midmorning and the house was empty so I had time to pack *everything* I wanted. Before I drove away with him, I rubbed shit into every pillow in the house except for Tunde's. My journey with him hadn't ended yet.

THE FIRST THINGS THAT STRUCK ME about Baba Segi's house were the soiled curtains. The layer of dust on them was so thick that Grandma would have sliced the veins in my neck if she ever came home to find hers looking like that. Except her *imported voile curtains* wouldn't have been that way; the *house girl* would have washed them as soon as she felt the pinch of the red harmattan winds!

The walls of Baba Segi's house were stained too. Everything was grubby but the wives were the worst of all—the aging toad and the shameless goat! One ruled the pond, the other played with its shadow all day! And how they stank! If I'd really wanted to punish them, I would have turned round and returned to Grandma's house immediately, but I decided to show mercy, especially after Baba Segi showed me my room. I was twenty-three yet I'd never had my own room before; I'd slept between my parents until the day they died. I looked at the double bed and tested the softness of the mattress with both palms. I would have been a fool not to lie on it, even if it was for just one night. I now know why rich people sleep longer than paupers. When I woke up the next morning, I felt like I was suspended in midair. It was as if I had reached my heaven. Not even God himself could have made me leave Baba Segi's house after that.

The next morning, Iya Tope brought breakfast into my room. Her fingers touched the face of the plate as she placed it on the bedside table. There was no way I could eat it so for two days all I did was sleep and wake, wake and sleep, harboring unbearable hunger pangs. On the third day, I stood up from my slumber knowing I'd die if I didn't eat. I found the kitchen and scrubbed every inch of it. The wives stepped around me in hushed curiosity. I finished at eight o'clock in the evening. Then I sat on the floor and finished a plate of yam. I cleaned and cooked the yam myself.

That night, Baba Segi came to me. He sat on my bed and grabbed my breasts. I thought it was all quite amusing until he jumped between my legs and tried to force his penis into me. "I am still wearing my underwear," I told him.

He wasn't like Tunde at all. There was no sucking, no licking, no nuzzling, no moistening. Baba Segi was heavy; everything about him was clumsy and awkward. He heaved and hoed, poured his water into me and collapsed onto my breasts. Tunde never did that; he always shook his water onto my belly. I looked forward to the day our paths would cross again at meet-roads. For months, I cleaned. I knew I would find Tunde when the time was right.

One day, that fat frog Iya Segi asked if I'd noticed that Iya Tope had left *all* the housecleaning to me. The truth was that I didn't want to share the washing and cleaning with Iya Tope. Sometimes I had to clench my fists to resist the urge to drag her to the backyard, brush her yellowing teeth, wipe her nose and scrub her from top to bottom. When I asked Iya Segi what she wanted me to do about the information she'd given me, she lifted both palms and insisted she was only telling me because she'd taken a liking to me. "Thank you," I said, staring her dead in the eye.

Let me tell you now, I don't like people who think they can outsmart me. Grandma used to throw skirts into the laundry basket with money in the pockets, hoping I'd steal it so she could accuse me. I wasn't that stupid! Then she'd leave her jewelry box open and leave one ring in it. One! As if I didn't know she stored the rest of her jewelry in a vanity case in the wardrobe! The day I left their house, I took complete sets with me. I took a heavy cross too. If I was going to be a Christian, I would need a crucifix. The most stupid thing was what Grandma did about the underwear though. She'd creep up behind me and ask me to lift my skirt so she could see my underwear. She did this every time her daughters reported that their underwear was missing. Why would I *wear* stolen underwear? They were buried in the big sack of rice in the pantry! I hate it when people think they can outsmart me.

The frog was relentless. She taught me tricks that helped me get the better of the goat. "Do this for Baba Segi," she'd say. "It will make him love you more."

"More than he loves you?" I'd ask.

Then she'd make that sound in her throat. *Kruuk kruuk.* Just like a frog.

"I didn't think so." Although the idea of becoming the wife who could get anything she wanted from Baba Segi was attractive to me, the prize was less so. Baba Segi was like a flatulent pig. Grandma would have scolded him; she would have rubbed chili powder around his anus.

Remember I said there was a road ahead for me and Tunde? Well, one day, I trailed him from Grandma's house to his workplace. When he saw me running toward him, he burst into laughter. He laughed until tears fell from his eyes. "Bravo!" he kept shouting. He says many strange things that I don't understand. He took me to a hotel not far from his

workplace and said renting a room for two hours in the afternoon was called short time. It was good to have him back
between my thighs, especially after two nights with Baba
Segi, whose penis was so big that two men could share it and
still be well endowed. Where he used his gbam-gbam-gbam
like a hammer, Tunde used his like a forefinger; he bent and
turned until it stroked all the right places. During one of our
frequent short-time sessions, I told Tunde that I was married
to Baba Segi. He didn't seem surprised at all. He just smiled.
"It can only make our time sweeter," he said.

One night when Baba Segi was busy pummeling Iya
Tope, Iya Segi came to my room and told me how children
were born in Baba Segi's household. She said it as if the solution wasn't out of choice but necessity. When she left my
room, I smiled to myself. I was already pregnant. Six months
later, Baba Segi and I brought Femi home from the hospital.
"He is very big for a child born three months early," his first
wife sneered. I told her the ways of God were mysterious and
snatched my newborn son from her arms.

Don't get me wrong. I don't hate Baba Segi; on the contrary, I have several reasons to be thankful to him. He gave
me a place of refuge when the wicked of the world were ready
to swallow me whole. You see, when the world owes you as
much as it owes me, you need a base from which you can call
in your debts. In return for his kindness, I have worked tire-
lessly to make him happy. I cook his favorite meals the way
Grandma taught me. The people in this household are easy to
please: cook them a hearty meal and they worship you.

In the years I lived in Baba Segi's house, I never forgot the evil my uncle did to me. I was reminded of it every day. Every day the children come home from school and talk about science and math, my head is flooded with anger. They use words like "biology" and "geometry," words I don't understand. Words I would have understood if my uncle had sent me to school. If he'd remembered the kindness with which my parents dealt with him, he would have seen to it that I became a greater person than I am today. I would have been rich and powerful, not a third wife in an illiterate man's home. My uncle deprived me of opportunities. And Grandma too. Thieves—that's what they are! Filchers of fortune. I won't rest until they are punished. In the Bible, God said, "Vengeance is mine." If God can delight in vengeance, how much more a poor soul like me who has been misused by the world? I must have revenge. Only then will I accept that there was a reason for all my suffering.

Last week, I returned to my village. If in your mind you are asking what for, then it means you haven't been listening to my words. I returned to Oke'gbo; Tunde took me. He said he wanted to help me make my dreams come true. I have often told him how I came to work for his mother for fifteen years. My story moves him and he asks me if I mind that he sheds a tear or two. True enough, he sheds them, and they are never more than the two agreed on. He says my life is a beautiful tragedy, though I don't know what that means.

I waited in the barn they had built for their goats. Two she-goats. Ha! That was the extent of their livestock. The scent of the miserable creatures nearly killed me so I kicked them until they limped off my land. My uncle was the first to come out through the back door. He had a large cloth wound round his waist. Staring into the clouds, he brushed his teeth with a chewing stick and spat intermittently. He was already using a walking stick. That is what wickedness does: you age before your time. His wife wasn't much better. When she came out to brush her teeth, she sat knees wide apart on a concrete block. Her eyes were open yet she sounded like she was snoring. Glutton!

Their children began to wake up and came out to greet their parents before commencing their morning chores. One of them came to the barn to feed the goats. When he couldn't find them, he scattered yam peel all over my yard. He looked like my father: tall and gangly, the back of his head pointed like the top half of an egg. His name was Maleek; he flinched when he heard his father's voice thundering through the house. My uncle had developed a big voice in my absence.

Seeing the young boy reminded me that I hadn't come there to harm anyone, just to claim what was mine. What do you do when something that is yours is claimed by someone else? You destroy it! You take it apart so devastatingly that it can never be put together again. My fingers brushed the fifty-liter keg of kerosene. My palm itched to turn the lid but I waited. The longer you wait for revenge, the sweeter it is.

Before long, the children marched out of the house in red stripes on khaki. So he let his own children go to school!

The injustice! Tears came to my eyes but I blinked them back. Soon, my uncle too slapped the road with his slippers, an old hoe hooked over his shoulder. No doubt, he was going to *my* farmland. My heart thumped with anticipation as I crept out of my hiding place. There was no real need to crouch and hide as we still didn't have neighbors. My father said he built our house away from the village so we would be shielded from the world's envious eyes.

Starting from the backyard, I poured kerosene along the walls. I poured some on the concrete bench my mother placed her baskets on. I poured some on the doormat we used to scrape mud from our feet. The paupers hadn't bought anything or changed anything. Everything was as my father left it. I sprinkled kerosene over all I could see.

My uncle's wife didn't recognize me when she opened the door. "Did you know the Bible says 'Touch not my anointed'?" I asked.

At first, she looked at me with interest, but when she saw my eyes burning, she retreated into the house. "We are Muslims in this household," she replied.

"I am *telling* you what the Bible says because you have done worse than touch; you have *bruised* God's anointed!"

I barged past her and locked us both in. I put the key in my bra and poured kerosene on the clothes in the wardrobes, the baskets of food. I emptied the keg onto the over-worn shoes stacked in a corner. I even upturned the kerosene stoves for good measure. It took a lot for me to swallow my laughter when she started banging on the door, shouting, "Don't kill me!" *Don-key* me, more like. That would have been closer to the truth!

How quickly fire eats! I ran outside and could see that the insides of the house were half-consumed. Flames burst through the windows and the bungalow looked like a blackened shell. You thought I killed her, didn't you? I went seeking revenge, not death. I let her out of the front door, yelling and tearing at her scarf. She didn't know whether to summon her husband or brave the flames. I prayed that her most precious possessions were aflame, forever beyond reach, destroyed before her very eyes. A few villagers were running toward the furnace. They ran right past me without even glancing in my direction. When I reached the end of the road, Tunde was waiting in his air-conditioned car. He was bent over the steering wheel, laughing. "Bravo," he spluttered, when he caught his breath.

TUNDE ISN'T LIKE MOST MEN; he calls himself a hedonist. He says he lives for worldly pleasures. Who wouldn't like to live for pleasure? Only some were denied them for fifteen years. Tunde's lips are constantly wrapped around a cigarette and he drinks beer until he is blind. He says he wants to die both under and inside a woman who is not his wife. He says the years with his mother have made me weak, and that if I had any guts, I would live freely like he does. He is wrong; I am not weak at all. It's just that my journey with him isn't com-

THE SECRET LIVES OF THE FOUR WIVES ◈ 153

plete yet. And only when it is will I be truly free. But I can't
tell him that.

I am waiting for the day when my sons will be grown up,
the day they can stand tall and walk proud. I don't treat my
children the way the other wives treat theirs. I don't beat them
or scold them. My babies won't suffer like their mother did;
they will have pain-free lives. They will eat what they want
and wash their hands when they want. The family knows that
the quickest way to see the red of my eyes is to let me come
home and find one of my children weeping. They understand
that my children aren't like the other children in Baba Segi's
household. They weren't sired by some riffraff. I made sure
of that. *Their* father lives in a house with a garden and a gas
cooker. Their father's mother is wealthy and respected. She
doesn't have paupers as friends. She wears the best gold and
the most elaborately embroidered lace. She would do everything to ensure her only son marries well and that his children are of good stock. Nothing makes me praise the Lord
more than this: one day, I will walk into her house with her
grandsons. I will look her in the eye and tell her that they are
Tunde's children. Then I'll see what Grandma will do.

Things are different in this house now. For five years,
Baba Segi loved me the most. I was better than his other
wives and he didn't hide this in the way he behaved toward
me. He would pretend he had an evening fever so he wouldn't
have to endure Iya Segi's bed. Then he would sneak into mine
at night so he could be with me. He took *me* out to visit his
friends. He liked the way I dressed so I alone accompanied

him to parties. He loved the way I cooked, the way I looked. Who wouldn't? I may be thirty but my limbs are quicker than a child's. My stomach bears no signs of labor; my breasts are full. I can't walk down the street without people wanting me. I couldn't even walk across the sitting room without Baba Segi salivating, but everything changed the day the monkey stepped into this house.

Baba Segi found a monkey whose teeth had been cut on sorrow and he forgot about me. I cannot accept it. I will not accept it! How can anyone accept being pushed aside for a woman who stores blemished bowls? Let me tell you what makes me laugh the most: the day we planted the *ogun* in her room, she declared to the world she would give her husband a son! What a fool! The biggest thing that will come out of her is a good, hefty shit. The toad hates her so *she* won't tell her the secret. The pygmy goat fears us so *she* won't tell. And she won't hear anything from me. I want her gone. I want my place back and I will get it.

THREE DAYS AFTER IYA SEGI and I decided what we were going to do, the toad came to the kitchen. At first, I thought she had just come to beg for food. It was Kole's fourth birthday and I was preparing a feast. All the children were buzzing with anticipation and wondering what dish I would dazzle them with that year. Even the other wives know what these days mean to me so they leave the kitchen and hover around for the meal.

Iya Segi tiptoed into the kitchen. "What are you making, Iya Femi? The ghost has left the house," she whispered.

"Jollof rice and chicken. Baba Segi came to my room last night but he didn't touch me. Before I could give him the *eja kika* I had prepared for him, he was fast asleep, or so he wanted me to think. For a man who cannot sleep without snoring," I said, "I didn't hear a sound from his mouth. That witch has cast a spell on him. If we are not careful, he won't sleep with us unless he asks her first."

"The gods forbid it! *We* forbid it! We will not let it happen. Look what I have brought you." Iya Segi slipped me a small plastic bag bound several times over with a rubber band.

"Iya Segi, you have the heart of a lion and the wisdom of a tortoise. What better day to bring that rat to justice!"

"Keep your voice down." Iya Segi peered out of the back door. "Iya Tope must not hear of this. Who knows where her weakness is leading her?"

"Yes, it is between us. *We* must settle this matter. And God will help us."

"Listen to me. Place Bolanle's portion outside her bedroom door like we normally do when she doesn't join us. When she returns this evening, we will greet her as if all is well so she does not suspect anything."

"How quickly does it work? Will we have cause to rejoice by tomorrow morning?"

"Mr. Taju said the medicine man who sold it to him promised immediate results. He said it was collected from the fangs of a cobra. Taju lied that it was for easing life out of an ailing dog. When the poison turns her belly, Baba Segi will be forced to take her to her father's house."

"You can count on me, Iya Segi. Evildoers should get what they deserve. The Bible says so."

As soon as Iya Segi left the kitchen, I tore at the bundle impatiently. The Lord is going to use me to conquer my enemy. The mantle of justice has fallen on me. Ha! I am blessed.

CHAPTER FOURTEEN
HOMEWARD

Bolanle

I KNEW IT WAS Kole's birthday when I woke up this morning but rather than congratulate mother and son, I slipped out of the house and headed to the diagnostic clinic to collect the results of my blood tests. On the way there, I bought Kole a remote-control car. Boxed and gift-wrapped, the toy was heavier than I thought it would be so I changed hands every time my wrist ached. I didn't want to return to Baba Segi's house yet. I was perturbed by the rat-head episode and I felt an unmistakable homeward draw. I decided to go to my parents' house.

If I wasn't so embarrassed, I would have visited my friends, if only to apologize. I'd hidden in my bedroom when Baba Segi told them that their foolishness was not welcome in our home.

"Is it not obvious to you that Bolanle has decided to choose the more virtuous path in life? You should both take her example," Baba Segi said. "What woman wants to be known as a harlot?" Yemisi gasped in disbelief. As she left, she stopped by the corridor mouth and shouted, "Let Bolanle know that people are like water. And the same waters that the streams divide meet again in the great ocean. Bolanle! You hear me?" I wept with shame.

I also wanted to go home because rumors had a way of growing feet. I reasoned that it was probably best that I tell my mother about the mysterious goings-on in my home with my own mouth. The last thing I wanted was for her to blame the decline in my morals on my father's genes. I could practically hear her: "She has become a medicine man's whore like your sister," or, "She has developed a hunger for blood like your mother did, before God clutched her to His bosom to give me rest."

I'd bumped into Segun's guard in Dugbe market a few days before and he'd mentioned that my mother complained of an unbearable throbbing in her temples. I hadn't been too bothered by this; Mama emptied sachets of Alabukun into her mouth so often when I was a child that Lara and I thought that was what all mothers did.

Anyway, today was a weekday so unless Mama was taking the day off work, I was certain I'd have to leave a get-well-soon note. That way, I could avoid the update on the progress my university friends were making in their high-flying jobs as bankers, businesswomen and lecturers, the life I should have had if I hadn't married Baba Segi. Well, none of my friends had been horribly defiled so it didn't bother me.

Today, I didn't think I could stomach any lectures. I wasn't in the mood to have my failures dangled before my eyes; I was already ashamed of them, more so in the last few weeks.

I reasoned that Mama would be glad we wouldn't have to speak to each other too. She never visited me at Baba Segi's house, but every so often a nameless visitor would drop off a branch of *awin*—bait to get me back home to wait for God to show me my *true* husband. At least she still remembered how much I loved *awin*.

When I reached the T-junction, everything seemed smaller. The road seemed narrower and the tar was eroded by flooding. When Segun's father was alive, he would tar it every January, but since his death, his wife had warned the tenants that if *they* couldn't contribute funds to arrest the deterioration, they'd better be content with parking their cars at the junction and forget *her* road was there.

My parents lived in one of eight two-bedroom bungalows on a small plot of land. A tall fence separated the tenants from the landlords, who occupied a sprawling multilevel structure surrounded by horticultural splendor. Every member of Segun's family, sisters included, had their own little suite within the building. Only Segun's had a door that opened onto the gardens. Everyone else used the magnificent awning that spooned people in and out of the main door.

I walked through the gate to the bungalows and was immediately struck by the weeds that had grown around the section of fence that my parents' bungalow leaned against. Given that Mama cleaned religiously for fear of being associated with dirt, I was surprised to see bits of paper strewn around our doorway. Mama would not have let that pass when I was living at home; she would have called me into her room and made known her disgust that I was going the way of my father's shameless siblings.

I could hear my heart thumping when I knocked on the door. I'd already started searching my bag for a notepad and pen with one hand when I heard a voice from within. I pushed the door open and followed the aroma of boiled okra to the kitchen. I stepped quietly through the sitting room, avoiding a pile of stale, unwashed clothes to find Mama straddling a low stool in the living room.

"Bolanle?"

"Yes, Mama." I was taken aback as she had her back to me. I didn't think my name would jump to her lips so readily.

"A mother never forgets her daughter's footsteps." She was sifting *elubo* into a wide-mouthed basin. "I sent for you as soon as it happened."

"As soon as what happened?" I moved closer to her and knelt to embrace her. When she turned to face me, I flung handbag and birthday present in opposite directions. It looked as if one side of her face had first been doused with oil, then set alight. From her left brow to her chin, every feature drooped like melting plastic. Her left eye was weeping, her left nostril running. There was a line of saliva dribbling down the left corner of her mouth. "Mama!" I spluttered as tears gathered in my eyes.

"The doctors say it is Bell's palsy or perhaps a very mild

stroke. Calm down. Is this not my voice that you're hearing? I am not dead. At least not yet." Her voice was the same but an octave higher. Her words seemed to spill from the corner of her mouth with a slight slur.

I tried to swallow but my mouth was suddenly dry. I feared she would hear me forcing a gulp. Mama let out a long breath and droplets of spit flew from her lips. "I sent your sister to you but she said she would rather drown than stop at your husband's house." She must have seen the shock on my face. "Your sister is not what she used to be. No, that is a lie; she is exactly what she used to be." She tried to stand but her left thigh shuddered and shook. "There is no room for me in her mind; it's just one man after the other. We do not know which one it is at any given time." She sighed. "She *too* says she's found herself a husband."

It may not have been an intended poniard but it hurt all the same. "Mama, when did this happen?"

"Just six days ago. I was slaving at work as I have always done—a mother must continue to do her duty to her children—when suddenly, I realized I couldn't hear what my colleagues were saying. I could see their mouths moving but I couldn't hear their voices. The last thing I felt was the cold tiles I have been begging my boss to change. He could at least use some of the government money he embezzles to make his surroundings pleasing to the eye. His home must be just as dirty. Anyway, when I came to, I found myself in a bed at UCH. They said I should stay but I threatened to jump off the balcony if they did not let me return home." She looked around and shook her head. "Just look how Lara has been living; the house looks like it has been taken over by harlots. You know how lazy she is! Well, I have gathered all the dirty clothes together for her to deal with. She thought I would die in the hospital but Eledumare did not permit it. She is stuck with me!" She motioned for us to sit on the cane armchairs. "The doctor said my blood pressure was exceptionally high. What does he expect? My life has been unsettled, in recent years." Another barb.

"Everyone chooses their path in life, Mama." I couldn't let that one go, no matter how much her face had dissolved.

She tried to raise her eyebrows but only the right one responded. She was surprised at my audacity, I could tell. I held out my hand to help her to a chair but she wouldn't take it; she preferred to limp on ahead. I sat opposite her, nervous as hell. Mama had always unnerved me. When I was in primary school, the journey home from school at the end of term was torture. I counted each step to make it take as long as possible, knowing that I had Mama to contend with. She would usher me into the house as if I was a visitor and ask me to kneel half an arm's length away so she wouldn't have to stretch if the need arose for her to slap me. After half an hour of waiting for her to digest every number and analyze every word written on the report, she would fold it up and look at me intensely. The words that followed tore me apart. Because there was maybe one subject I hadn't topped the class in, Mama would look at me over her glasses and tell me I wasn't her child. "My child comes first in everything," she'd say, "because I didn't raise a dullard." The one time that I protested that I had at least come first in everything else, she dug her nails into the back of my ears and twisted my earlobes until they burned. After that, she sat me down and asked me to write her a letter explaining why I had failed to beat the boy, whose father was English, in English literature. Both ears burning, I tried to work out what to write given she'd insisted that the only acceptable explanation was that the boy had two heads. While waiting for my letter, she would move on to Lara and whip her for her consistent, all-round failure. Then she would ask why Lara couldn't be more like me. Lara soon learned to doctor her report cards. I never had the guts. I was the long sufferer. I wanted to be perfect for Mama. It was on nights like those that I prayed for my father to come home early, but it was as if he knew what awaited him at home. When he did return after midnight, he would be too drunk to save us from Mama's madness.

BEFORE MAMA FLOPPED ONTO THE cushions on the cane arm-chair, she did what looked like a jig: left turn, foot forward, arms akimbo, arms down, flop. The cushions broke her fall and she patted them in gratitude. They were the same ones she'd made for her New Year ritual in 1992, nine years before. I was sixteen, and well into the second year of lifelessness. Mama liked to change at least one thing in our home; she said a new year wasn't truly new unless you made it new by buy-ing a new water jug or new curtains. Every Christmas, she troubled my father for money and he always gave in in the end. That year, however, my father had spent all his money replenishing his supply of gin. We all saw the cartons in the hallway but Mama kept asking all the same. On the twenty-third of December, Mama dragged me and Lara around Dugbe market and begged every fabric seller to pity her and her children by giving us their off-cuts for Christmas dresses. Mama had instructed us not to wear shoes and to put on the shabbiest dress we had. Lara almost died of shame and kept saying she needed the toilet. It didn't bother me at all because my dress reflected the way I felt. My tattered hemming captured my innermost feelings accurately. I stood by Mama and together we trawled the entire market until, at last, we bundled the rags onto our laps and took a taxi home.

From the moment we opened the front door, Mama decided she wasn't sleeping and neither were we. She made us cut along her unsteady lines with a rusty pair of scissors while she carefully threaded the old sewing machine she'd dragged out of storage. And while she swayed over the needle, she told us to stand behind her and watch while she thought up ridiculous chores to send us on. One by one, she sewed the silk to the taffeta, the polyester to the wool, the cotton to the velvet, until she plumped eight patchwork cushions and set them into their cane frames. Lara, who I'd thought was slumbering on her feet, burst into tears. She was always better at expressing herself; I just stood there praying for my father to come home and wipe the smug look off Mama's face. He swaggered in at one A.M. He didn't look drunk, just mellow.

So mellow that he patted my head without asking why I was up so late. He had a soft smile on his face and his eyes had a glossy film.

"Won't you sit down?" Mama pointed at one of the armchairs.

Baba noticed the difference right away but still he settled himself in his seat without commenting on the shambles Mama had turned our living room into.

"The cushions look very interesting."

Interesting? I thought. Not enchanting, provocative, affecting, alluring, striking, arresting, captivating, intriguing, enthralling, entrancing or riveting. What was *interesting* was that, for someone who loved words, "interesting" was the best he could come up with.

"I will never be able to bring my friends home again!" Lara yelled, startling everyone. I just stood there listening to my father hum happily to himself. Mama rolled her head back. I couldn't tell if she was hiding tears or resting. You could never tell with Mama.

"THE OKRA SMELLS AS IF it is cooked. Won't you help your poor mother? Or have you come to rejoice over my misfortune?" Her voice returned me to the present.

I dashed to the kitchen before she finished so her words hit the back of my head and fell to the floor. It wouldn't surprise me if she were making hideous faces behind my back so she could feel a sense of victory.

"Hmm," she exhaled when I returned to my seat. "Maybe God has decided that it is time to relieve me of my sadness. *Trust and obey for there's no other way to be happy in Jesus but to trust and obey.*" The song oozed from her lopsided mouth; it lacked melody and sincerity. She'd never been a churchgoer. Mama used God at her own convenience.

"God wouldn't take you without letting you see your children's children. That's what all mothers pray for, isn't it?" It was all I could think to say.

"Oh, really? Tell me, is it the one from that buffoon you call a husband that I should look forward to? Because if it is those ones you speak of, I pray that God keeps them in his bosom."

All the air inside me escaped through my mouth.

"How could you expect me to look forward to such grandchildren? Have you never paused to wonder how my heart stopped when you brought a married man to visit me? Or how long the dagger he dipped into my throat was when he told us that you had been courting for months? Under my roof, Bolanle! Under my roof! My house was burning and I didn't smell the smoke!"

"I should've told you earlier, Mama." I didn't want to upset her. I thought, given her illness, she might be inspired to forgive me.

"And now your sister has followed the path you opened for her. What is left for me to live for? You know, I *want* God to take me so I can look him in the eye and ask why he gave me such wicked children."

"Mama, I do not want to quarrel."

"Even if we lie to each other every week, there will come a day when we must look each other in the eye and speak the truth. Bolanle, you are the biggest disappointment the world has seen. You are ruined! Damaged! Destroyed!"

This time, she aimed well. She hit me in a soft spot. So painful was it that I raised my palms to my face and pressed out tears like pus from a wound.

She hadn't finished yet. She stopped to catch her breath and continued. "Has it been so hard for you and your sister to honor me? All I wanted was for you both to do well. But no! You want your mother to die of sadness. Let me tell you, Bolanle, I don't just sit here; I beg God daily to forgive my sins, even though I don't know what they could be. I have asked myself a million times: what evil sins have I committed to bring curses upon myself? But hear this: a child who says her mother will not have rest will also be ravaged by insomnia. There is a punishment for wickedness and we will all stand before our maker one day!" Mama leaned her head back into the headrest.

My tears pleased her enormously.

"And now she cries. She cries but she doesn't think to redeem herself. She cries but she will return to her copulation. Of what use are such tears when—"

"Mama, stop! Please! Stop!"

"Stop what? Does the truth deafen your ears?"

"I know I failed you but there is so much you didn't know."

"The truth has never said that it should not be uttered. Hear the truth now and repent. Reward your mother for all the hard work she did for you! Other than that, there is nothing more to know!"

The chipped skirting board caught my eye. There was a crack in the wall above it and a row of ants headed toward a piece of bread lying by the fridge door. I held on to the frame of the cane chair. The stuffing from the cushions brushed against the back of my hand. "I was raped, Mama! Did you know *that*? I was raped when I was fifteen years old." I'd never shouted at my mother but I heard a strident tone I'd never dared use before.

"Raped? This is not a time to tell wicked lies. Such a thing could not have happened to *my* child."

I took a moment to collect myself, knowing she was watching me, daring me to talk without first retracting my words. "You are right, Mama, I am ruined, damaged, destroyed. I am all those things you ever said. My life was wrecked and I didn't know how to fix it. I *still* don't know."

"No!" She jerked her head from side to side. Her voice fizzled into a whisper. "You couldn't have been raped. No daughter of mine could have been raped. That is not the way I brought you up."

"No one brings their daughter up to be raped." I closed my eyes and told her what happened. There was no point sparing her the details; it was time she heard them. When I reached the part where the stranger put a pillow over my head, Mama snatched her scarf from her head and began to rock slowly in her seat. I didn't stop; I wanted my mother to hear it all. I didn't want to carry it alone anymore.

Tear after tear rolled down one eye alone. "Why didn't you tell me so I could seek out this beast and cut out his insides?"

"I wanted to be your perfect daughter. I didn't want to disappoint you."

"Hush, child, what mother can hate the child she labored to bring to the world? Ah! The blood that runs through my veins is full of sorrow." She paused to wipe her tears with her wrapper. "Was I so distant? Was I so deaf? Ah! This world and its violent surprises!"

It wasn't the time to answer those questions. I wasn't going to give her the chance to justify her behavior. I wanted to tell her about me. "Mama, you were living with an empty shell. Everything was scraped out of me. I was inside out."

"Is this why you allowed yourself to be seduced by that buffoon?" Distraught though she was, Mama couldn't cast aside her anger over my marriage. I didn't expect her to; it wasn't her style. She had to win.

"I wasn't seduced. *That buffoon* was prepared to take me as I was. He didn't ask me any questions. Neither did he know a past he could compare my present with. I was lost and didn't want to do anything with my life. He was prepared to take me like that. All he wanted was for me to be his wife. Imagine how appealing that was to me!"

Apart from the business with Segun and the abortion, which was best not mentioned, I told her everything. I told her about the wives and the rodent skull. I told her I was seeing a doctor because I hadn't been able to conceive. Mama listened and nodded her head, all the time observing my face: the tiny crow's-feet at the corner of my eyes, the shallow creases on the skin around my mouth. When I was finished, she asked me if I was hungry. She looked more sympathetic than I had ever seen her, but even so, the words "I told you so" were written all over her face. Only a fool would have expected reparation. Mama didn't do things that way.

Before I left, I soaked all the dirty laundry. I made some *eba* and when I sat down to dish the food into separate bowls, Mama insisted that we eat out of the same one. When I returned to the sitting room after washing the dirty dishes, Mama was snoring quietly, so I looked into my old bedroom. It was a complete mess. Why did I expect different? I wasn't there to clean up after Lara anymore.

The cardboard boxes in which I'd carefully folded my old clothes had been ripped open. Some of the contents were strewn around the room, others stuffed back in. She'd given the beautiful women on the Mills and Boon novels mustaches. One of my old diaries lay under the bed. Lara would have pushed it there. Perhaps she did that so Mama wouldn't find it. It was carelessly hidden all the same. Thank goodness I had given the people in it the names of trees. I picked it up and put it in my bag; I'd throw it in the bin on my way out. Before I left, Mama gave me a firm one-armed embrace. It was awkward because I couldn't remember that she ever held me with tenderness. There always seemed to be pain involved when she touched me, so the feel of her arm on my back, the warmth of her cheek against mine, was memorable in its own way.

WHEN I RETURNED TO BABA SEGI'S house that evening, I noted that it was that lovely phase of dusk when the sky filled with orange clouds as if a paintbrush had been rinsed in it. There was a looseness about my stride. At university, my friends had joked that I walked upright, to curb the tiniest provocative waggle. It's true. I sucked my buttocks in and clinched my knees together, but for a different reason. I reasoned that if I strengthened my thigh muscles, it would make it difficult for anyone to force my legs apart like they did in my dreams. That evening, I let my arms dangle at my sides. I set my hips free and my neck sought the source of every sound, the way children did until their mothers slapped the backs of their heads into the direction they were going in. I saw the night guard approaching and greeted him before he got to me. He smiled but it disappeared all too quickly and a scrawny hand scratched a bald head. He was probably baffled by my lack of poise; I was normally so well pulled together.

The aroma of fresh palm wine was rich and intoxicating, so I looked in the direction of the nearby shack. I wanted to see the large pregnant gourd buzzing with the hum of inebriated bees as young men dipped into it, drowning themselves in its sweetness. Leaning and slouching over them were women who had braved neighborhood gossip to be there. They sat there in the distance, laughing and sipping from halved cala-bashes. I smiled to myself and hurried on, tickled by the play-ful finger of young love.

I heard the footsteps gaining on me but I ignored them. I didn't want to turn and find it was just some poor woman rushing home clutching a Bible and a toddler. Apart from that, I was determined not to let anything knock me off my high. I hadn't felt such liberty in a long time. It was only when a voice breathlessly shouted, "Wait, please," that I swung round.

"Good evening, Segi." She didn't just want me to slow down; she wanted me to stop.

She slowed down before she reached me, urging me to stop. "Auntie, please don't tell. Mama will kill me."

I exhaled. My exhilaration vanished and a sense of wea-riness came over me. Not more household intrigue! Could I bear it? "Don't tell her what?"

"Don't tell my mother that you saw me at the palm wine shed. Don't tell my father you saw me with a boy." Segi flung her fingers into the air as if to shake wetness from them. She was hopping from foot to foot and her mouth was open in supplication.

My heart went out to her. "I won't say a word." I must have given in too easily. Either that or she just didn't believe me.

"Please, Auntie Bolanle. Please. I beg you, Auntie. I'll do anything."

"So now you want to bribe me?" I asked. It occurred to me that although Segi had always been civil, she had never addressed me as "Auntie" before. She'd always just blurted whatever she had to say. And now, this rain of affectionate "Auntie"s.

"No. I'm not trying to bribe you. I'm *begging* you, Auntie. Don't make my father disown me. Please."

Maybe some other person would've derived joy from seeing her so distraught, but I didn't. Neither, contrary to the young girl's thinking, did I feel I now had a punch I could take at will. I felt sorry for her. Only eight years before, I'd have done anything to get to Segun's room so I could satisfy the mysterious rush of blood to my groin. "I give you my word; I won't tell anyone."

Segi looked up at me and wiped away tears that had not yet dropped to her cheeks. "Thank you, Auntie. It was a silly mistake. I have never been there before but this boy has taken over my mind. When I sit down, I think of him. When I eat, he is there, on my mind. Sometimes I fear Mama will look at me and read my innermost thoughts."

"What's his name?"

"Goke. He is eighteen. He is a student at Ibadan Polytechnic, studying to become a surveyor." She wanted me to be impressed.

I indulged her. "Really? Where did you meet him?"

"His mother sells snacks outside our school. Sometimes he comes to help her."

"Is he handsome?"

"Well, you saw him, didn't you? All the girls in my class are jealous of me."

"He didn't look bad at all." I was by now too far gone to

admit that I hadn't seen Segi nor the man she was with.

"But why did he invite you to the palm wine shack? Doesn't he know how old you are?"

"I told him I didn't want to go there but he said he wanted to show me off to his friends."

"Did *you* enjoy being there?"

"Not particularly. His friends were telling very dirty jokes. I was just happy to be near him so I could look at his face."

"And have you looked at more than his face?"

"Auntie!" Segi covered her eyes with her fingers. "I swear I have not seen any more. He said he would teach me how to kiss like a woman tonight but I left him and ran after you. I am sure all his friends are laughing at me now." She sighed and looked over her shoulder.

"Then they are foolish. Anyone who laughs at you for showing your family respect is a fool. How would *you* be feeling now if you'd just sat there?"

"My heart would be in my mouth. I wouldn't have been able to relax." Segi put her arm through mine as the thought created new dread in her mind.

"Good. So even though you left him at the shack, you have peace of mind . . . which means you did the right thing. A real woman must always do the things *she* wants to do, and in her own time too. You must never allow yourself to be rushed into doing things you're not ready for." We stepped onto the veranda of Baba Segi's house together, the same foot at the same time.

Iya Tope was the only adult in the sitting room. As soon as we strolled in, her nostrils flared like damp shorts on the washing line. She opened her mouth to speak but no words came out. She just stared, forgetting to blink, then blinking a flurry. She turned to the children happily scoffing their food but it was clear that her mind was burdened.

Segi touched the forehead of each sibling she encountered. Most of them were sucking on chicken bones, their cheeks dotted with half grains of jollof rice. Akin looked up at us, smiled and returned to the sports column of yesterday's newspaper. Ever since Baba Segi tried to strangle me, he'd flattened himself behind curtains and cupboards whenever I walked by.

"What sort of things were you talking about?" Segi asked as we walked through the corridor to my bedroom. Ordinarily Segi would have gone straight to her mother's bedroom and then to the bedroom she shared with Akin to change her clothes, but on this occasion, she didn't do either; she linked her arm in mine, determined not to leave my side.

The bedroom was as I had left it except there was a cream-colored bowl on the dressing table. The handle on the lid was a puckered rosebud. "Iya Femi has saved me some birthday chicken." I fanned the aroma toward Segi with the lid and replaced it.

"Well, aren't you going to eat it?" Without waiting for the go-ahead, Segi dipped her fingers into the bowl and lifted out a peppered wing cut deep into the shoulder. A generous chunk of flesh half-covered by dimpled skin hung from it. Segi placed a palm underneath to catch the oil and sank her teeth into it. She closed her eyes so she could savor the stock trickling down her throat.

"I just had dinner with my mother. You eat it. It's chicken and I've never been a fowl person." I surrendered the entire bowl to Segi's eager hands.

"There are three big pieces here. I could comfortably throw the lot into one nostril. I'll finish it for you and lick the bowl. If only I'd known you were this generous—" Segi spluttered with her mouth full.

"You can have them all!" I laughed.

"You were saying earlier not to rush things . . . ?"

I watched Segi wolf down the chicken. She didn't appear to chew at all. For someone who rarely spoke to me or sat with me, I was amused by Segi's disregard for protocol. I wondered if she'd be as friendly when her mother was around.

As if Iya Segi had heard my thoughts, her voice suddenly rang through the walls. She inquired if Segi was back from her walk and Femi eagerly informed her that Segi was locked away in my room. Eager to get to the bottom of the unfathomable intercourse, Iya Segi went to the mouth of the corridor and yelled her daughter's name.

"I'd better go now," Segi said, steeping each finger into her mouth and swiveling her tongue around it. I passed her a paper napkin.

"Please say thank you to Iya Femi for me. And give this

birthday present to Kole." I handed her the colorfully wrapped box and flopped onto the bed. I arched my back and tried to find sleep but I couldn't. My mother's face kept inching before my eyes. Besides, the silence was unsettling, there was a backdrop—a long whistle somewhere beyond my window, beyond the garden and the fence.

CHAPTER FIFTEEN
NIGHT NOISES

IT WAS JUST LIKE it was when she slept in the same room as Lara. She'd lain there for what seemed like hours before she realized she was being kept awake by the night's noises. The air was steamed with an aphrodisiac. Every toad for miles was croaking its finest *woo* song, and in the Alao house, crickets serenaded one another in harmonized duets. It was the exact location of this noise that Bolanle was trying to decipher when she realized she was fully clothed. She changed into her nightgown and got on her knees. As she crawled along the walls, she pressed the nozzle of the insect killer at the narrow gap between the wall and the wooden skirting board. She could taste the insecticide at the back of her throat.

Iya Segi's room was just a few yards down the corridor and Bolanle could hear her voice filtering through the walls into her room. It was angry, like the buzzing of a frustrated bee against a closed window. Bolanle heard her name each time Iya Segi accused her daughter of shamelessness. Equally aggravating was Segi's silence at the end of every question, which seemed to cause her mother much frustration. It was only after her mother told her to go to her room that Segi opened her mouth. "Do not be annoyed, Mama," she said.

The words did not carry the remorse her mother was looking for. "Just get out!" Iya Segi snapped.

"Yes, Mama."

Bolanle heard Segi shuffle out of her mother's bedroom.

Around two A.M., a chilling scream pierced the silence in all the rooms of the house. It wasn't high pitched—more like the sorrowfully low notes of a trombone—but it went on for an uncomfortable length of time. Bolanle sat up with a jolt and leaped off her bed. She wrapped her cover cloth around her shoulders and raced out of her bedroom.

Baba Segi, Iya Femi, Segi and Akin were all in the sitting room. Iya Segi was there too but standing in the far corner, with her fist in her mouth, shivering. Black bra straps had fallen onto fat upper arms and her wrapper was bundled together around her waist.

From where she was standing, all Bolanle could see were Segi's feet lying on the floor. They flexed and contracted as if she was in the throes of an epileptic fit. Her father was on his knees next to her, staring at her as if to absorb her pain. He kept touching her legs and arms, addressing her in a mix of prayers, pleas and promises. "Don't leave me, my daughter. Don't let me mourn you. It is not the order of things in our world. Tell the gods you want to stay here with me. Tell them you are not ready to walk the path of the ancestors. Tell them there are those who love you here, in our world. Tell them your father loves you. Tell them for me, Segi. My daughter, I will buy you gold. I will buy you the finest lace. First fruit of my loins, do not disregard my words." It was a pitiful sight. He tried to blink back his tears but they created dark spots on Segi's nightdress. Iya Segi kept peeking at Segi from behind the head tie she had draped over her face.

Iya Tope ran into the room carrying the shirt that matched the trousers Baba Segi was wearing. Her entire front was covered in undigested chicken streaked with blood. A stench pursued her but she wasn't bothered by it; she was entirely focused on retrieving the keys of the pickup from the nail.

Bolanle scanned the faces of all those present but not one pair of eyes responded to her inquiring brow. Instead, they were wet with foreboding. Iya Femi sat in her armchair jiggling her foot. Her eyelids were heavy with sleep and resentment. *Her* children didn't get this much attention when they had a fever. Why did the entire household have to be disturbed on account of Segi's vomiting? She ate far too much anyway.

It was when Iya Tope and Akin carried Segi to the pickup that Bolanle got a chance to see her face. She looked like she was sucking her cheeks in, like they'd been deflated. Every so often, a torrent of toddler-like gibberish escaped her throat. Her crooked fingers were drawn into semi-fists. Her palms looked as if the blood beneath the skin had receded into her wrists. Just before they bundled her into the pickup, her body was wrenched by a sudden urge to vomit. The force of it was so overpowering that she soiled herself.

Baba Segi settled himself into the driver's seat. Opting for lucidity over maternal unpredictability, he commanded Iya Tope to get in and sit next to Segi. "Watch over Iya Segi and the children!" he shouted to Iya Femi before he drove off.

Bolanle went to the kitchen to fetch Iya Segi and Iya Femi some cold drinking water from the fridge. She brought out two glasses on a tray and presented one of them to Iya Segi. Iya Segi slapped saucer and glass onto the carpet and pulled Bolanle's face close to hers.

"What have you done to my daughter? Answer me, witch! What have you inflicted on my daughter?" Iya Segi grabbed Bolanle by the sleeve, knocking the tray to the floor.

"Mama, no!" Akin shouted.

Iya Segi turned to her son. "If you don't want your mother to curse you, find your way to your bed. Now!" With the boy out of earshot, she burrowed her nails deeper into Bolanle's shoulder.

"I didn't do *anything* to her," Bolanle shouted. She didn't know whether to wrench herself from Iya Segi's clutch or offer herself as a sacrifice. Iya Femi lay her head on the head-rest of her armchair, put her feet on a footstool and folded her arms, watching.

"What did you *say* to her? What curses did you put on her?" Iya Segi's words were laced with garlic. She chewed six cloves every night as part of her constitutional maintenance.

"I didn't say anything to her!"

"Why did you force her into your room then? My daughter has never kept secrets from me but tonight she behaved as if she was born without ears! Tell me what you did to her!"

"Iya Segi, please, you are hurting me. Let me go to my room."

Iya Segi pushed Bolanle with all the strength in her muscular arms. The smaller woman fell backward and landed bottom-first on a stool before toppling over and knocking her head on the cold terrazzo, just missing the edge of the rug. Although Bolanle heard the sound of bone grazing stone, she jumped to her feet in case Iya Segi decided to pounce. Unstable on her feet, Bolanle touched the back of her head and brought her hand within view; it was moist with blood. "Look what you have done to me!" she whispered.

At this, Iya Femi pointed at Bolanle, threw her head back and burst into peals of laughter. She held her belly and rocked on her seat. Then, as suddenly as she started, she stopped. "What *she* has done to you? How lucky you are that Iya Segi did not decapitate you and pound your head in the mortar! You are indeed an evil spirit. Get thee behind us, Satan! Leave our home!" Iya Femi flicked her wrists and shooed her.

"But what have I done to make you hate me? What have I ever done to hurt any of you?"

"Ha! The exact words of the witch who was caught drying her hands after her neighbor's child was found floating in the compound well." Iya Femi paused. "Sooner than you think, we will be rid of your evil spirit."

Bolanle raised her hands. "I don't understand this! One minute you are giving me generous portions of chicken from your son's birthday celebrations, the next, you call me an evil spirit. What am I to make of all this? Which is it exactly?"

"You will know soon enough! Don't be in a hurry, evil spirit." Iya Femi let her laughter loose again.

"Then it is good that I did not eat it. I'm glad it was Segi who ate it all. I am glad my lips did not touch food that was offered to me from hands that hate me. I am glad that—"

Iya Segi, who had slipped back into her trance, sat up. "Did you say Segi ate your chicken?"

"Yes, she wanted it and I let her have it. I am not full of hate. Why should I deprive her of anything when she is a child, and my husband's daughter?" Before they could humiliate her further, Bolanle ran to her bedroom and locked the door behind her.

After a few moments of silence, Iya Segi sank into her seat as if she was being softened, feet first, in a pot of boiling water. She only stopped when her back was where her bottom should have been. "Ah! Iya Femi, what have we done with our own hands?"

"I told you the woman was a witch. Why was it tonight of all nights that Segi went to her room? She must have used spiritual water to wash her eyes. She must have known and forced Segi to eat the chicken."

Both women looked at each other. They both knew no force was required where Segi's appetite was concerned. "Did you use all of the powder? Perhaps it will not have the potency Taju said it would have."

"Every grain of it. As you instructed. Don't worry, I know what to do. Early tomorrow morning, I will go to the prophets in my church. They will fast and pray for three days. I am not a prophet but God does not fail me. We will not lose a child in this household!"

"Did you say lose a child? Do you realize what has just come out of your mouth?" Iya Segi grabbed a stool by the leg.

The veins around the older wife's grip were set to burst; it looked like Iya Segi might hurl the mahogany stool. "I spoke foolishly, Iya Segi, like a child without wisdom." Iya Femi said a hurried good night and locked herself in her bedroom.

When morning came, the younger children sat around the corridor and didn't seem to know if they were awake or sleepwalking. They'd woken to find Iya Segi there as if she wasn't, head on fist, watching white clouds discolor the darkness. Iya Femi's room was locked, as was Bolanle's. Iya Tope was nowhere to be found. And to top it all, their beloved Segi was gone too.

Akin tried to persuade them that all was well and offered to make breakfast, but the corn pap he cooked was riddled with raw pellets and swam off the spoon. The children didn't complain; they sucked it off the spoon and sieved with their teeth. After a few minutes, Akin threw down his spoon and ordered them to pour it down the sink. It was Femi who saved the day. He sat by his mother's bedroom door and yelled until his throat hurt. For once, Akin didn't try to stop him, running to his own bedroom to pull a pillow over his head. Before long, an anxious Iya Femi surfaced and appeased the children with hot loaves of bread and tinned sardines.

Woken by Femi's screaming, Bolanle's thoughts immediately went to Segi. She sat up and felt the stinging from the nail marks on her shoulders. Her head ached. There was a large tie-dye bloodstain on her pillow and her shoulders were dotted with blood flakes. She sat in front of her dressing-table mirror and examined the back of her head with a compact. If I am not careful, I will die in this house, she thought. She cupped the clump of dried blood that clung to her hair and feathered it into the bin. Then she concealed the gash with a scarf and decided to wait for Baba Segi's return before leaving her bedroom.

The pickup ground the gravel and came to a halt at seven twenty-five. Iya Femi and the children rushed to the sliding door. Baba Segi's movements were slow and uncoordinated as he struggled to climb out of the pickup, followed by Iya Tope, whose face was drained of all emotion. They stumbled through the door to find Iya Segi motionless in her armchair, staring but not seeing. Iya Tope started pulling off her vomit-stained *buba* before she got to the corridor. Her lips were turned down. She looked as if she'd shed her skin too if she could. Baba Segi flopped onto his armchair like he always did. He let his eyes roll back, and then his head. He stretched out his legs before him and loosened his shoes from his feet. "She is not dead. The doctors say it is food poisoning. She confessed that she drank palm wine yesterday evening. Ah, these young girls!" He sighed. "As for me," he said, stretching, "I am exhausted!" His head lolled onto the headrest and he immediately began to snore like a wild hog.

Iya Segi heard the snoring, yet she turned to him with eyes full of relief. All night, she'd sat there wondering if her daughter might go from the hospital to the mortuary. As tradition dictated, she would never have been able to see her daughter's face again, never touch her fingers, never admire her hair. She was thankful for the news Baba Segi brought so she stood up and dragged herself to her bedroom.

For the rest of the week, there was no laughter in the Alao household. It was as if the grieving had been prescheduled and therefore impossible to cancel. The older children went to the back of the house and sobbed inconsolably while the younger children moped and sat in the corridor, refusing to wear a thread of clothing. They missed their sister and the fact that she was lying on a hospital bed where they couldn't see her made it unbearable. They missed Segi's laughter, her comforting words, the last bites of meat she gave them.

It was hardest for Akin. They'd slept in the same bedroom for nearly ten years and as he slunk around the house, Segi's absence swelled by the minute. He imagined that his siblings would soon begin to turn to him and the thought frightened him. He wasn't sure he could do the things his sister did so masterfully, so he carried his loneliness around with him with no one to turn to for comfort. Iya Tope was trying to run the household, his mother was still not herself and Iya Femi's bosom welcomed only her own children's heads. A number of times, Akin knocked quietly on Bolanle's door but ran away before she opened it.

CHAPTER SIXTEEN
NOTE

Iya Femi

G OD HAS TURNED HIS FACE from this house.
Last night Baba Segi brought news that threw the household into anguish. He told us that Segi's hair was falling out and that if she as much as brushed her finger against her ear, her hair dropped onto the pillow like the feathers from a fowl steeped in boiling water.

To the uninformed ear, this might have sounded trivial, but in our house, it fermented the stomach contents of all who heard it. Iya Tope cried out first because she spent much of her time nurturing Segi's hair. She wailed that she had plaited it since she joined this household. She doesn't have much to do with her life, you see.

I went to church after I heard but I was not uplifted. The candlelit altar and the candle-lighting pastor looked ridiculous. The prophet stared at my breasts for so long that I had to tell him not to defile me. It wasn't until I got home that I realized how much his evil spirit had followed me.

I sent Taju to Tunde's office this morning but instead of bringing money to raise my spirits, he returned with a photocopied note:

> *Following my mum's passing, I have decided to accept the position of U.S. rep.*
>
> *A big thank-you to those of you who made it to my mum's funeral at such short notice. For those of you that I didn't get the chance to say good-bye to, forgive me.*
>
> *My e-mail address remains the same so I look forward to hearing from you soon.*
>
> *Ever yours,*
> *Tunde Adeigbe*

I ask you: what is e-mail? And what is a U.S. rep? Ha! God! Is this your face? I could not stop the tears of anger that wet my face. I cried. So there is no Grandma to parade my sons in front of? Ha! Coward! She saw my triumph coming and decided to deny my victory! She begged the devil to spare her my revenge, my gloating, my head-splitting laughter! And my children. My sons! They might as well have been born to Baba Segi. All these years, wasted!

Ha! Tunde! So you have abandoned me without knowing your sons! Will I ever see you again? Why didn't you tell me you were going? Is that how small I was in your eyes? Did my spirit not speak to your conscience? How could I have been so stupid?

I am alone in this world and it is now that I know that I am an orphan. I have no one. Who will I speak to? Who will I walk with? Iya Tope does not want to know me and Iya Segi is mad with grief. Every time I see her, I remember the chicken spitting in the frying pan.

God, cover me with your spirit. Cover me so my enemies will not laugh at my shame. Send your angels to shield me with their wings. Avenge those who want to persecute your daughter. Rain brimstone and fire on their heads! Do not let the devil smite me in my time of shame!

CHAPTER SEVENTEEN

RESULTS

Bolanle

Dr. Dibia was shorter than most men but he made up for it with a big book. He had a short Afro and his thick lenses were framed with heavy rectangular rims. When I walked into his office, he asked me to sit down and made me wait for him to finish the page he was reading. "Pardon me," he said as he inserted a tattered leather bookmark between its pages. Only then did he pick up my file to mouth every word in it.

"So have you brought the test results?" He stretched out his hand without looking up at me and eagerly tore at the envelope with a steel letter opener.

While he read, I glanced at his desk. All his stationery was coordinated; the letter opener, the stapler and the staple remover were made from leather and shiny copper. When he'd finished, he summoned a nurse and instructed her to prepare me. I wondered if there was some reason why he avoided my eyes and concluded that he must be bashful. He muttered to himself as I lay waiting behind the white curtain. The nurse must have sensed my uneasiness because she reassured me that I was in good hands. "Dr. Dibia is one of the best in the country," she said.

Within a few moments, Dr. Dibia swooped the curtain aside and came at me with latex talons. He mumbled to himself as he prodded and pushed my belly. And when he moved between my legs to examine me internally, he gazed up at the ceiling and cocked his head sideways. It was only when he pressed my stomach down and swiveled his fingers around inside me that he looked inquiringly at my face for wincing and grimacing.

"Please relax," he said. "Make your knees flop sideways." Awkward though the experience was, he was gentle and there was no serious discomfort. When he was satisfied, he asked me to put on my clothes and returned to his table.

"From my examinations, the results of the scan and the blood tests, I cannot see any immediate reasons why you shouldn't be able to conceive. You have had one termination?" He lowered his frames and looked me in the eye for the first time. So he wasn't shy then.

I nodded. As if his colleague hadn't already grilled me on the when, where and who, he queried me again. This time I was alone so it was easier. "Nineteen ninety-two. In a small shed. A nurse, I think."

"A nurse?" He hit the table with his fist, making everything jump. "Did you hear that, Sister?"

"Yes, Doctor." Sister's voice came from behind the white curtain, where she was clearing the examination table in preparation for the next patient.

He looked back to me. "Well, all I can tell you is that you are a very lucky woman. An unqualified person has performed a major procedure on you and you have, seemingly, escaped unscathed." He looked at me for a few seconds and then softened his gaze abruptly. "Well, now that you are older and no doubt wiser, I hope you won't subject yourself to such butchery again." It sounded more like an order than candid advice.

I was just about to tell him I was in his office because I want to have a baby, not to dispose of one, when the nurse summoned him. "Doctor, I think you should see this."

The doctor excused himself and returned within seconds. "Mrs. Alao, there are some bloodstains on the examination table. Are you by any chance bleeding?" He fluttered his fingers in the direction of my face to indicate that he wasn't referring to my lower region.

I was puzzled for a moment but then I reached up and touched the back of my head. It was wet. "I slipped and hit my head on the floor. Hard." It came out like a question. Even I wouldn't have believed me.

The doctor sprang up from his seat and stood over me. "Do you mind if I take a look?"

I untied the scarf; the smell of stale blood swirled around my face and filled my nostrils.

"That's quite a gash you have there. Has it been seen to?"

"No, it's just a small—"

"Believe me, it's not a small anything." He returned to his seat. "Nurse will escort you to the A & E department from here. It will need a *proper* dressing." There was a glimmer of sympathy in his eyes when he spoke but it disappeared quickly. "Now, back to the matter at hand: I would like your husband to come in for some preliminary tests. Do you think he can make it next Monday?"

"I'll tell him," I said.

"Good." Dr. Dibia opened his appointment book and drew zigzags down the page with his finger. "Ten thirty A.M.?"

"That should be fine."

"It is important that he comes. I am sure that he'll understand that it takes two to make a baby."

"He has seven children already." I could be saucy too.

"Nevertheless!" He handed me an appointment card. "Right, straight to the A & E with you, Mrs. Alao." He said it like he didn't trust me, like he imagined I would run off with a bloodied head scarf.

The nurse appeared before he'd finished talking and flashed him a reassuring glance.

The female doctor who treated me was sympathetic. She said the wound was infected and slowly pressed an anti-tetanus injection into my right buttock. Then she carefully shaved the hair around the wound, all the time telling me that she didn't believe in taking off more hair than was necessary. Given that I was left with only three-quarters of what was on my head when I first sat before her, I wondered what styles she imagined I might comb it into.

Luckily, the wound didn't require round-the-head bandaging. She dressed it and held the gauze fast with strips of surgical tape. Dr. Dibia's nurse returned with a clean scarf. "Anything donated to the charity box has been laundered first," she said as she handed it to me.

I left the hospital grounds wondering if modern medicine was making a mockery of my childlessness. I didn't feel the sense of relief I should have. If there was nothing wrong with me, why was my belly not rounded and taut? Dr. Dibia must have missed something! The doctor at the ultrasound center must have missed something!

I got to the gate of my parents' compound to find a heavy-duty padlock hanging from it. There were six new doorbells on the pillar, each one labeled. Another of the landlady's modern innovations, I thought, wondering how my mother would cope with having to walk out to open the gate every time their bell rang? I pressed the bell that had AKANBI printed on it.

My father soon appeared dangling a bunch of keys from his forefinger. "Bolanle, it is only eyes that have special powers that see you these days." His face was smeared with that mellow smile of his and I wondered if he was truly glad to see me or if his cheeriness was gin induced. He normally had at least four shots warming his belly by midmorning.

"I was here just a few days ago, Baba," I replied, feigning indignation at his accusation.

"And before then?" He mockingly held his head back to take a good look at me. "I am not as old as I look, you know." He liked these games. When we were children, he liked to amuse himself by making us articulate our hatred for things using new words. "I loathe bread and despise onions," I would say. Lara would follow with "I just don't like Mama at all," which made my father fall over laughing. The visitor game was his favorite by far. If he ever missed a visitor while he was out, he would ask us to describe them. Of course, we would rattle on about the obvious features but Baba would ask us if the visitor's left arm was shorter than the other, or if he had a mole buried in his mustache. Our stammering greatly tickled him. He would tell us to keep our eyes peeled the next time and send us off to buy lollipops. He was the only man who could have coped with Mama; any other would have strangled her or deserted her. He'd long ago come to terms with his emasculation and it seemed he was more at ease without responsibility.

"You are right, Father. I have not been the most dutiful daughter but my life has been filled with uncertainties lately."

"Yes, I heard. Your mother was much distressed by it. Such ruthlessness! Such callousness! Wives without the worthiness of wifeliness!" It was never enough to just state something simply. For him, the more syllables the better. And since his wife didn't seem to appreciate his soliloquies, he spent his big words on his children. He used them during assembly at the school where he'd taught history for twenty-seven years and the look of bewilderment on his colleagues' faces gave him immeasurable pleasure. It wasn't that he was much of an intellectual; he just had the peculiar hobby of memorizing words in the *Roget's Thesaurus* he'd thumbed three times over.

I watched Baba battle with the padlock as he spoke. I was glad Mama hadn't told him I was raped; she wouldn't have wanted me enjoying that much sympathy. Besides, she would have worried about appearing inadequate, or worse, sloppy. Baba put his arm around me as soon as I stepped into the compound so I wouldn't squat to greet him. He didn't like the business of kneeling and prostrating; he said it was ungainly and superficial. He drew me close and whispered into my ear, "Lara is home and a battle is raging. It's a good thing that you've come because I was beginning to think I should escape."

We walked indoors, arms linked, and I thought how unfamiliar it felt to be so close to him. The smell of him didn't conjure any fond memories. Gin had stolen Baba from our childhood and when there wasn't any, he did what he did best: he escaped.

I braced myself for Lara's resentment. Our chance meetings were never pleasant; she tried hard to offend me but I always restrained myself. I felt sorry for Lara. There was a part of me that believed I'd failed her. I should have stuck up for her when Mama ripped her already-fragile confidence to pieces. Mama was at it again now but her voice didn't have the old potency; it wavered, dipping into deep somberness and then breaking into a high-pitched urgency. Her breathing was uncoordinated and got in the way of the things she wanted to say.

Lara kissed her teeth when she saw me. "So you decided to summon your favorite and gang up on me."

"Actually, they had no idea I was coming. I just dropped in to visit my family and see how my mother was faring. Believe it or not, I didn't know she'd had a stroke until last week because no one bothered to tell me." I looked Lara in the eye and as my gaze traveled downward, I saw an unusually rotund midsection. "Are you—"

"Yes, she is! You see what woe has befallen me? She has allowed that common musician to climb on top of her and pump her full of child."

"Is it the fact that he is a musician that bothers you, Mama, or the fact that I am pregnant and not pursuing your dreams? Woe indeed! You'd think I had nothing better to do."

I looked from one woman to the other. Lara had inherited Mama's venom: by the time she was seventeen, she was taking her on in full-blown shouting matches while I hid in the next room, incapable of calming either temper. They were so alike, determined to get what they wanted at any cost, and stubborn as hell.

"Lara, that's no way to talk to your mother." Baba knew he had to say something to her before her brazenness was ascribed to our gene pool.

"What mother? She has never been a mother to me! You'd think I was after her husband, the way she's victimized me.

Do this! Study this! Go to university! Only marry a man who does this! When will you stop trying to make me live the life you failed to live? Can't you just be happy with yours?"

"I may think about stopping after I have slapped that ungrateful mouth of yours, you imbecile!"

"Slap it now, Mama." Lara shifted to the edge of her chair and turned her cheek toward her mother. "Slap it as you have always slapped it. Slap it to your heart's content! Go on. Slap it! Jump at it! What difference has it ever made?"

"Iya Bolanle, there will be no need for that!" If there was one thing Baba couldn't bear, it was what he called gratuitous brutality. Every time Mama beat us when we were younger, Lara and I prayed for him to come to our rescue and ward off Mama's palm, but he would look away, unable to watch. We fantasized about him standing up to her and warning her never to inflict pain on his children, but it never happened that way. Baba would issue a quiet cautionary word and vanish, leaving his words by the wayside.

Three times Mama tried to push herself off her seat but each time, she fell backward. Her eyes were set on Lara. When she became breathless, she launched into Papa as if her inability to lift herself was *his* fault. "Just listen to your pathetic self. What do you know about how to bring up a child? You call yourself a father but keep mute until all dignity is beyond us. If not for the mother who has slaved for them, where would they be today?" She snorted and shook her head in disgust.

"Oh, dear! Poor Mama!" Like our mother, Lara had perfected her sarcasm. "Imagine!" she continued. "All that slaving wasted. And you thought you'd be able to dictate who I'd marry and how I'd live my life! Well, I'm sorry, *I* didn't beg you to slave for me. You should have done that for Bolanle alone."

I could have cut Lara down to size. I could have called her a dunce and made her burst into angry tears, but instead I chose to be sensible—the one quality she despised in me. "*Who* is it that Lara wants to marry, Mama? And why are you so unhappy with him?"

"Is it not a guitar player with knotted hair? He prances around in jeans that are torn at the knees and every time he comes here, the smell of cigarettes fills the entire house. And he speaks like those Jamaicans too—'no, man,' 'yes, man.' I had to ask him yesterday: is it that I look like a man to you? And what did he do? He laughed in my face."

Baba covered his mouth with his palm but his eyes bulged with amusement.

"As it happens, Mama, his mother *is* Jamaican. Yes, he has knotted hair and smells of cigarettes. But you know what? I like him that way and I am the one who will have to live with him." My sister scratched her belly.

There was an awkward silence.

"Mama, there is just one thing." Everyone turned to listen to me. "And I want you to consider the implications of your words before you utter them. This child that Lara is carrying, what do you want her to do to it?"

Baba, who was already putting on his shoes, stopped and sat upright. The room went so quiet that everyone heard the

ticking of the wall clock. Mama looked away, sensing that
she'd been cornered. Twice she made to open her mouth to
speak but closed it again. It was as if the actual existence of
a child, though unborn, had only then dawned on her. This
wasn't just another of Lara's frivolities but a fetus that would
one day speak, walk and laugh. And if I was indeed barren, this might be her only chance to carry a child born to
her daughter. She'd sat there slicing the manhood from the
father of what might be her only grandchild. She whimpered
and looked from one face to the other. Even Lara could not
endure the sight of Mama hitching her leg against the chair
leg, like a dog scratching its belly; she crawled to Mama's feet
and buried her face in Mama's lap. Mama didn't say anything;
she placed her hand on Lara's head and brushed her hair back
with her fingertips.

When Lara returned to her seat, she looked at me and
mouthed the words "thank you." Baba brought the knuckles of both thumbs to his lips and closed his eyes. There was
discomfiture at first but before long, we were talking. We
talked about the scarcity of kerosene and how distressing the
queues at the filling stations were. We all laughed when Baba
described his frustration over the endless yelping of the neighbor's puppy. He declared that he was plotting to kidnap it and
dump it in a faraway village. Mama laughed so much that she
held her forehead and quaked in her seat. It was a deep-belly
laugh with a hum at the end of it. It was an unfamiliar sound
yet I had heard it a long time ago, long before Baba developed
a passion for Gordon's. An image came to me of the four of us

in the same room: Mama pregnant with Lara, Baba clapping his hands and me dancing around the room for their entertainment. A happy family.

I looked at everyone's lips and noted how their voices had suddenly become crisp, clear and melodious, no longer the muffled echoes my ears had become attuned to. That afternoon, I said good-bye without telling Mama about Segi's illness or my hospital visit. I didn't want to raise false hope. Things were still inconclusive and I knew there were challenges ahead. How to tell Baba Segi about the appointment, for instance. It didn't seem the right time to bring up such things.

As I started up the street, a familiar car screeched to a halt beside me. Segun was driving and his mother was in the front seat. They honked for the guard to swing the gates open. Even though she must have been nearing sixty, Segun's mother's skin glistened like the flesh of a pawpaw sliced open. Her nose was straight and her neck long and distinguished.

"Aren't you one of the Akanbi girls? What's your name again?" she asked, pointing a slim finger at me. She spoke with her teeth clenched so it was only her lips that moved; she didn't want to appear like she was making any real effort.

Segun responded before I could. "Her name is Bolanle. Surely you remember?"

His mother shot him a disapproving side glance. "How is your mother? Is she better?"

"Much better. Thank you, Ma." It was strange. I could look at her. I could speak to her. The panic wasn't there. There was no stuttering and my voice came out exactly as I'd intended.

"Good. What do you do now?" She examined her silver nail paint, clearly not interested. *She* was so rich, she didn't need to do anything. She wanted to remind me of that.

"Nothing at the moment but I am thinking of getting a job. If I can't find the sort of thing I want, I'll improve my prospects by going back to university for a master's degree."

Both sets of eyes in the car widened, Segun's from astonishment at my self-confidence, his mother's from cynicism. Segun recovered first. "All the best then." With that, he pushed the shift stick into first gear. His mother giggled and laughed all the way into their beautiful driveway.

Her laughter rang in my ears long after she'd stopped mocking me and rubbishing my aspirations. But instead of feeling ridiculed, I felt strong and defiant. You weren't laughing the night armed robbers told you to pull your ears and do frog jumps, I thought to myself.

My mind immediately took me to that night when the gentle winds brought squalls of dust and everyone shut their windows anticipating rain. It was one of those nights when, even though it was cool, everyone looked forward to sleeping with a light cloth.

Segun had asked that I come to his bedroom that night. He was whistling the tune to "Casanova," which meant the coast was clear. If things looked risky, he whistled Anita Baker's "Watch Your Step."

"That boy has evil in him. The way he whistles behind the wall is eerie. Maybe he's communicating with ghosts in the spirit world." My mother bent her ear in the direction of the whistling.

I quickly ran to my bedroom so Mama wouldn't catch my eye. I could keep secrets but I could never tell barefaced lies. It amazed me daily that she hadn't smelled Segun on my skin or noticed how much weight I lost after the abortion. I'd tried hard to stop relating what had been scraped from my belly to the little humans that gurgled on their mothers' backs. The relationship between the two haunted me.

At the time, Segun was already in his third year at university and I was still waiting for my admission letter. He often brought girls home and holed them up in his room over weekends. His father liked this; he liked that his son was a virile ladies' man. His mother, on the other hand, referred to his lady friends as whores. "What kind of daughter tells her parents she is going to university and then goes around sleeping in men's houses. It's disgraceful!" she would say, and mop sweat off her nose with an embroidered handkerchief.

That night, I changed into my pajamas and jumped under my cover cloth with a Mills and Boon. I wanted everyone to think I had turned in early, knowing Lara would follow suit. She often copied me so it didn't appear that she lacked initiative and common sense. I was her role model, then. If only she knew! Her footsteps came just after ten minutes, and she quickly mummified herself with her cover cloth, dead to the world.

I sneaked out of our bedroom and stopped by my parents' door. I listened for sounds but there was none except my father's snoring. No doubt Mama was sleeping with a pillow over her head. I unlocked the back door and tiptoed toward the drainage system at the back of the compound. I took a bucket with me to fool anyone who saw me slinking around; there were endless things a young woman could be using a bucket for, and luckily, a rendezvous with the landlord's son wasn't one of them.

On our side of the fence, the concrete blocks weren't planed or painted so I dug my toes into the ridges and climbed to the top. As I lowered myself on the other side, Segun's guard dog licked my feet. I giggled as I landed on their manicured lawn.

Segun's door was open. He always kept it open for me. He was sitting shirtless on his bed, reading an old *Time* magazine. He flicked cigarette ash into an ashtray he'd balanced on his thigh. When he heard me come in, he put the magazine aside. "Are you staying the whole night?" he asked.

"No, I left our kitchen door open. I don't think I should risk it."

"You're scared!"

"And you're not?" I folded my arms.

He grunted and walked into his en suite bathroom. There was a coral bath in the corner and a matching toilet and bidet.

"My father hasn't come home yet. I can't believe he is doing all this shit. Vincent saw him at the Cotton Club buying pizzas for two scantily dressed girls." He pushed the bathroom door open with his big toe. "Does he ever stop to think how that looks? *I* could have been with Vincent. *I* could have been sitting down having a drink with *my* friends and we would all have seen my father traipse in with a girl on each sleeve." He stopped talking when he started urinating and did not resume until he had shaken off the last drop.

"Maybe he's at a business meeting with his partners or something." I didn't like it when he was tetchy so I thought of things that would calm his nerves.

"You could call it that," he spluttered. "It is *business* for the girls and my father is obviously a willing *partner*." He took up his toothbrush from the metal cup with a clang.

His wit was greatly sharpened when he was irritable. I covered my mouth so he wouldn't hear me chuckling. "He'll be home soon. He always comes home."

"Yes, he does. Dead drunk. Last week, dawn found him in the driver's seat. He had driven into the compound, locked himself in the car and slumped onto the steering wheel. The night guard was beside himself with worry, not knowing whether he was dead or alive or going to suffocate." Segun brushed his teeth for a while and spat into the sink. "It is a miracle he can find his way home at night."

Segun always had the air conditioner on full blast, so by the time he had shaved, I was lying under the duvet. He snuggled in beside me and we lay there for several minutes. His mind was far away but I found the feel of his skin comforting; his body filled all the parts where mine caved in. If sex was the price I had to pay to be close to someone's skin, it was fine by me. I waited. I knew he would speak soon. And when he did, it would be something about his father.

"Here he comes now," Segun said, springing up to turn off his air conditioner. He was still frozen on the spot, listening out, when we heard two muffled gunshots, one after the other. It was obvious that they came from nearby. Segun flew into the bathroom to get his dressing gown; I bolted, gripped with fear.

"I'm going out there," Segun announced, pulling on his jeans.

"Don't be a fool. We should hide."

"My *father* is out there!"

"You think he wants you to get killed?"

He thought for a minute and somehow my crazy logic made sense to him. He didn't suspect that all I wanted was for him to stay with me.

"Where shall we hide?" he asked.

"Outside. Let's hide outside in case they come in."

"No. They could be on their way here already. This is the only way if they can't get through the front door. It's bulletproof."

"Let's hide in the bathroom then. We can climb into the ceiling through the tiles."

I used his clasped fingers as a step, then Segun hoisted himself up after me and replaced the polystyrene tiles. There were hundreds of holes in them so we could see into the bathroom. Since the bathroom door was open, we could see into the bedroom too. Segun grimaced when he realized he'd left the lights on.

The bedroom door lock was suddenly splintered by bullets and a short, stout man in a sleeveless football shirt kicked the door open with his foot. "Bring the idiot so he can lead us to the safe," he snarled. Even though the bathroom door was wide open, he split it in half with bullets. Two men dressed in black denim dragged Segun's father by the collar of his shirt. He could hardly walk. His face was swollen and he was bleeding profusely from a gash on his forehead. There was a dark circular stain on his trousers and blood trailed his every step. Segun covered his mouth with both palms; his eyes looked like they would drop out of his head.

"Which way?" A fourth man slapped Segun's father across the back of the head and pushed him in the direction of the veranda that led to the main building. Although I was just as frightened, I was captivated by the tears that rolled down Segun's face. All the years I had known him, he'd never cried. Not even when took me to the nurse to abort the child he imagined was his. Even though he could see how terrified I was, he blamed me for not insisting that he go out to buy a condom. Not once did he comfort me or acknowledge the tragedy of the occasion.

I REACHED OUT MY HAND to him but he pretended not to see it. He wished I wasn't there. Not to save me from the terrible things I was seeing but because he was embarrassed that I, a common tenant, was witnessing such a personal family tragedy. It was at that moment that I realized that I meant very little to him. I might as well have been another dusty wooden lintel. I thought perhaps I wasn't worthy of him.

There was silence all around but we knew it wasn't safe to come down from our hiding place. Segun developed cramps in his legs but he gritted his teeth. After what seemed like hours, Segun's mother entered the room carrying a metal safe on her head. She was wearing a long nightdress and one of the men in black denim kept poking her buttocks with the point of a machete. She looked around the room and went toward the outside door. On her way back from depositing the safe in her husband's new BMW, the armed robber asked her to pull at her ears and leap like a frog. She hopped as best as she could in turquoise silk, egged on by a rusty iron blade. She was crying and I could tell that her tears had nothing to do with the humiliation. She kept shuddering like something had shaken her to her core. I knew Segun's father was dead but I didn't say a thing.

The robbers left at four A.M. with thousands of dollars in cash and trinkets they'd found in another safe cleverly tucked behind the picture of Segun's grandmother. As soon as we heard two cars screeching up the road, Segun dislodged the tiles and jumped to the floor. He didn't wait to help me to my feet; he just sprinted down the veranda to the main entrance.

I crept out of the house and climbed back to my side of the fence. As I picked up my bucket and made for the well, I thought of the disaster I could have caused by leaving the door open. If the robbers had decided to go to our compound too, it would have been easy for them. I might as well have invited them into our home, not that we had anything of great value. I placed the bucket of water in the center of the kitchen floor and crawled into my bed. The entire house was quiet. If Mama asked me anything in the morning, I'd try to lie.

I didn't need to. By the time I woke up, the entire neighborhood was grief stricken. Every eye within the vicinity was bloodshot and there were cars parked all the way up our street. Like all the tenants, my parents went to the landlord's house to register their condolences but they were not allowed into the property. The house was full of dignitaries and they didn't want paupers dirtying their Persian rugs.

I didn't see Segun for days. On the day of the funeral I stood by our gate for hours so I could catch a glimpse of him. As the funeral cortege drove to the burial ground, he looked in my direction but looked straight ahead when he saw me. Not a pursed lip or a raised eyebrow in acknowledgment of my vigil.

CHAPTER EIGHTEEN
SEED

THE TRAFFIC ON SANGO ROAD had slowed to intermittent jerking. "She seems happy and restful now," Baba Segi continued to his driver. "The nightmares are gone; we have much to be grateful for." He was determined to embrace optimism.

Taju massaged the steering wheel each time they stopped and started. There was a funeral at the local cemetery and a few young men were gathered at the gates singing dirges. Brandy was downed by the mouthful and empty bottles dotted the ground around the cemetery gate. The men had black bands tied around their uncombed hair. One of them carried a framed picture of a young man with a neat part and a plastered smile. It bore all the pretention of a studio portrait; it must have been the third or fourth pose at least. A few moments later, a university van full of young women squeezed through the traffic and deposited its occupants at the mouth of the cemetery.

Cars slowed and stared, their passengers' eyes full of sympathy. They knew all too well that it was important to be slightly inebriated before entering the cemetery; a little something was needed to numb the mind and dull the senses. It was no secret that the cemetery was full. Every yard of earth had been disturbed, every foot unearthed. Nevertheless, coffins went in and gloved pallbearers came out, having deposited their burdens into three-foot graves.

Corpses were forced into unsavory unions. Reckless men were laid to rest on chaste widows; children on top of elderly men; girls on top of women who were too young to be their mothers. Nature in its omniscience would not accept these copulations: the shallow graves were ravaged by dogs and what the dogs rejected, the heavy rains returned to the residential area on the other side of the road.

As Taju drove past the cemetery gates, the clouds gathered into fists. Baba Segi, who had stopped to gape at the mourners, spat out of the window. "So it is the specialist who wants to see me?"

"Yes," Bolanle said.

"Now, that is a man who has sense in his head. He understands that a woman must have a master that she submits to. Unlike that imbecile we saw the other day, he clearly understands the significance of a husband!"

Bolanle decided it was better to leave things vague. It had

been hard enough summoning the courage to invite him. In fact, the telling was only made possible by Baba Segi's late-night visit to his daughter.

"Is she sleeping through the night now?" he'd asked as he swung the bedroom door open.

Bolanle was wiping beads of sweat from Segi's forehead. "Speak quietly, please; she has only just fallen asleep."

Baba Segi lowered his voice to a whisper. "Is she sleeping through the night now?"

"No. She wakes up every few hours, when the pain is unbearable."

"Is the medicine not working?" He reached out to touch his daughter's head but snatched back his hand, afraid he would upset her slumber. "Perhaps we should take her back to the hospital." He looked to Bolanle for an answer.

"You could, but you yourself said that the doctors predicted her recovery might be slow. Speaking of which, Dr. Dibia has asked to see you. He's the doctor I saw when I went for my appointment at UCH. He said it's important that he speaks to you." It went down perfectly.

"So you went for the appointment?" He hadn't expected that she would take the initiative.

"Yes, and I took the results of the tests. He said it was important to see you. Tomorrow, in fact."

"But why didn't you tell me before?"

"What sense does it make to treat ringworm when the body is consumed with leprosy? Segi's condition has overtaken all our minds."

Baba Segi exhaled deeply. "You are right. Well, if the doctor calls, then I must answer. *All* the diseases of the body must be treated." He tiptoed toward the door.

"The appointment is at ten thirty."

"May we wake well!"

A few half truths, a few untold truths, and the deed was done.

Dr. Dibia was not in a hospitable mood; when Baba Segi and Bolanle walked into his consultation room. He was digging the lid of his pen into his ear, as if something had jumped in when he wasn't looking, just to annoy him.

"Good morning, Doctor." Baba Segi hoped to impose his high spirits upon him.

"Please sit. I take it you are Mr. Alao?" He looked at the clean pen top with disgust and threw it in the bin.

"Yes. *I* am the husband." He drew his hands to his bosom. "And *this* is the wife who cannot conceive." He pointed two forefingers at Bolanle as if there was a slight chance that the doctor might mistake one for the other.

"Good, good. Now that I know who's who, let me tell you why you are here. Now, in order to arrive at a conclusive prognosis about your wife's inability to conceive, it's important that couples hoping to become parents are examined together. We've already administered some tests on Mrs. Alao, so now you need to do some initial tests too. This will help us determine how we might overcome the difficulties." He avoided using the word "problems."

"I hope you're not insinuating that *I* might be the cause of these difficulties." Baba Segi glanced at Bolanle, then moved his face as close to the doctor's as the table would allow. "Listen, Doctor, I have many children. I have sons; I have daughters. The only thing God has not blessed me with is twins. Mind you, there is still time. So, tell me." He paused. "Are the tests you want to do on me not a waste of time?"

Dr. Dibia reclined into his seat and took off his glasses. He looked intently at Baba Segi while his glasses swung from his finger like the wand of a metronome. "Mr. Alao, did you see that queue out there?"

"Yes. There are many people waiting outside the door."

"Good. Do you know why they are there?"

"Is it not to see you?" Baba Segi didn't know where he was going but he was suspicious all the same.

"Indeed they are. But they are also there because they have a common belief."

Baba Segi opened his mouth to talk but the doctor raised a solitary finger and stopped him before he started. "They believe that I know what I am doing. They *believe* that I don't just sit here making things up. They *believe* that when I ask them to do something, it is because *I* believe it is for their own good. After all, I did not drag them here from their homes, did I?"

"Well—"

"There are no wells, no buts, no arguments, no questioning of my understanding of obstetrics and gynecology." He turned to Bolanle. "Mrs. Alao, if *you* seek a solution, perhaps you can advise your husband. A sperm count has to be done. This involves us taking a sample of your husband's sperm and examining it in a lab. The hospital labs are open until twelve. The sooner the sample is taken, the better." He scrawled on a yellow form and handed it to her, together with a small transparent container. His whole manner made it clear that he'd appointed her as the go-between.

"Thank you, Doctor."

"And how is the head?"

"Much better." She patted her scarf discreetly and flashed the doctor an embarrassed grin.

The harmattan winds had been brutal the year before and the walls were smeared with a film of warm terra-cotta. The windows were so high that even the exceptionally tall Baba Segi couldn't survey the hospital grounds. But then, like the room, they'd been glossed over with dull, off-white paint. A twenty-inch TV/video combo sat on a mobile stand; there was a large tub of Vaseline on a shelf beneath it.

Baba Segi held his penis in his hand as if it was a hefty bill he had not expected to pay. His eyes were on the man in the video who was dipping his tongue into a woman's pubis. He was both surprised and disgusted that his member responded to what looked alarmingly like taboo. As his member grew in his hand, he squeezed hard to admonish it. But the swelling didn't stop, so *he* didn't stop squeezing. He watched the blond woman gag on her partner's penis.

"Unthinkable!" Baba Segi's mouth filled with saliva. He looked from his penis to the small container. He examined his testicles and gave them a gentle prod, hoping that something would make its way out but there was nothing but a clear trickle. When he couldn't stand it anymore, he zipped up his trousers and unlocked the door. Bolanle was still sitting on a bench at the end of the corridor, her chin pressed into the crook of her palm. A nurse sitting nearby blew gum bubbles as she thumbed her way through a pile of forms.

"Sister!" Baba Segi called, decidedly opting for the less awkward conversation. Bolanle looked up but Baba Segi pointed to the nurse and motioned for her to come over.

"Can I help you, sir?" The nurse cautiously held the door open with her foot.

"I can't do this! There is only one way a man should shed body water, and that is the way I have done it all my life. I don't understand how to do it like this. I don't even know how to hold it!"

"Sir, it's easier than you think." The nurse wondered how it was that men, with all their talk of conquering women, had not mastered the art of pleasuring themselves? You'd think women were their dustbins. "Did you watch the video? It helps."

"I couldn't bear it. How can anyone respond to that filth?" He inhaled sharply and suppressed his urge to spit.

"Then maybe it will help if you see how it's done first." She wedged the door open with a metal Coke top and marched toward the TV. She stopped the video and pressed rewind. "All you have to do is copy everything the man in the video does. Try not to think too much about what you are doing. Let your mind go to . . . yes . . . let your mind go to that young wife of yours. Imagine you are with her."

Silence.

She pressed play and the video started. The nurse averted her eyes and made to leave the room but before she closed the door, she turned and said, "Mr. Alao, there is some Vaseline under the TV. Some men say it happens quicker when they use it." As the nurse walked back to her desk, she popped a small pink bubble with a click of her tongue.

The Vaseline was full of holes where it had been poked by desperate fingers. Baba Segi scooped a little less than a handful and smeared it over the fat flap of flesh that floundered at his groin. There was a naked Chinese man in the video and as he watched a woman dancing around a pole, he grabbed his penis and stroked it. Baba Segi followed suit. When the woman at the pole approached him, he pointed his penis in her direction and massaged firmly. Baba Segi too pointed his penis in her direction and mimicked the man's movements. Before long, Baba Segi's toes began to curl. He felt like he was lying on a mattress on wheels that was zooming down a steep hill. The wild and wonderful buildup to the orgasm made him shudder.

The man in the video told the woman to kneel down before him, at which point the expression on his face changed and he became enraged. He thrust his member into his half-open fist and rolled his eyes to the ceiling. Baba Segi would have emulated him had his own eyes been open. He had dreamed up his own fantasy: Bolanle naked, on her knees, begging for his seed. As the man in the video erupted all over the dancer's face, Baba Segi, who had never had the need to aim, added his own splodge to the far wall while the container lay patiently beneath his testicles.

As his breathing returned to normal, he looked around, not knowing what to do. If it is seed they want, they will get it, he said to himself. He waited for coordination to return to his fingers and then used the rim of the container to scrape the last dribbles of semen from the tip of his penis. He secured the lid and sat back down. What would Teacher say if he saw me here, heaving like a pursued duiker? What would Taju say if he heard that I, Chief Alao, was filling a plastic container with my body water? What would Iya Segi say if she saw me whipping myself? One by one, the looks of disappointment on the faces of family, friends and employees tormented him. When he'd worked his way through everyone, he straightened his clothes with moist palms and fled the room, the video, the dancer and the memory of what he had done there.

Just outside, Bolanle was pacing the corridor. "Is it done?" she asked, more concerned about the sperm sample than the patches that had merged into one at his crotch.

"I have done the best I can do." Baba Segi couldn't look her in the eye; his fantasy clung to the walls of his mind and embarrassed him.

When they returned to Dr. Dibia's consultation room, Bolanle knew there was something going on. The bubble-blowing nurse had rushed the results back to the doctor in a sealed envelope. But rather than invite his patients in, Dr. Dibia scurried out, open envelope in hand, forcing his arms into the twisted sleeves of his lab coat.

A few minutes later, he returned with the better-groomed Dr. Usman in tow. It was the look that Dr. Usman gave her that gave it away. He may not even have known that a look had passed between them. All he'd meant to do was glance at her but he squinted and rearranged his lips so they formed a straighter line. It was definitely a look, a sympathetic one.

Back in Dr. Dibia's consultation room, the debate on Baba Segi's fate was well under way.

"I think telling him would put the women in his household at risk. She came in with a nasty gash on the back of her head last week."

"But we don't know *he* did that. I didn't pick up on any domestic violence. He seemed more possessive than aggressive. You know? More of a lover than a fighter?"

"As far as *he's* concerned, it's his wife who's got serious problems. It would have been a different matter if he had low sperm count, but there's nothing! Not a solitary sperm swimming around!"

"Probably had mumps in his teens. I'll bet any money he's never had a vaccination in his life."

Dr. Dibia rapped the table with the tips of all eight fingers. He wasn't interested in Dr. Usman's betting; he wanted to know where to go from where he was. "This just doesn't add up. I think I'm going to need to talk to his other wives."

"Yep, that makes sense. Just say it's part of the investigation. He can't argue with that."

"So you agree that I shouldn't tell him the results yet?"

"I think that's reasonable." Dr. Usman stood up, eager to return to his own department.

"But what about the girl? Doesn't she deserve to know?"

"A few more days won't do her any harm." With this, he waved and shut the door behind him.

Bolanle and Baba Segi found themselves in the same chairs they'd sat on that morning, except now the air conditioner was on. The smell of the cheap lemon air freshener filled the room. Bolanle immediately noticed that there was a marked difference in Dr. Dibia's demeanor: he was now disturbingly well mannered. As soon as Bolanle saw him stand up to receive them, she expected the worst. She looked at Baba Segi to see if they were thinking alike but he was sleepily scratching dry saliva from the corners of his lips; he'd nodded off outside Dr. Dibia's consultation room.

The doctor flashed eight small teeth. "The investigation is incomplete," he began.

Baba Segi was immediately riled by this statement: his nostrils flared and his eyes resembled overpowered torches. "Even the gods could not make me repeat that . . . that . . . immoral act. I will not!" He snapped his fingers over his head in defiance.

"That's quite all right, Mr. Alao. I'm not asking you to provide another semen sample. In fact, I don't need anything else from *you,* not for now at least. It is your other wives we need to see, or maybe just one of them. You choose." Maybe he'll respond to empowerment, Dr. Dibia thought.

"Why? You have seen Bolanle. You have seen me. Why

do you need to see another wife?" Baba Segi decided to play hard-to-get; he wanted to get his own back for the doctor's earlier discourteousness.

"Well, you know, before you wrap leaves around liquidized beans, one must ensure that the ingredients are complete."

"Indeed! Or you would be left with a plain lump of *moyin-moyin*." Baba Segi completed the saying.

Dr. Dibia smiled. The traditional shit always worked on the older farts. "Well, exactly. Consider the invitation I am extending to your wives as a boiled egg, not half, not quarter, but a whole one which will complete this bounteous recipe."

"Ha, Doctor! I see you like good things. I too like the very best for my stomach and I will bring you the wife who sees to it that that is what I get." Baba Segi beamed. "Write down her name—Mrs. Labake Alao."

"Perhaps on Wednesday? I normally teach on Wednesdays but I could squeeze her in at nine thirty." He handed the appointment card to Baba Segi. "See you on Wednesday. And, please, don't leave that wonderful wife of yours at home!" It was meant as a joke and it was received as one.

Baba Segi guffawed all the way down the newly mopped corridor, all the way down the narrow stairs and all the way back to the pickup.

CHAPTER NINETEEN
BABA SEGI

I REMEMBER A SAYING from my childhood: only a foolish man falls into a trap prepared with his own hands. It is because of what happened to my father that these words were on everyone's lips. My father was a hunter and he caught his foot in the snare he'd laid for an antelope. They say he heard the squawk of a wild guinea fowl and ran after it, forgetting what was before him. His ear led him to an early death; he was barely twenty. He didn't wait to see my face or hold my little feet. He died lashing about at the bottom of a burrow. They say he was already buried when they found him; there was no point in digging him up to bury him again so they just shoveled more earth onto his body.

No other man would marry my mother for they feared that they might also die in a grave intended for a lesser beast. But they *were* all lesser beasts, all unworthy of her. My mother tied fabric and dyed it indigo. The soles of her feet were always black and as a child I would sit for hours removing the black residue from her toenails. By the time I was twelve, I wished she would cut off her toes. Not because I hated her but because my arms ached and Mama was never satisfied. I think she just liked me to touch her feet.

When I was seventeen, I prayed that the gods would forgive me for all the evil thoughts I had ever had about my mother, because without her I would not be here today. She was a mother of mothers to me. She nursed me through an illness that reduced me to an infant—I lost my ability to walk or talk. They said it was my father's spirit, that it had come to take me, but I knew that was a lie. Why would any father want to do that?

It all started with a headache. I was fetching firewood from the forest one day, when my head started to throb at the *ewuje*. It was as if the bones that had merged were being forced apart. I managed to stagger home. My mother had her hands deep in dye but when saw me coming, she ran to my aid. If she hadn't, I would have broken my skull on a stone. She carried me into our house and lay me down on a mat. My body was covered in dye but I didn't know it. It was as if a witch had set my belly on fire. With every hour that passed, the flames rose to my throat. They say I screamed "fire" until sleep smothered it.

It was when I realized my trousers had been changed that I knew another day had dawned. My T-shirt had not been touched and it was when I looked in the small mirror in the corner of the room that I understood why. It looked like I had stuffed two mangoes in the curve where my neck meets my face. So swollen was my neck that my mother sighed every time she laid eyes on me.

The way my daughter is now, that was the way I was for weeks: of no use to myself or anyone. There were days when my eyes would close from pain, rendering me deaf and dumb. My legs would curl like caterpillars and my arms would have nothing to do with me. My mother would frantically bathe me in cold water only to stand and marvel when steam began to rise from my head.

I have been where Segi is now and I know the only thing that will save her is the arm of one that she chooses. That was how it was for me. It was my mother I wanted. I hope you understand why I didn't discourage her from sleeping in Bolanle's room. True, no one can love a daughter like her mother, but illness is not only about motherly devotion; it's about the choices of she who ails. Anything different could hasten Segi's journey to the gods. I will not bury my own child. Help me say amen.

Back to my own illness. Mama said there was a spirit that snuck behind the door every time she entered the room. She said she could feel its presence. She whispered in my ear that the smell of her husband's sweat was unmistakable, so she called the medicine man to come and banish it.

"Do not let *him* take my son from me," she pleaded. "Make him return to his resting place." She knew the dangers of calling a spirit by its name.

The old medicine man whispered to the cowries and

threw them in the center of the cloth they came wrapped in. "Hmm. This spirit has come for revenge."

"But what have I done to anger it?"

"It is not you; it is the boy."

"What has the boy done?"

"He walks on his grave like the chief who strides the palace and neglects to pay his respects to the king."

"But the boy does not even know where he was buried. The men refused to take even *me* there!"

"It is not your place or mine to question the spirits. Tell your son to abandon the forests or he will leave the land of the living. And as soon as he is of age, send him away from here to protect his own unborn sons."

"I have heard your words and they are full of wisdom. Take these yards of cloth for your wives." My mother handed him a pile of beautifully embroidered tie-dyed fabric.

As soon as he stooped through the threshold, Mama knelt beside me and held my right hand in both of hers. "Son, did you hear the words of the wise man?"

"Only some," I said, but I'd heard everything.

"Then listen. Soon, you must go far from here. Go to Ibadan, where forests are few and palaces are plentiful. Go far from these roots that threaten to knot themselves round your feet and drag you into their tombs."

The swelling around my neck went down within weeks. I swore to my mother that I would never go to the forests again, not to fetch firewood, nor even to hunt. But they say a hunter's child is not trained but born. Though I resisted, the leaves of the forests beckoned to me. The roots formed a path and branches begged me to perch upon them. Before I knew it, I was pressing my ears against solemn trees, listening to the hoot of guinea fowls I would never set eyes on. My disappearances did not go unnoticed. My mother heard my feet stomping on the doorsill and she knew straightaway that I was disobeying her. One day, she tied a wad of notes in a handkerchief, placed it in my pocket and sent me off to Ibadan with journey mercies. I was to work as an apprentice in a store where they sold plumbing materials.

I worked for many years not knowing the scent of women until the spirit of Ayikara found me and sucked me into its belly. That is how I met Teacher—the noble one whose rays of wisdom have guided me through darkness. If the gods took the form of men, they would fight for Teacher's body. It was he who told me that I should return home and marry the woman my mother had found for me, lest the women of Ayikara bitter my blood with their bile. It was Teacher who pointed me in the direction of the medicine man when it seemed Iya Segi's back would be permanently gummed to our matrimonial mat. Within months, she was forced on her side, her belly bulbous like the back end of an earthen pot drunk on rainwater. Segi, my daughter, was named by my mother. My mother looked into her face and died a contented death.

Lust points its finger at every man and soon after I married, the women of Ayikara began to look like princesses and goddesses. I was happy to have these women on the side, but Teacher said, "Two women at home are better than ten in a bush. They are Jezebels. A man whose house is full of birth will never want for mirth." And this from a man whose penis they say has never known the moistness of a woman! You see, the gods are always merciful: what they took away from the bottom they added to the top. The man is full of wisdom. I took a second wife, a peace offering from a desperate farmer. I took the third because she offered herself with humility. What kind of human being rejects the fullness of a woman? Would the gods themselves not have been angered if I had forgone the opportunity to show mercy upon another human being?

I chose Bolanle, I cannot lie; I set my mind on her, the way a thirsty child sets his eyes on a cup filling from a spout. Teacher said I was right to possess her. He bought me two shots of whiskey and patted me on the shoulder. Not a fleck of jealousy, not a speck of envy. I tell you, the man is to be admired.

CHAPTER TWENTY
HOMECOMING

Iya Segi

THERE IS SOMETHING SPECIAL about a mother bathing her child, so I have decided to bathe my daughter. I want to wipe away that woman's handprints and reclaim my daughter. This Segi was not the daughter who left that night.

We had been waiting impatiently for her return. The children's foreheads were pressed against the glass sliding door. I could not sit so I perched on the edge of my armchair. When the pickup drove into the compound, the windscreen brought a piece of the sun with it. The children jumped up and down as if their feet were made of rubber. Baba Segi had hardly opened the door of the pickup when they covered Segi with their hands. They all wanted to touch my Segi, as if to confirm that it was really her. Segi looked at them all and touched their foreheads the way she liked to do. She smiled but her lips were cracked and full of pus. Her father carried her into the sitting room and eased her into his armchair. Iya Tope rushed to her side and propped her up with cushions but as soon as her back touched them, her head dropped onto the armrest.

She looked like a ghost. Her face had lost its fullness and her forehead was full of scales. Her eyeballs were yellow like they had been bathed in urine. Even her breasts were flattened against her chest. What used to be firm, supple skin sagged like beaten leather. All her hair was gone; her scalp shone like a marble.

I went to my daughter and knelt down before her. I put one hand to her bosom and I caressed Segi's head with the other. It was as if she was deafened by the sound but my daughter did not want to tell me to stop. She looked at me and said, "Mama, I am here. I am alive."

"Yes, my child," I told her. "You left me but you have returned." I stood and turned to all the faces around us. "My daughter has returned." My voice was no louder than a whisper but it reached every ear. Even Taju wept tears of joy on the veranda.

I would not have left her side but Baba Segi asked for his food. "My belly is ringing its bell," he said. "Bring food for me *and* my daughter. This is a day of joy. The doctors said it was the speed with which we rushed her to the hospital that saved her life. She was at death's door but the gods took mercy on me and sent her back. A million slaves and a thousand servants cannot equal the value of a child. When a man dies, only his children can truly mourn him. The gods have saved me from burying my daughter and I am grateful. Let everybody in the house drink a bottle of Coca-Cola!"

The children skipped around the room with glee. Seeing my husband in such high spirits gave me great hope. His affection for Segi was clear and unwavering.

When I returned with his food, I found Bolanle in the sitting room. She was at my daughter's side. She touched Segi's cheek with the tip of her finger. To my surprise, Segi clutched Bolanle's hand and drew it to her breast. They traded words I could not hear. That was when Segi spoke the words that burned my heart. "My father," she said, "it would please me greatly if you allow me to recuperate in Auntie Bolanle's room."

A whirlwind may as well have blown into the room and rained hailstones on all who were present. Every eye turned to me. What could I do when I knew it was my daughter's sickness that was speaking? Whatever Bolanle had done to bewitch her was still working, but it was not the time to fight. Bolanle shook her head and covered her face with her hand.

It was the rumbling from Baba Segi's belly that broke the silence. He looked fondly into his daughter's eyes. "As you wish, my daughter," he said. "As you wish." He also knew it was not the time to ask questions but he did not just leave the matter like that. He called me to his side and told me to bring my ear. When I knelt by him, he said, "Your child will always be your child, and you will always be her mother."

THE FIRST THING I DID before preparing bathwater was to make sure Bolanle had left the house. I did not want anyone to come between us. I was a woman and I knew where to sponge and where not to apply any pressure at all. I knew also that there would be no scrubbing. Segi was molting like a viper and the new skin was tender and raw.

I took off all her clothes and helped her onto the stool that I had placed in the bath. She sat there like a hunchback and I poured bowlfuls of tepid water down her back.

"Daughter, why don't you speak to me?" I asked.

Segi raised her head to look at me. Her eyes were accusing eyes but she said nothing. I could tell that her stomach was full of words.

"Is it your hair? Is that why you are so silent? It will grow back, you'll see."

Segi shook her head from right to left and bowed her head.

"Then it must be your breasts. The fullness will return."

Segi looked at her breasts and lifted them one at a time as if she was weighing them.

"Then why won't you talk to me? There is no shame in illness."

"Is there shame in death?" She did not even have the strength to clear her throat.

"Daughter, why would you say such a thing?" I was perplexed. "You will not die. I will not mourn my own child."

"But other mothers can mourn their daughters. That would please you, wouldn't it?"

"What goes on in other homes is no concern of mine, Segi. *You* are my concern."

"No, Mama. What I asked was if it would please you if another mother had to mourn her daughter." She coughed and grabbed the pail for support. Blood trickled from one of her nostrils.

I reached out to rinse away the blood but Segi brushed my hand aside.

"Mama, the doctors said I was poisoned. They said I could have died. Why would there be poison in our house? It was the food I ate the night I went to Auntie Bolanle's room, wasn't it?"

I dropped the small washbowl into the pail and reached for a towel. "Segi, do not delve into matters that do not concern you!" I said firmly.

Segi stood up and stretched out her arms, exhibiting what remained of her. "Mama, look at me and tell me again that this matter does not concern me."

I looked away and swallowed the lump in my throat. Segi looked like she had been in the ground for weeks. Her skin clung to her bones. "You are provoking me, Segi."

"Then let the daughter who provokes you die!" she said. "If someone in this house is serving poisonous food and my own mother will not find out who it is, how is my life worth living?"

"Let me cover you, child. The wind has teeth today." I tried to spread the towel around Segi's shoulders but she flung it into the bucket with all the strength in her wasted arms.

"No, let me die!" she screamed. By the time she closed her mouth, she was breathless and spent.

"The food was not meant for you, child! It wasn't meant for you!" It was as if I had gone mad. She watched me as I tore my dress from the neck to the hem. I slapped the walls and scratched my face. I boxed my breasts and pulled my hair. I could not control myself.

Segi knelt in the bathtub, slowly shaking her head. Then, as quietly as when she started, she said, "Mama, I am cold. Please bring me a dry towel."

CHAPTER TWENTY-ONE
WASHING DAY

Iya Tope

Iya Segi decided to bathe her daughter today. It is good because since Segi went to the hospital, both she and Iya Femi have been behaving as if they do not remember how to be mothers.

Akin came to my room and told me that their school uniforms were dirty. I told him to take the washing bowls outside. I gave them soap and sat outside with them. There was sadness in the home and it is good for them to do something that they normally enjoy. Like all children, they like to play with water.

They formed a ring around a giant heap of laundry and squatted before the white basins but they did not talk like they used to. Segi was not there to flick soap suds at them. She was not there to start the songs they all knew and loved to sing.

Femi was still angry because his mother wouldn't give him money for sweets, so he sank his hands in his basin and refused to scrub. Like his mother, he only thinks about himself. He just sat there with snot running from his nose. Every so often, he stretched out the tip of his tongue and licked the mucous into his mouth.

Any other time, the other children would have ignored him, but Akin stood up from his basin and slapped him across the face. The older boy left a streak of soap suds across Femi's cheek. When he recovered from the shock, he began rubbing his clothes together.

It is a wonder that a good boy like Akin could have come out of Iya Segi's belly. I have been watching him since he was young. One day, he will grow up to be a good father. He does not spoil the children like Segi does. He cares for them but he is firm. He knows what is wrong and what is just. I remember one day when they were all sitting at the dining table to do their homework. That day, Bolanle passed and asked if they needed any help but Segi's voice was unyielding. When it is Bolanle, she knows how to raise her shoulders, but she lets the children ride her like a donkey. No, she said. That is my job, she said. Who would have thought that one day Bolanle would suckle her? This world is full of mysteries!

So on that day by the dining table, Femi started his usual stubbornness. First, he sat and looked at his pencil as if he did not know what to do with it. Then he started to cry like an eight-day-old baby. He said he didn't understand anything, not even his name. He shifted his seat close to Segi and begged her to do his homework for him. Why wouldn't he expect people to do everything for him when his mother gives before he asks? Iya Femi has ruined him. He is so rotten that maggots fall from his body!

If Akin had not been there that day, Segi would have abandoned her own work to write for him. She would have held his hand and written the answers. Akin did not allow it. He looked hard at his sister and told her to leave. "That boy does not deserve the caressing you give him," he said.

Segi laughed and told him that not everyone was lucky enough to be born with great cleverness. Akin did not stop. He hardened his face at Femi. "How is it that you manage to remember every character on every TV program and the name of every football player, yet your brain falls asleep when you are asked to write one-two-three?" he asked.

What wisdom from a young head, I thought.

Segi warned Akin to keep his voice down so that Iya Femi didn't come through the door to give him a tongue lashing.

"If she comes, I will tell her how lazy her son is," he said. His voice did not shake. He was not afraid. I marveled at his courage because even I, a wife, could not consider saying such words to Iya Femi. That Akin will grow up to be a good man.

BEFORE THE SUN CAME DOWN, Iya Segi called a meeting. Without looking up, she told Iya Femi and me about the bathroom talk with Segi. If I said I understood what she was saying, I would be lying. Where would Segi get the boldness to speak to her mother that way? But the more she spoke, the clearer the work of their hands became. So *they* did it! They stole Segi's spirit! If only I were braver. If I knew how to stop my tears, I wouldn't have cried so many. I listened to Iya Segi's words but I could not say anything. Words would not form in my tongue. I could only pray that the gods would open the eyes of mercy on our home.

All the time Iya Segi was speaking, I could see that Iya Femi's palms were itching. When she couldn't keep the question down anymore, she turned to Iya Segi. "Tell me," she said. "How do we know that she will not tell her father what you said? Since she's been back from the hospital, she refuses to eat unless her father is seated before her. And who knows what she may tell Bolanle? Or have you forgotten that they sleep together? I only ask this because we might as well start packing our belongings now."

"We deserve to be thrown onto the streets," I said. "There isn't one thing that flies to the skies that will not eventually drop with rain. Our time here is finished."

"Speak for yourself, Iya Tope." I could not believe that Iya Femi's mouth could be so sharp after all the evil she had done. "If you want to sweep the streets with your children, start packing," she said. "Is it not Iya Segi who has divulged our secrets to her daughter? Since it was she who killed us, she will have to bury us. And besides, how do you know that it is not prison you will go to? Segi is the egg of Baba Segi's eye."

"No, Iya Femi. *You* will go to prison," I said. I do not know where I got the boldness but I spoke my mind for once. "Was I there when you were cooking your enemy's last meal? Don't you dare drag me into your murderous plot! If you had God in you, you'd be praying for the child who barely clings to life. But no, you sit here wondering how to remain in the house that you have used your hands to burn! How many times have you visited Segi to ask her where she aches? How many times have you inquired how she hears, now that her right ear is deaf? Never! You prefer to hide than to do a good deed that may wipe away your sins! Continue hiding," I told her. "You are not worthy of that child you have soiled." I left them there in the sitting room. My words were for Iya Segi's ears as well.

CHAPTER TWENTY-TWO
VICTOR

Bolanle

THE WIVES SIGH AND STARE into emptiness. They act as if a fist of stone has been stuffed into their throats. They don't swallow; they just sit and stare. They don't even seem to be bothered with *me* anymore, which is in itself confusing. I liked it better when they were predictable. Now I can't tell who has left food outside my door. It used to be so easy. Iya Femi always left the burned scum from the bottom of the pot and topped it with a small piece of meat that had been chewed off at the corners, while Iya Tope left a mound of dazzling white rice with an extra cube of beef hidden underneath. Now there are just two identical plates of food—one for me and one for Segi.

I suppose it is Segi's illness. She has not put on any weight and blood trickles from her nose relentlessly. I would never say so but her breath is foul, even when it is exhaled from her nostrils. It's a stubborn, unpleasant smell. It hangs in my room at night and I can hardly breathe. It bitters the back of the throat and clings to the beddings as if the corpse of a small beast is buried there. It's as if Segi is rotting from the inside out.

She has hidden a small mirror under her pillow and she weeps every time she looks at it. A few days ago, she asked me to swear on my life that I wouldn't tell Baba Segi about it. Perhaps a few weeks ago I would have obliged her, but now I can't bring myself to swear on my life. Not for her, not now, not for anyone. I just said, "I swear," and that was all there was to it.

When she's asleep, I can't help but look at her. I feel like I know what troubles her. The illness has ravaged her and left her bare. She has lost control of her body yet she wouldn't know what to do if she regained it. She knows the illness will do with her as it pleases, cease only when it decides to. It's strange, but Segi makes me feel strong. When I'm in her presence, I feel a sturdiness within me. Her fear makes me feel like there is nothing more for me to be afraid of. She said an odd thing yesterday. She said, "Auntie, you are a victor." I thought she was hallucinating. "Victor?" I asked, but she had drifted into one of her three-minute naps. She wakes from them a little agitated, asking questions like "Where are my wings?" I left the victor matter alone and did not return to it.

Victor. Nobody has called me a victor before. Even as a name, it's forceful, packed with hard, uncompromising consonants. It's impossible to say it without snarling and baring your teeth. I liked that she'd said it, even if it was born of some abstract notion.

She says the oddest things to her father too. Sometimes, she talks but no sounds come out of her mouth. Then when he tires and heads for the door, her voice returns. "Won't you hear what I have to say, Father?" she asks. Baba Segi returns to her side and the wordless chatter begins again.

"The doctors say it is to be expected," he mutters, his voice heavy with gloom.

CHAPTER TWENTY-THREE
OUT

Iya Segi sat calmly in the pickup but there was madness crawling beneath her skin. She had heard that people on the verge of traipsing naked into the streets often complained of a persistent march of ants all over their bodies. The truth was that it was Baba Segi's joy that nibbled at her limbs, his smile, pure and trusting, like that of the lamb skipping to the slaughterhouse.

The instructions had not been complicated: take this appointment card; wake up early on Wednesday morning; dress yourself and accompany me to the doctors; if they ask you any questions, keep nothing from them.

Iya Segi had etched out her own plan. There would be no questions, only answers. She wouldn't wait for the long rope of truth to be pulled from her; she would volunteer it willingly and without persuasion, even if it made Baba Segi force his head through the hospital walls. The truth, they say, can-

THE SECRET LIVES OF THE FOUR WIVES ❖ 243

not hide itself forever. Even if it conceals itself at the bottom of a well, one day, drought will reveal it. Bolanle's barrenness had brought drought.

Both doctors were waiting in the consultation room. Breaking the news to Baba Segi was a tricky task and Dr. Dibia wasn't entirely sure how to go about it. Did he just say it matter-of-factly? Bend his tone as if someone had died? Or was he to say it like Baba Segi should be grateful that he was born in the age of medical advancement? After all, he could have gone through his life not knowing.

As Dr. Usman reached for the door handle, Dr. Dibia said he might learn something if he stayed and listened in. Dr. Usman smelled the fear behind his colleague's arrogance so he retraced his steps to the examining table and folded his arms. He concealed a wry smile when Dr. Dibia poked his head out of the door to invite Baba Segi and Iya Segi in.

"Doctors, this is my first wife. No man could have a better one." His face shone with pride.

"Very good. Mrs. Alao, thank you for coming. Please sit comfortably." Dr. Dibia was slightly embarrassed by his patient's effervescence. Things would have been so much easier if he had been in a more subdued mood. He decided to dive right in. "Mrs. Alao, I'm sure you are aware of the investigation we have been doing into the younger Mrs. Alao's difficulties with conceiving."

"Mrs. *Bolanle* Alao," Dr. Usman offered.

Iya Segi carefully undid the knot in her head-tie and unraveled it to reveal a head of uneven, graying hair. Then she painstakingly folded the scarf into eight equal parts and laid it carefully on the doctor's table so it jutted out no further than any of the books. With equal precision, she stood and dropped to her knees. The doctors looked at each other. Baba Segi's cheerfulness dissolved into embarrassment.

"My lord"—she turned to her husband—"words do not decide whether or not they will be uttered but our people say the day always comes when words themselves will have their say." Her gaze returned to the doctors.

Again, the doctors glanced at each other. Dr. Dibia sat back in his chair and sniffed, making his glasses slide down the bridge of his nose.

"*I* know the reason why Bolanle has not conceived," she continued, "and it is not one that a thousand doctors can cure. Yam cannot cook itself. It needs a careful hand that will slice it and expose it to raging heat."

Baba Segi gasped in confusion.

"I am not quite sure I understand you." Dr. Dibia wanted Iya Segi to spell things out for her husband.

"That is because you are young and do not know the ways of the world. I was a young wife when I found myself in a cloud of sadness. I was childless and restless. Every time I saw a mother rocking a baby on her back, my nipples would itch to be suckled. My husband and I tried everything. He did not let my thighs rest but leaped between them every time dusk descended upon us. Even his mother was hungry for his seed to become fruit. Then, I had an idea. It was a sinful idea but I knew it would bring my sadness to an end. In fact, it was more than an idea; it promised to be a solution. If my husband did not have seed, then what harm could it do to seek it elsewhere?" She shrugged her shoulders. "So, I found seed and planted it in my belly."

Baba Segi turned his side to his wife and looked at her through one eye only. His arm was raised in defense as if to shield him from the odious suggestions hidden in her parables.

"Are you saying your husband is not the biological father of your first child?" Dr. Dibia asked. Eureka!

"Not my first, not my second."

Baba Segi ducked as if someone had taken a swing at his face. "Woe! It cannot be!"

"And the other wives? What about *their* children?" Dr. Dibia asked. It might as well come out in one big gush; better that than in dribs and drabs.

"I misled them. Perhaps if I had not shown the second one my way, this shame would have come out sooner. But you see, they were so desperate to be fruitful. They knew that my husband valued children above all things, so when I saw their desperation, I took pity on them and shared my secret. They also followed the same path."

Baba Segi whined like a dog caught wolfing down his master's dinner.

"So you are saying *none* of Mr. Alao's children are his?"

"Not one of them." She reached out her hand to touch her husband but he leaped from it.

Dr. Usman stood up straight. "Mrs. Alao, you have said

quite enough. Thank you. Perhaps it is better that you head home now." He could see that Baba Segi was set to explode.

Iya Segi rose and left the room with peace in her eyes.

Baba Segi's head was bowed, bent right over like a dying branch before it offers its leaves to the next gust of wind. His tears hit the floor with a quiet splat.

"Is there anything we can offer you, sir? A soft drink, perhaps?" Dr. Dibia asked.

Dr. Usman mouthed the words "Let's leave him" to his colleague and tiptoed out of the room. Dr. Dibia took all the sharp instruments from his table and hurried after him.

CHAPTER TWENTY-FOUR
TAJU

THE RICH HAVE FAT BELLIES. They swagger until the world swings to one side. They see more food and they lunge at it. They have a permanent hunger, you see. For the poor, it's different. They've never known the taste of fullness, so they scramble for leftovers, not because they are hungry but because they want to know fullness, the contentment that makes the rich think the world is theirs.

I like to speak in parables. I spend a few minutes of every day pondering the unequal balance of this world. Except most of the time, my parables are too complicated, too subtle, misleading even. I want to turn them around in my head but my boss returns and I must turn my mind to the road. I am not paid to be a thinker. I am a driver.

I shouldn't love this job like I do; every hair on my body should reject it after what happened to my brother. "The bus drove him to his death and you have set your palms on the same wheel," my mother cries. She means it as a cautionary tale but I tell her I drive a pickup, not a bus.

You see, Faruku—the brother she speaks of—was a son worth weeping for. His skin was so yellow that he should have been born at a time when the cold harmattan winds did not ruffle the sands. He wore his shirt open to his belly button and silver chains hung from his neck. Women sought to be with him; men thought him slick—a dandy. He thought he was slick too; he sported a wry smile and his tongue would grow taut and hover between his lips when he spoke to women.

Like most young men did when they were reaching the age of wisdom, Faruku left our village to seek his fortune in Ibadan. Most of the men from Olugbon did the same: they worked or trained all week and only returned to the village on weekends to visit their families. Faruku showed he was our father's son and did something special: he trained as a driver and before long, he got a job driving public buses for a well-known transport company. I won't mention the name of this company because you are likely to know it. Everyone knows the owner.

Sometimes he would drive his bus to our village and throw up the mud that had caked and set over the dust roads. He would show off the bus's gleaming burgundy and dart carelessly through shrubs and trees. He loved this reckless fun and so did we. Along with the other children, I would run after the bus screaming with excitement while our mothers and fathers rushed to the door mouths to wave. It was hard not to want to *be* him with his shirt loose, flying like a sail, a matchstick fixed to the corner of his wry smile.

The women couldn't wait for him to return on Saturday morning. From Monday to Friday, they showered me with gifts in the hope that I would put in a good word for them. I took their gifts but said nothing. Faruku would make my mouth bleed if he thought I was overreaching myself again. From the day he caught me peeping through his keyhole, he reminded me regularly that I was only nine and he was twelve years older than me. I don't hold any of his beatings against him. No. He didn't knock my head against the hard mud walls to hurt my feelings; he did it to put me in my place. Whether it worked or not was a different matter, as peeping through his keyhole was already a habit. Faruku's keyhole held many pleasures. If anything, I learned the workings of a woman's body.

Faruku could have any woman. They would chase him yet he'd make them feel that he was hot and sweaty from exertion. They wanted him and he obliged them, sporting his wry smile as they squatted over his body. I tell you, when a woman wants you, it is better to surrender and let her take you. Afterward, you will feel like a polished coin. Women couldn't get enough of that yellow skin of his. They couldn't rest until their breasts were pressed against it, their thighs wrapped around it, their toes curled upon it.

On this particular weekend, Latundun hadn't knocked on our front door like she'd done for the last three Saturdays. This was unusual as loose women tended to circulate more efficiently. Faruku kept going to the door to see if she'd arrived, but by afternoon he was restless. He gave me one naira and sent me to find her. "And if she doesn't follow you straightaway, get on your knees and beg until she does or see what you'll get!" he snapped as he weighed his balls. I put my slippers on and wondered what was so special about her. To me, she'd been no different from all others. A child simply couldn't understand these things, you see.

Latundun gave me her hand and let me drag her and her orange-peel smell into our home. Of course, she had no idea that I'd seen the droop of her breasts or her backside up. Thrice, to be exact. Those times were all I could think of when she touched my hair, fondled my neck and prodded my forehead, then she disappeared behind Faruku's door. By the time I fit my eye into the keyhole, I was well and truly primed. I was shocked to see Latundun lying there like a slug. But then, as Faruku lifted himself from her, I glimpsed what it was that made men despise her when she went with other men. Curled between her thighs was a flawless snail. Her lips were beautifully defined halves encasing perfect pink. So lost was I in the wonder of the pulsating snail that I forgot to look out for Faruku. He flung the door open and found me standing there with my hand twitching in my shorts. He ignored Latundun's protestation and kicked me until I was doubled over. I dared not cry out. If our father heard what I'd done, he would make us both sleep in the rain.

A few months later, Faruku appeared through the corn in the backyard. He was shoeless, sweating from every pore.

One arm was clearly broken and blood stained his fingertips. My mother called me into her room and told me to keep his arrival a secret. Her reason was simple: Faruku's bus had driven him to his death. I thought she must be mad because I knew my brother was alive, albeit distressed. I'd heard him crying in his bedroom, seen him performing absolution as if his sins had to be scraped from his skin.

The truth came later, weeks after the men in a gray Volvo had barged into our home, stripped Faruku naked and roasted him in full view of everyone in the village. It turned out that, after a night of heavy drinking, Faruku had nodded off at the wheel and driven a busload of passengers into a concrete electricity pole. He killed them all and fled the scene before the police arrived. He'd come home to share what time he had left with his family and his God; he must have known he was little more than a dead man praying.

The men in the gray Volvo threw four worn tires over his head, sprinkled his hair with gasoline and set him alight. All that yellow skin that the women desired fried and sizzled in its own fat. Our mother watched and even when smoke stung her eyes, she just kept telling hysterical onlookers in her told-you-so voice that it was the bus that drove him to his death. Faruku's head eventually stopped its manic nodding, at which point Mama's strength failed her. She collapsed to the warm earth like an old linen cloth.

We buried Faruku in the cornfields, but we did not mark the grave. It wasn't a resting place anyone wanted to remember, but it was secretly comforting for Mama to know he was near. I cried until my eyes nearly dropped out of my head. Where were the police? Why was there no investigation, no newspaper articles? Do you know why? I'll tell you: the rich own this world and the poor are nothing. My view of the world was altered greatly in those weeks. It was the women who surprised me the most. When Faruku was alive, they would not let me rest, but as soon as his body disappeared beneath the soil, they turned their affection to other men, and their younger brothers. It was as if his yellow skin had never existed. They avoided my eyes when they saw me, even Latundun. Women are such fickle creatures! They will eventually destroy this world with their slippery, slimy snails.

I told myself that Faruku's death would not be in vain and that I would become everything the world had denied him. Despite being known as younger-brother-of-the-murderer-driver, I wanted to become a driver too. I moved to Ibadan at the age of nineteen, a time when Latundun and her ilk were sprouting gray hairs and dragging callused heels around the village. I responded to a roadside advert and was employed by a man who was starting his own business with money he got from I don't know where. What business is that of mine? As long as my salary is put in my hand at the end of every month, nothing else concerns me.

As soon as I saw my boss, I knew he thought of himself as a rich man. He talked like one, acted like one. He still does. In turn, I play my part as the driver, the poor driver, the driver whose belly will never know fullness. He has been good to me but therein lies my problem—I pity him. What do you expect after we have sat buttock to buttock nearly every day for going on eighteen years? I swear, the only thing worse than a rich man is one who seeks to be a good man.

A few months after I started working for him, he told me his wife was having trouble conceiving but I said nothing. Days afterward, the wife too started talking to me about her problems. I didn't say anything to her either but she started giving me gifts and making eyes at me. She told me she didn't know anybody in Ibadan and she needed a friend. I told her to consider opening a shop alongside other women. Isn't that the way women make friends and start their idle gossiping?

Anyway, one day, my boss sent me home to collect a parcel he had left in her care. It was a hot afternoon and my mouth was dry. She was home when I arrived and she let me sit indoors. When she returned from her bedroom, she found me in her husband's chair. I was a little frivolous in those days but what else would you expect from a young man who didn't own an armchair? Instead of chiding me, she asked me to remain in the chair and laughed. Next thing I knew, she was sitting on top of me, riding me like a horse. I cannot say I resisted, but remember, my boss's wife is not a woman of modest proportions. She pinned me down with the strength of three men. I thought maybe I should tell her to stop but she covered my mouth with her hand, or maybe I covered my own mouth. It all happened so long ago. I don't remember things clearly now. All I know is that it was like stealing the fattest chicken breast from a rich man's dining table.

After that, whenever my boss sent me to his home on

various errands, I found myself sitting in that armchair being ridden like a new saddle. I don't know what I liked more, the fan above our heads, my boss's armchair or the riding I received in it. Within a few months, her belly swelled like a boil. Boils are very painful. Even after they have burst, they itch and itch.

I don't know whether the child, Segi, is mine. Only a mother knows who the father of her child is. All I know is that two years later, I found myself in the chair again. I swear, I should have been born a horse. I sometimes imagined that my boss's wife was Latundun. Ha! Even now, when I stop at a beer shack to eat snail, I fork it and nibble gently, as a small tribute. Don't mock me, please.

Iya Femi asks me to deliver messages to a man in Bodija. The rich and their surplus! I didn't even have to ask before Tunde stuffed my hand with money. Iya Femi couldn't have felt worse than me when Tunde traveled. It was as if my own brother died. My boss is not that generous. After he gives me my salary, he removes his eyes until the next month. He doesn't know that I eat freely from his kitchen. I eat his beef, his tripe, his kidney, his liver, his tongue—all the things that my wife's pots dream of but never cook. My children think it is terrifying when stew is not riddled with small strips of cowhide. Maybe it is better that they do not taste what their mouths will never be accustomed to.

Iya Segi's second child was a boy. He does not resemble his father. Sometimes, when I look at him and close my eyes, I think my young son will grow up and look like him. If you think I care about that it means you have not heard a word I have said! What would I do with Baba Segi's son when I can barely feed the ones I have? My life is simple and I want to keep it that way. The lot of poor men is to get what they can and go, quietly.

Judge me if you want to. Call me disloyal! I think I have acted as honorably as a poor man could. If you can't accept that, I leave you to your mischievous thoughts. When I tire of this job, I will leave. There are always adverts for good drivers. Like I said, my life is simple and I want to keep it that way.

Taju heard the sound of vomiting but only realized the source of it when Baba Segi staggered to the open door of the pickup. His breakfast had formed a colorful bib on his gleaming white shirt. "Take me to Teacher!" he ordered. His eyes were bloodshot, as if he'd been weeping blood.

A few minutes before, Taju had seen Iya Segi leaving the building. Her feet were all over the place like an inebriated dancer's; she blew her nose into the head scarf she clutched. Taju's first instinct was to hide but he resisted and walked toward her. "Iya Segi! Are you not going back with us?" he asked.

"No, I am going home by myself, Taju. My husband knows." Her shame was complete; the mere sight of Taju made her filthy.

"Your husband knows what?"

"That his children are not his children."

"Did you mention my name?"

Iya Segi stopped in her tracks and jerked her head backward. "Have you taken leave of your senses? I have one foot in my husband's house and one foot out of it and all you can ask is whether or not I mentioned your name?" She resumed her usual matriarchal tone. "I told my husband about his children. How does that concern you?"

"I'm sorry if I appear thoughtless but I also have a family to feed. I work in your household, so if there is something that could bring my employment to an end, is it not right that I should be warned? My boss has been good to me." He knew she knew what he was talking about and he wasn't going to give her the satisfaction of thinking he thought she didn't.

"Perhaps you do not understand me, Taju. The question of whether or not you will be relieved of your duties is between you and your boss."

"I was just thinking that—"

"No, Taju. Don't think. Face your driving. That is your job, is it not?" Iya Segi swung her whole body round and stormed off in the direction of the hospital gates.

Taju scratched his scalp with his toothpick and headed back to the pickup. He felt exposed, like the skin of his stomach had been chafed away by the breeze. His innards were an unpleasant spectacle and he knew straightaway that it was not a sight he could live with.

———

"SIR, ARE YOU ALL RIGHT?" Taju inquired as Baba Segi collapsed himself into the window seat.

"Just drive!"

Taju waited for the wind to fill his collar. "There is something I've been meaning to tell you." He cleared his throat nervously. "I have to travel to Olugbon. My mother has taken ill; my relatives say there is death in her eyes."

"When are you going?" Baba Segi didn't look his way. He remembered that he'd given Taju money for his mother's funeral two years before.

"I can't say. I received the message this morning."

"I take it you want your salary early then?" So Taju was leaving.

"Any financial assistance would be greatly appreciated, sir."

They say when one god is aggrieved he invites other gods to join him in seeking vengeance. Baba Segi felt as if ten winds were whirling in his head. He felt the force of wrath and wondered what he had done to make the gods smite him. "Just take me to Teacher. I will pay you when we get there, if you want."

"Thank you, sir." There was no gratitude in his voice, just disquiet. He mulled over Iya Segi's confession. Only a fool asks who struck a match when he sees billows of smoke on his rooftop. Iya Segi had brought an end to an eighteen-year companionship. He glanced at his boss, sitting there, stinking of vomit, but he did not feel any guilt. There was fear but no guilt. Baba Segi was twice his height and thrice his weight.

He had seen him handle Bolanle; they didn't call him a leopard because he had spots.

In silence, they drove. Baba Segi ignored the flies that were drawn to the stench of his garments. Ordinarily, he would have slapped them off, but today he sat still and let them feed on him. Baba Segi was practicing being dead. He took intermittent deep breaths and wondered if life could drain from him if he drew one deep enough.

When Baba Segi put the money in Taju's hand, he clutched his driver's small fingers and looked deep into his face. Taju flinched and pulled away but Baba Segi didn't relinquish his fingertips. "Will you not give me my keys before you go?" He was completely unaware that Taju's bladder was brimming. He took the keys and gave Taju his hand back. "Go well," he urged.

"Thank you, sir." Taju did not look back but marched across the road with long, swift strides.

Baba Segi returned to Teacher's shack, wishing that his thick legs would buckle under him. He saw the ugliness of his surroundings: the bowed buildings; the shattered planks held together by moisture rising from festering gutters; the uneven roads that sighed dust clouds every time a car upset their calm. "No! This is not the place," he repeated to himself.

There was a woman outside Teacher's shack. Her thighs were bandaged in a micromini denim skirt and her breasts bound in a fuchsia boob tube that matched her lipstick. Any other day, Baba Segi would have made a snide comment about the rigidity with which she paced. "Can you breathe all right?" he might have asked, feigning concern. Or he might have said, "If I didn't have a home full of wives and children, I would make you my bride." It would have been said with a trivial, superior air, of course. To this, the woman would have replied, "Is it the way I walk you are interested in or the way I fuck?" Or she might have responded to his condescension with a loud hiss that would pursue him all the way to his destination. Ayikara women were desperate but they spat in the face of insolence. Today, Baba Segi's eyes were dim with melancholy; his wit would not be roused. He sniffed past the woman and bowed into Teacher's shack.

The small space was full of men eager to drink the afternoon away. Many of them were already well on their way. The night guards defied sleep. They leaned their staffs on the wooden walls and dipped their fingers into their glasses to remove dead insects. Some had made guzzling whiskey their purpose for the day, as it had been the day before, and the day before that. They were all huddled together on low stools playing checkers and laughing at unrelated anecdotes. Baba Segi was irritated by their disregard for life's many tragedies. Angry beads of sweat collected at his brow, careered through the furrows and formed tears at the tip of his nose. Teacher rose and beckoned to him.

"My life is ruined." Baba Segi wiped his forehead with his palm. "I feel like I am in a pit of quicksand. All is dark, Teacher. All is dark."

"Where there is hope, there is life." Teacher absorbed his tale with compassion and contentment. A sense of comradeship brewed within him; it was comforting to hear that another man had been stripped of his manhood. If *he* could live in the knowledge that his penis would never prise apart a woman's lips, why couldn't Baba Segi live with his predicament? At least he could soften a woman with his hardness.

"Where is the hope?"

"There is a rainbow at the mouth of every tunnel."

"I don't understand."

"Hmm." Teacher got up and refilled the glass that Baba Segi had emptied. "What I will say to you will seem like the words of a madman, but you must consider them." He cast his shimmering eyes on Baba Segi's face and murmured, "It is time for you to let the deceivers who have brought bastards into your home return to their father's homes."

Baba Segi clasped his hands together and bunched them under his chin. His head became heavy quite suddenly. "Just send them away like one shoos chickens?"

"It is the only honorable thing to do." Teacher continued, his eyes widening at the thought of Baba Segi frequenting his shack and spending his money there. "As you spread your mat in this life, so you must lie on it." He paused. "Unless"—he pointed at Baba Segi until his fingertip was within an inch of his nose—"you want a home full of children that are yours in name alone."

"A curse! That would be a curse!" The thought disturbed Baba Segi greatly.

Teacher raised his hands in triumph. "Listen to me. When the missionaries left me behind, the thing that made me bitterest was that I had taken them to be my fathers. They plucked me from my father's home when I was a young boy and made me feel like I was their own. But when the time came for them to return to their country, they abandoned me here, like a cockerel casts the shells of groundnuts aside." He sipped his whiskey and looked dismally at the clouds of smoke that blew upward from half-parted lips and partly extinguished cigarette butts. "For three years I despaired, unable to accept my lot. Orphans are miserable people, you know?" The rooftop of the next building caught his eye. "It was not until I returned to my blood father that my misery was washed away. What I am trying to say is that your father will always be your father, even when life forces you to find a father in strangers."

"Are you saying that my children will one day seek their true fathers? That all I have been is a temporary caretaker?" Baba Segi spat the last few words out as if they'd burned his tongue.

"Indeed, my friend. You have been no more than a doorkeeper. The day those children can open doors themselves, they will depart and you will be left with nothing but your loss."

Baba Segi nodded. "Teacher, your wisdom humbles me."

"Don't say that, Baba . . . er . . . my friend. Pride makes men tumble before they fall." Mission accomplished, Teacher took a satisfying slug of his brew and scratched his chin.

CHAPTER TWENTY-SIX
SILENCE

WITH EACH PASSING HOUR, the silence in the Alao house grew until it was so sharp it stung the eye and drew saltwater from the nose. The wives sat in their armchairs, waiting for Baba Segi to return and determine their fates. Each one thought of words with which to blame the others but their throats were parched with worry. Every so often, their minds would stray to their children, tucked away in their beds, oblivious to the uncertainty of their futures, unaware of the possibility that tonight might be the last time they slept in their own beds.

Bolanle sat on the floor with Segi's head resting on her shoulders. She had seen Iya Segi return home with red eyes and a snot-stained head scarf but she couldn't make sense of the grief on the other wives' faces. There was regret and remorse, but why? Segi too had absorbed this air of dread. She had become perplexed and her temperature had risen briefly.

Bolanle had swathed her all over with a damp cloth and she seemed more rested now. Still, she refused to go to bed. Every time a car revved up their street, she would lift her head and ask, "Is my father back?" at which the older wives looked at one another, unable to respond.

Finally, just before the clock struck eleven, the pickup rolled into the compound. The engine stopped abruptly and the door slammed. Segi straightened her neck.

"He has arrived," her mother said, plugging her daughter's mouth.

The stones fled Baba Segi's unsteady footsteps. He battled with the sliding door and stumbled into the building, carrying the stench of vomit and stale whiskey.

Bolanle rose to greet him but Baba Segi didn't see her or Segi. "So the witches have gathered for blood!" he slurred, glaring at the other wives, who were seated with their heads bowed. "Go back to tell the evil spirits who sent you and tell them I wasn't home when you stopped by." He tore off his soiled shirt and dashed it to the floor.

"Segi has been waiting for you," Bolanle entreated, hoping that talk of his sick daughter might sober him a little.

"Is she? Tell me why she waits for me. You wives, tell me why!" he yelled, pointing his lips in the direction of his wives.

"Baba Segi, let us not do it this way." Iya Segi thought she might bring reason, the way she'd always done.

Baba Segi was not having her reason tonight. He lunged at her and raised his arm until it almost touched the ceiling fan. Then, with one smooth sweep, he brought it down onto her jaw. Everyone jumped, including Segi, who was groaning. Her father hadn't acknowledged her and she thought she might impress him by lifting her head off the floor.

"May the dogs eat your mouth!" Baba Segi towered over Iya Segi. "What mouth do you have to tell me how to do anything? You, who have brought bastard children into my home! You have used me! Wounded me!" His voice lowered to a growl. "But let me tell you, the lion has roared, the dog has barked, the mouse has squeaked. Enough is enough!"

Iya Segi's face rested on the arm of her seat where the force of the slap had sent it. The other wives were silent, half-waiting for Baba Segi to turn on them as well.

Then Iya Femi had a brainwave and decided to sing her signature tune. "It was the devil!" she proclaimed, kneeling in supplication on the cold terrazzo floor.

"Yes, it was the devil, and I am tired of doing his job for him. He must come and take his offspring from my house!" Baba Segi straightened as if he dared the devil to disobey him.

"Baba Segi, what has brought all this on?"

Bolanle's voice made him swing round. Surprisingly, his face softened. "What has caused this? I will tell you. In fact, I should thank you first, because had it not been for you, I would never have discovered the deceit I have been living with for all these years." He winced. "It was revealed in the hospital today that none of my children are my children. I found out, just today, that the children I have nurtured and called mine were sired by men *my* wives lay on their backs for." As he said this, he coughed up phlegm and aimed what he had collected at Iya Femi. He aimed well; it flew through the air and landed on her forehead with a splatter. She dared not raise her sleeve to wipe it.

Baba Segi paced the room and returned to his chair, knocking the head scarf off Iya Tope's head on the way. Her reflexes served her. Like a child who had spotted a snake on her beddings, she leaped off her chair and pressed herself into the corner of the room. "Harlot!" he said accusingly. He eyed her with disgust. Then, with one nod, he was dead to the world.

Bolanle's eyes were still traveling from wife to wife when a thudding intruded on her curiosity. The back of Segi's bald head was rhythmically slapping the bare terrazzo flooring. Her eyes had rolled upward, revealing ripe, yellow eyeballs. Her tongue hung out of the side of her mouth, clasped into place by clenched teeth.

Iya Segi woke from her slap-induced slumber and raced to her daughter's side. She wrapped her arms around Segi's belly and hoisted her into a sitting position.

"Segi! Segi!" Iya Tope yelled. It was a beseeching bawl to a child dancing on the rim of a yawning well.

Bolanle ran to the kitchen to fetch a bowl of water and returned with trembling hands. Iya Tope dipped her hands into the bowl and sprinkled droplets on Segi's face while Iya Femi rubbed the young girl's left hand, hoping to restore warmth to it. The jittering eased into a rigidity that made Segi's toes lengthen and spread like a rake's fingers. Her arms straightened at the elbows and her neck extended out of her shoulders. Her face held a look of pain so glorious that it brought tears to the eyes of all four women. Then, after a long, deep breath, Segi exhaled all the life within her. All the tension and agony was suddenly gone from her face, leaving her slightly open eyes staring at the stool beyond her blood-less toenails.

Iya Segi immediately withdrew her arm from behind her daughter's neck. She rose slowly to her feet and stepped backward, her eyes never leaving her daughter's lifeless body. Even when her back touched the wall, she was not convinced she couldn't take another step back.

"I have seen what a mother's eyes must never see," she gasped, as if someone had asked. She took a determined bow but before Iya Tope could restrain her, she slammed the back of her head into the wall. She didn't blink. Nor did she flinch. She would have gone for a second slam had Iya Tope's arms not held her in a headlock. Iya Femi joined in and before long, the three of them were rolling around on the floor in a tan-gled ball of arms and feet.

Bolanle, who had been staring at Segi's face, untied the wrapper from her bosom and laid it gently over Segi's body.

"Cover her face!" Iya Tope yelled. "A mother must not see her child's eyes after life has left them!"

Bolanle lifted the cloth at the hem and pulled it over Segi's face, thus unveiling delicate yellow feet. She marveled at the handsomeness of each toe and turned to the sound of Baba Segi's strident snoring.

Every so often, a grunt escaped Baba Segi's mouth, but the women of the Alao household could not sleep. When fatigue threatened to take them, grief prodded them awake and tears rolled down their faces in an unending stream. Also, since none of them had the courage to move Segi's body, their children woke to find her stiffened beneath a tie-dye wrapper in the center of the sitting room. The older children huddled in twos and watched the younger ones defeat the urge to ask why their sister had a cloth over her head. Akin sat by his sister's feet and stared and sobbed.

At about six A.M., Baba Segi blinked and was confronted by ten pairs of probing, bloodshot eyes. He shut his eyes as if to do a private appraisal of the situation but when he opened them again his gaze moved from the veiled mound on the floor to Iya Segi's face. Without speaking, he hauled himself out of his chair and headed for his bedroom, followed by a stream of warm urine.

He must have believed no one could hear him because he let out consecutive howls so haunting that the neighbors hurried to their gates. By the time Akin had found the keys and let them in, Baba Segi had returned to his seat fully dressed, except his trousers were inside out. No one cared to mention it. Careful to avoid the mound in the center of the room, he fixed his eyes on one of the visibly concerned neighbors and asked where he could buy a coffin. His words were punctuated by hiccups.

"They sell them by the roadside between Sabo and Orita-merin. But please, Baba Segi, my husband will go and buy it."

As if the directions were all she'd uttered, Baba Segi walked out, leaving his family gaping at the hem of his trousers.

A doctor was called to certify Segi dead and Iya Segi was led away to their neighbor's house. With fear and great sadness, the other wives prepared to change Segi's clothes. Halfway through the process, Iya Femi fled to the guest toilet and threatened to kill herself if anyone tried to persuade her to come out.

Akin helped to lift his sister's weightless body onto the soft cushioning of the small coffin. The neighbor drove carefully but the potholes made the coffin tip and slide against the metal. Akin held the varnished gray box through the entire journey to the cemetery.

Everything was arranged by the time they got there; a favor from another kind neighbor. Akin, Bolanle, Iya Tope and the neighbor lugged the coffin past the cemetery gates and forced it into a shallow grave between two headstones. The inscription on the one on the right had been grated away by the elements. Knowing his sister would be buried in an unmarked grave, Akin cast the words on the small marble slab to memory:

Dola Oladeji
Much loved & greatly missed

It wasn't much of a burial. It was taboo for parents to attend their children's funerals so there was no mother to wail for her. Understandably, also, there were no priests, no prayers, no graveside blessing to set her on her way. There was only a smirking gravedigger leaning against a tree, hoping to receive a sizable tip for a space well found and a grave hastily dug. Akin and Bolanle bowed away from Segi's gravesite, arm in arm, knock-kneed and dumb with sadness.

When they returned to their street, the words "may she be forgiven" echoed from every window and every door. Segi had defied the course of nature and spat out the milk from her mother's breast. It was a sin but a forgivable one. A verdict nevertheless left to the gods.

Together, they entered Baba Segi's bedroom, Bolanle one step behind Akin.

"Is it done?" he asked.

"It is," Bolanle replied, turning to leave. She didn't want to be there; she wanted to mourn in private.

Akin blinked back tears. "My father, I want to be a man about this but I fear I am weak."

Baba Segi looked at the tall, gangly boy sitting hunched on the edge of his bed. The word "father" made every other word echo. It was distinct and comforting to his ears.

"Akin, you are more than a man, for it is only a true man who acknowledges his weakness. Your sister will watch over you from the spirit world. Know this and let it strengthen you."

"Was there something I could have done, Baba? Was there some way I could have saved her?"

Baba Segi hummed uncomfortably and shook his head.

He felt tears heating the backs of his eyes. "You are not a god, so strike that from your mind. We are mere mortals who must humbly accept our destinies."

"Baba, I am tired but I am afraid to sleep. I don't want to wake up and remember she is no longer with me. Where will I find the strength to live on?"

"You will find the strength. We must all find the strength. That is the way it is for men: we wake up to find that things are not the way we imagined them. But what can we do?" Baba Segi's thoughts claimed him. He covered his mouth with his palm and looked up at the ceiling.

"My father, let me go and ensure that my brothers and sisters are fine. I have been away from the house for a few hours now."

"Before you go, child, I have some words for you." Baba Segi started abruptly, his eyes unnaturally eager. "Keep these words in your left hand lest you wash them away after eating with your right. When the time comes for you to marry, take one wife and one wife alone. And when she causes you pain, as all women do, remember it is better that your pain comes from one source alone. Listen to your wife's words, listen to the words she doesn't speak so that you will be prepared. A man must always be prepared."

"I hear you, Baba." Akin was baffled by his father's candidness but he suspected it was his grief talking. He was only thirteen and marriage was far from his mind. He saw that Baba Segi's eyes had closed so he rose from the mattress and tiptoed toward the door. As he placed his hand on the door handle, Baba Segi called his name and motioned for him to return to the place he had vacated. The older man reached out to place his hand on top of Akin's head. He pressed his fingers into his hair and stroked his face. "Go to your younger ones." He withdrew his hand and placed it flat on his chest.

CHAPTER TWENTY-SEVEN
STAYING POWER

No one expected Baba Segi to call a family meeting so early into the mourning period but he was pursued by his own tragedy. One part of him wanted to weep; the other wanted to scratch the tip of his contempt to release the hardening pus within. In the three weeks his family tiptoed around the house, muffling all the symptoms of healing, his discomfort had throbbed like a boil. When he couldn't take it any longer, he waited until the children had retired to their beds and instructed Iya Tope to summon the other wives.

Baba Segi sat in his chair, waiting, contemplating the manliest, most honorable way to present his proposal. Iya Segi arrived first, draped in black. She had tasted her first meal just hours before and already the pleasure of nourishment filled her with guilt. She had lost a considerable amount of weight and the folds of skin she dragged around slowed her pace. No one attempted to comfort her because she rejected it outright, preferring the solitude of her room or the silent reflection she engaged in when in company.

Iya Tope followed, her face creased with tiredness. As the second wife, the well-being of the children had now become her responsibility. A few steps behind her, Iya Femi, her head wrapped in a scarf, joined them. Segi's death had induced an epiphany. She had lost weight too, but hers was from fervent fasting. On the day of the burial, she had flushed her mobile phone down the toilet and burned all her flamboyant items of clothing. True to her character, she hid Grandma's gold under her bed and pretended she didn't remember it was there when she prayed.

Bolanle came in quietly and perched on a stool, her fingers linked to calm her nerves. For the first four nights after Segi passed away, she had jumped at the slightest rattle. This, coupled with the heaviness of Segi's breath in her bedroom, disturbed her. Every day for the last two weeks, she'd washed the walls down with Dettol, but in spite of the antiseptic, the bitterness remained.

Baba Segi's head was propped up by his fist. "I have called you today because I am full of words, words that threaten to tear my belly apart if they remain unsaid. This is a time of mourning, but a man must be mindful when weakness threatens to take him over." He looked at each wife and they stared back wondering if their flesh could endure any more misery. "I will not pretend the words that struck my ears at the hospital have not preyed on my mind the way hunger preys on the mind of a motherless child. I have been deeply wounded. It is not every day that a man discovers his life is a mere shadow and that there is a gulf between what he believes and reality. Neither is it every day that a man finds his children are not his own." He raised his eyebrows in resignation and paused as if to regain his composure. The words Teacher had forced into his belly were now stuck in his throat like large orange seeds; they refused to be swallowed but were reluctant to be spat out. He took a deep breath. "I want you to know that you can go. The door is open. I will not stop you."

"But where? Where? Go where?" Iya Femi was terrified.

"Wherever you please! I do not want to keep you here."

"But where will we go?"

"Perhaps the father of your children will take you," Baba Segi mumbled, shrugging his enormous shoulders.

"My lord." Iya Segi cleared her throat. "I have considered your words and they are wise. More than wise, they are justified."

Baba Segi nodded, half in appreciation that his words were understood and half in the knowledge that he knew Iya Segi could be trusted to conjure a faultless response to his proposition.

"You talk of the *father* of our children. *Who* is the father of our children? Who was the father of the child who now rots below the ground?" Her voice broke but she continued. "There is no other but *you*. *You* named her. *You* named every child in this house, every one. You have nurtured them so it is your name they will bear. You may say that there are other fathers but you are the only father they know. You alone have been their father, for it takes more than shedding seed to be a father."

The other wives puffed their chests out in agreement, all except Bolanle, who was deep in thought about Baba Segi's words.

Iya Segi continued, her voice cool like balm. "I have sat for many days now, faint with grief, but my sins have been at the very top of my chest, beating over all else. *I* take the sins of these women onto myself. Heap them on me and let me bear them for the rest of my days. If you want to punish us for our misdeeds, let me single-handedly carry the waste bucket. Send me into the marketplace with it and then let the world smell my misfortunes. I say this because it was I who led these women into the darkness that engulfs them now. It was *my* eagerness to bear children that destroyed them."

Baba Segi nodded in concurrence but he was silent. Arms that were earlier folded over his bosom dropped to his sides.

Iya Segi knew him better than everyone else who sat there silenced by angst, so she dealt her final card. "My lord, I know you want to send me off into the wilderness but I beseech you to have mercy on me. My eyes have already seen what no mother's eyes should see. Forgive me, for I seek nothing else but to stay by your side, serving you as I have done all these years. Consider that I have lost one child but there is only one remaining. I give that child to you. Take him! Own him! What do I know about bringing up a son? Which words will I use to chastise him? If your heart does not forgive *me*, my lord, take Akin. And if your heart accepts me to serve you, receive me also." With this, she lowered herself onto her knees, lay flat on the floor and reached out her hands until they held her husband's feet. "My lord," she whispered. "Let us not allow the world to see our shame. Let us keep our secrets from those who may seek to mock us."

She was good, Bolanle thought as she watched the other wives join her in her supplication. Only then did it all fall into place. Baba Segi's big testicles were empty and without seed.

CHAPTER TWENTY-EIGHT
BOLANLE

THE DECISION WAS EASY and was met, as I expected, with understanding. I knew Baba Segi didn't want me to leave but the recent revelations had left him without a viable alternative. It was more important to him, as Iya Segi had sussed, that his manhood be protected. An agreement was drawn: you can stay if you promise to be the wives *I* want you to be. He promptly banned them from leaving the house without his permission. Iya Segi was instructed to close down all her shops and relinquish every kobo she had saved to him. Iya Femi was forbidden to wear makeup and there would be no more church. God hears your heart no matter where you are, he'd said. Surprisingly, he didn't have any rules for Iya Tope. Rather, he came to favor her and now decided to spend most of his nights with her. In return, Baba Segi swore to buy them all the jewelry, all the lace, every luxury they needed and wanted, provided these were only worn within the four walls of his home.

On the day he called a meeting to lay down these new laws, everyone was given the opportunity to respond. Iya Segi sobbed silently and said she was just grateful for Baba Segi's graciousness. Iya Tope smiled; his words greatly satisfied her. Iya Femi launched into prayer and asked that God bless Baba Segi with the riches of Solomon. When it was my turn, I simply said I'd thought about it and decided to return to my parents' house.

Baba Segi was taken aback; he asked if he had offended me in any way. I told him he had not and explained that there was no point staying if I wouldn't be able to give him children. He listened attentively and promised that he would always be there to give me anything I ever needed. I saw the sadness in his eyes; it was as if it had just dawned on him that our paths had crossed for a purpose and we were never meant to be together.

Of course, I couldn't tell him that I felt as if I'd woken up from a dream of unspeakable self-flagellation. It started a few days after Segi died. I'd walk through the house and feel like I was in the midst of strangers, people from a different time in history, a different world. I didn't feel soiled anymore.

The other thing was that a young girl had died for sins that were not hers. Segi came to my mind too frequently. I couldn't get the picture of her dying next to me out of my head. Perhaps she would still be alive if I'd never come to

Baba Segi's home. Then again, Baba Segi would never have known about his wives and their deceit.

I will remember Baba Segi. I won't miss him but I will remember him. Perhaps on some days, I will remember him with fondness. I have learned many things from the years I spent under his roof. It was being in his house that shook me awake. I should be thankful for that.

The wives will be relieved by my departure, I know. Maybe not Iya Tope, but the other two will remember me as the wicked wind that upturned the tranquillity of their home. When they talk about me, they will console one another by calling me the uppity outsider, the one who couldn't cut it as an Alao wife. I will remember them as inmates, because what really separates us is that I have rejoined my life's path; they are going nowhere.

One after the other, they offered to help me gather my belongings, but I told them I could manage. There wasn't much left to pack anyway; much of it was never unpacked. Akin offered too. Even if I'd said no, he wouldn't have listened. He helped me load up the waiting taxi. He stood alone by the gate and waved until I was out of sight.

Don't think I can't see the challenges ahead of me. People will say I am a secondhand woman. Men will hurt and ridicule me but I won't let them hold me back. I will remain in the land of the living. I am back now and the world is spread before me like an egg cracked open.

A⁺

AUTHOR
INSIGHTS,
EXTRAS &
MORE...

FROM

LOLA
SHONEYIN

AND

WM

WILLIAM MORROW

Questions for Discussion

1. It is normal practice in Nigeria for wives to be known as "Iya" followed by the name of their first child. "Iya" in this context means "mother of." What does this say about the identity of women in a traditional Nigerian setting, and how do you think this might impact women who are unable to produce children?

2. From the outset, the wives decide not to let Bolanle in on their secret, largely because her educational background makes them feel inferior. This turned out to be a disastrous decision on the wives' part. From your assessment of Bolanle's character, how do you think she would have reacted if she had been told?

3. Baba Segi insists on everyone in his household being present during "family time." Is this a normal occurrence in Western homes? Why do you think Baba Segi introduced this as part of the daily routine?

4. The circumstances that led the four women to become Baba Segi's wives are very different. How much say did they have in the matter and what alternatives do you think were open to them? Did any of the wives make the right decision? What would you have done if you were in their situations?

5. The novel explores the issue of gender and how society defines a woman's role from childhood. To what extent

does Iya Segi defy these set roles? And in what ways does she wield power over her family? Why do you think, after making more money than she could imagine, Iya Segi remained married to Baba Segi?

6. In the chapter "Rat Head," Baba Segi attempts to strangle Bolanle. This is out of character for a man who, in the beginning of the novel, said, "We must not manhandle our women." What was it about this particular situation that led him to behave so irrationally? What does this tell you about the role of superstition and the fear of the supernatural in Nigerian society?

7. Although many people find Iya Tope to be passive, we learn from "Iya Tope" that it is she in fact who goes through the most liberating internal changes. Do you agree? How important would you say sexual pleasure is for the different wives?

8. Iya Femi comes across as bitter and vengeful, even after her religious encounter. Would you say some of her actions are justified? To what extent did the death of her parents change her destiny?

9. In the beginning of the novel, it is clear that Bolanle does not love Baba Segi. Do you think her feelings toward him changed through the course of the novel? If the other wives had been more accommodating, do you think Bolanle would have endured the marriage? Would your answer be different if she had been able to "give" Baba Segi a child?

10. Baba Segi loved his children dearly. He doted on every one of them, sent them to good schools, and ensured that they lived comfortably. After discovering the "secret," however, do you think his feelings toward his children changed? His reputation, ego, and the physical presence of children

in his household are all very important to Baba Segi, but which is most important?

11. Some reviewers have stated that everyone "won" in the end. Do you agree with this? Who, in your opinion, are the true victors?

Interview with Lola Shoneyin

You've spent a lot of time outside your native country, Nigeria, so why did you choose polygamy as the topic of your first novel?

I feel very lucky to have been able to drift relatively comfortably between two cultures for most of my life. I left Nigeria for boarding school in Edinburgh, Scotland, when I was six years old, so I have spent many years of dreaming about Nigeria, fantasizing about it. And even though some communities have not yet made much progress with the ways that they nurture girls into womanhood, it is a country of men who worship women—their mothers anyway! During the time that I have spent in Nigeria, my mum, who is quite the storyteller, has never spared me the harrowing details of her childhood, growing up as the second child in a polygamous palace of five wives and twenty-four children. My paternal grandfather was the traditional ruler of Iperu-Remo. Women threw themselves at him, and he eagerly received them.

Then, when I was fourteen, I fell hopelessly in love with Anne, my brother's girlfriend. I warmed to her because she was unperturbed by the sick and often highly offensive sense of humor that we, my five brothers and I, intimidated outsiders with. She was a house officer at the local teaching hospital that you'll have read about in the novel, and I enjoyed nothing more than hearing stories about all the strange things that happened at the hospital. It was she who told me the story of a man who had dragged his fourth wife into a hospital, screaming about her barrenness. I was completely engrossed with this story and when I later learned the outcome of the medical examination, I knew I had to write it. I knew even then that it was a story I would one day tell.

Does the setting, Ibadan, have any particular significance for you?

I was born in Ibadan and spent many years of my life in the dusty, ancient city. Many of the stories in the novel were experienced by people who also lived in Ibadan. The rape scene, for instance, actually took place in Bodija, Ibadan, as described in the novel. My description of the cemetery is based on my personal experiences. The book is full of little snippets from my own life as a girl in Ibadan, becoming a woman. For instance, the gravestone in the novel bears the name of a young friend of mine. She was nineteen when she died in a motor accident. In Yoruba culture, parents are not allowed to see the bodies of their children. Nor are they allowed to know where their children are buried—a horrible, senseless tradition. We, the friends of the family, had to send her on her final journey. We paid for a fresh grave, but the grave digger showed us to a three-foot grave. So she was buried on top of a stranger, an elderly lady. I wrote the woman's name down so I would never forget. In the novel, one of the characters is buried, at the same cemetery, on top of Dola Oladeji, my friend.

Ibadan used to be the cultural capital of Nigeria but now it's just full of sad anecdotes, little of the joy the city gave me.

You are better known as a poet than as a writer of fiction. How easy was it to transition from poetry to prose?

I feel very lucky that I can switch from one to the other with relative ease. The energy required for writing these two forms is totally different. I am never confused about what genre I am going to engage in; I know straight away whether it's going to be poetry or fiction and I just fall in.

Do you have a preference?

Poetry is a lot easier for me to write, although the gestation period for poems can sometimes be longer than what you would observe with prose. I like the exactness and economy of words in poems.

It's the difference between having a small golden nugget and carrying around a box of gold dust. That's what prose is like for me. You have a chance to spread yourself around a bit more, explore characters, start a joke, and not feel like you've got to get the punch line in immediately.

Would I be correct in saying that a lot of your work is about and for women?

I do like the thought of writing *for* women but that wasn't what I set out to do. Every author's dream is to reach as wide an audience as possible—man, woman, gay, straight, African, Asian, Western, Middle Eastern, etc. With regard to my work being "about" women though, this is probably true. Coming from a family of five boys, I came late to loving women. I spent the first eleven years of my life hoping I'd wake up one day to find that my voice was lower. And although I had several strong alpha females in my family, I didn't trust their strength because they wept too often and their tears were induced by men. It wasn't until my teenage years that I started fully appreciating what it meant to be a woman, so I developed a sort of crusader complex. It's always been important that I speak out for women. It makes my existence worthwhile.

What is it about women that prompts you to want to write about them?

Well, as I got older, I started to see that what I had imagined was weakness in women was not weakness at all but a very raw survival instinct. In Nigeria, for instance, many women opt for polygamy for financial security. Even more disturbing is the fact that the status of a junior wife in a polygamous household is higher than that of a single woman, no matter how accomplished she is. As a result, from a very young age, women aspire to marriage and motherhood; an education, a career, financial independence are viewed as masculine aspirations. I am often saddened by the fact that a woman's achievements are filtered through who she is romantically or sexually involved with. Nothing intimidates men more than the idea of an older, successful, single woman. They often have to label her a whore to comfort themselves. Institutions like polygamy were employed to dominate women. After deprecating them, the next phase for men is to try to marry the women.

Why do you think polygamy still exists in Nigeria?

The northern part of Nigeria has a large Muslim population, and there are Muslim communities among the Yorubas in southwest Nigeria, which is where I'm from. My paternal grandfather was a Muslim and so was my father until he converted to Christianity at fifteen years old. Islam allows for a man to take up to four wives, provided he can treat them with equity. I think many men fail to see the irony here. Even among one's own siblings, one tends to have favorites and so how much more competition will there be with women who look different, act differently, and are likely to have different skills and strengths. Polygamy is about power, sex, and greed—a man's ability to have multiple sexual partners who would do anything for his attention. Recently, a Nigerian senator took on a fourteen-year-old Egyptian bride (the daughter of his Egyptian driver) as his fourth wife, after divorcing his teenage wife. Women's groups and pro-child activists were up in arms about it, especially since the marriage took place at the largest mosque in the capital city, with other federal senators in attendance. The polygamist senator immediately used Prophet Mohammed as his yardstick, ignoring the implications of sex with a minor. It's completely disgusting when religion is used to defend the indefensible, but that is what you will often find. Polygamous marriages do a lot of damage to womenfolk and, by extension, their children. Polygamy can turn the sweetest, most agreeable women into paranoid, volatile wrecks. As can be seen in the novel, the competition is brutal and can lead to devastating consequences.

What kind of reaction have you had in Nigeria?

It's been interesting. Some men have come out to say that the novel is antifeminist, which is a low blow. Others have said that their polygamous family is fine, thank you very much. To this, of course, I say, "Sure it is. How about I ask one of your wives?" This is exactly why it was so important to tell the story in multiple narrative voices. I wanted readers to hear from the women themselves. These are the perspectives we don't often get. Every wife in a polygamous home knows that she can't trust anyone, sometimes not even her own children. Female readers have been very supportive and very complimentary, even the ones in polygamous homes. At a few of the readings I've done, they come up close and tell me how pleased they are that I have told their story. It doesn't get any better than that.

Distance

And do you think that love itself, Living in such an ugly house,
Can prosper long?

—Edna St. Vincent Millay

The ring of red on the coaster dries
I taste your robust Shiraz
so your blood can break my bread.
My lips leave a mark on your glass.

I flatter the guests,
fret about the salt in the stew.
My husband will not look at me.
He knows, he knows it's you.

Across the table, you touch my lip-print,
circle the length of my smile
from the centre to the corners,
fingering every grove.

I want to reach for you
above the shaken salt,
press your palm into mine
but no, this is not the time.

The wine sours in my mouth
when you reach for your coat.
Soon, you will leave me by the door,
stroking your kiss and wanting more.

Jide Alakija

LOLA SHONEYIN lives in Abuja, Nigeria, where she teaches English and drama at an international school. She is married, with four children and three dogs.

Lola Shoneyin

12~11